Edward Backhouse Eastwick

Journal of a Diplomates Three years Residence in Persia

Vol. 2

SALZWASSER
VERLAG

Edward Backhouse Eastwick

Journal of a Diplomates Three years Residence in Persia

Vol. 2

Reprint of the original, first published in 1864.

1st Edition 2022 | ISBN: 978-3-75259-234-4

Verlag (Publisher): Salzwasser Verlag GmbH, Zeilweg 44, 60439 Frankfurt, Deutschland
Vertretungsberechtigt (Authorized to represent): E. Roepke, Zeilweg 44, 60439 Frankfurt, Deutschland
Druck (Print): Books on Demand GmbH, In de Tarpen 42, 22848 Norderstedt, Deutschland

JOURNAL OF A DIPLOMATE'S

THREE YEARS' RESIDENCE

IN PERSIA

BY

EDWARD B. EASTWICK, F.R.S, F.S.A.,

OF THE MIDDLE TEMPLE,

LATE H.M.'S CHARGÉ D'AFFAIRES AT THE COURT OF TEHRAN;

MEMBER OF THE ROYAL ASIATIC SOCIETY OF GREAT BRITAIN; OF THE ASIATIC SOCIETY
OF PARIS, AND OF THE ORIENTAL SOCIETY OF GERMANY; HONORARY MEMBER
OF THE ETHNOGRAPHICAL SOCIETY OF FRANCE, MEMBER OF THE
PHILOLOGICAL SOCIETY OF LONDON, AND FELLOW OF THE
SOCIETY OF NORTHERN ANTIQUARIES.

VOL. II.

LONDON:

SMITH, ELDER AND CO., 65, CORNHILL.

CONTENTS OF VOLUME II.

CHAPTER VII.

Contents.

APPENDICES.

JOURNAL

OF A

DIPLOMATE'S THREE YEARS' RESIDENCE IN PERSIA.

CHAPTER I.

Social Atmosphere of Resht—Departure for the Caspian—The Grand Vazír humbled, or Pride will have a Fall—The Via Scelerata—Lagoon of Enzelli—Sháhrukh Mirza—Leave Enzelli for the Sturgeon Fisheries and the Port of Ashurádah.

The European society at Resht consisted, when I was there, of several Russians and Germans, a few Greeks, and the English Consul. The Russians, of course, preponderate in numbers and influence, for they hold entire villages, by right of mortgage, and have many hundred protégés in Ghilán. The Russian Consul has double the pay of the British. M. Zenovieff was consul at the time of my visit.

He was not more than twenty-five years of age, but an excellent linguist, and a most gentlemanly, agreeable person, as well as a good man of business. The consulate is entirely ruled by the Russian envoy at Tehran, and how completely Russian subordinates are in the hands of their Chief was shown in a droll way some time after my visit, when M. Zenovieff had been succeeded by a M. P——, and the Russian envoy by a new chargé d'affaires. On the arrival of this chief at Tehran, one of the Mission, in joke, wrote a terrible account of the new régime to the acting consul at Resht, and said he advised him to be on his guard, for there was no saying to what length the tyranny of the chargé d'affaires might go. Poor P—— took the matter so seriously to heart that he forthwith prepared an application to be allowed to resign, and his anxiety threw him into a fever before the next post could arrive and bring a second letter, in which the joke was explained.

The Ghilánis are so bigoted that they will not associate at all with the Europeans, and ebullitions of fanaticism are by no means rare. In fact, in May, 1861, a very serious disturbance took place about a frail fair one, who was said to have visited the Russian consulate. The head of the religious party among the Muhammedans at first doomed her to be buried alive, but afterwards commuted the punishment to a hundred blows, and the Russian servant, who acted Mercury on the occasion, was handed over to the tender mercies of Islám. It is strange that, in spite of the massacre of the entire Russian embassy, with the ambassador Grüboedoff himself, at Tehran : in spite of the Kábul massacre, which the English in a measure brought down on themselves by their immoralities, Christian Europe should be sometimes even now disgraced in Eastern countries by the profligacy of its representatives, and, stranger still, that Christian governments should wink at such profligacy, though they know that bloodshed and war may be the result.

The antipathy between the natives and the Europeans was not the only leaven at work at Resht at the time of my visit, but I had at least the satisfaction of leaving things smoother than I found them, when, on a sunny 1st of April, I bade adieu to the town. In obedience to the advice of those who knew the road we had to travel, we had sent back our own horses to

Tehran, and now bestrode ugly little ponies that had learned, by long experience, how to keep stepping for hours together, from one row of holes a yard deep into another. We cut but a sorry figure on these wretched little animals, and even the innumerable beggars, who had assembled to see us depart, and who were being gratified with showers of small coins, were in doubt whether to cheer or hiss us. But there is no escape from these ugly quadrupeds, and his Holiness the Pope, or the Emperor of China, if he visited Resht, would be obliged to make a similar Guy of himself by mounting them. It is said that it is the fear of having to ride a Resht pony, which has kept the Shah from coming to the town. Certain it is that a former Grand Vazír, some years ago, when he came to Resht, resolved not so to demean himself, and insisted upon bestriding, as usual, a superb charger, with housings of gold. So his Eminence rode forth, looking as haughty as possible, and not so much as deigning to cast his eyes down upon the lean ground that was to bear the load of his dignity. All this was mighty well for the few hundred yards of made road, but, when the ruts were reached, alas for the prancing steed and the golden housings, and alas for his Eminence the Grand Vazír! Splash, splash, slip, slip, and down goes steed and rider in the mud. So pride was sobered, and the fiery steed was discarded for the little Resht pony, and his Eminence the Vazír was fain to crawl along the Via Scelerata like other mortals.

It was 10 A.M. when we reached the outskirts of the town, and there we took leave of our friends, and entered the famous road to Parí bazár. I say entered, for that is exactly what we did—we entered a lane of water, in general about a yard deep, with a thick jungle on either side. Along this pleasant path our ponies splashed and stumbled for half a mile, when we came to the ruts, which consisted of row upon row of holes, succeeding each other interminably. Here our experienced beasts plodded continuously on, dragging out one leg, and poking in the other, in a slow, monotonous fashion, most piteous to see.

Weary of this road, we dismounted, but our servants, with the usual Persian affection for horse-back, stuck to the saddle. Luckily for us the hot sun had dried patches of ground here and there, and

from one to other of these we scrambled, while all
around us was mud and water, and forest. It was
the Dismal Swamp, in *Dred*. On our right flowed
the Resht river, a rapid, turbid stream, fifteen feet
deep, with a high bank, and so full of fish, the
sufid máhí, or white fish, that we saw men hauling
them out with nets, literally, by cart-loads, many
being from three to seven pounds weight. On our
left were deep water-courses, swarming with snakes,
tortoises, and all sorts of slimy creatures. Once
or twice we came to great mulberry plantations, with
sheds in which silk-worms were stored, but in general
a thorny jungle hemmed us in, brushed against our
faces, and pushed us into the mud. This jungle is
full of wild beasts, and tigers often kill cattle even at
Parí bázár. It was 1 P.M. when we reached this
place on foot. Our servants and the things did not
come up for some time, so that we had ample leisure
to admire the beauties of our rendezvous. As to the
etymology of the name I am doubtful. If it be
Parí bazár, the bazár of fairies, I can only say it
is the strangest place for Oberon and Titania imagi-
nation could picture. Even Puck would hardly

delight to lead hapless travellers astray in such a locality, more fit for carcase-eating ghouls and goblins dire, than for gentle fairies.

While we sate bedraggled and bedevilled at the brick Custom-house, which with a shed or two forms the bazár, our domestics made their appearance, not looking like sober domestics, but like very scared and angry wild-fowl indeed. From their rent garments and mud-bespattered exterior it was easy to judge of the state of their inner man. But we were not left long in doubt as to their feelings, for no sooner was the last rut cleared, than such a storm of words arose, that I fancied myself in the hubbub of King Agramante's camp. Every one of them had been down scores of times, according to his own deposition, volunteered on oath, and accompanied by the most animated gestures. "*Ai Gor i piderat,*" said my servant Riza, addressing his pony, "am I a son of Adam, or a bag, that thou dost chuck me from thy back every moment?" In revenge for his falls, Riza deducted a túmán from the pay of the chárvadárs, who let us the horses, and on my ordering it to be restored,

Rustam, the Consul's servant, under our very eyes, abstracted four of the ten kíráns. A bold strong fellow he was that Rustam; but neither his strength nor his courage availed him shortly after, when he tried to swim the White River. It would seem as if the curse of the poor chárvadár whom he had defrauded weighed him down, for he sank, though his money was saved.

About 1 P.M. we embarked in a dirty open boat, or barge, at Parí bazár, and by 3 P.M. got to the Enzelli Lagoon, in Persian *Murdáb*, or dead water,—a salt, or rather brackish lake, extending twelve miles from north to south, and thirty from east to west. It was a dreary, desolate scene, and one at times not without its dangers. The country being quite flat all round the Lagoon, the wind in storms sweeps without a check over the water, which, shallow as it is, perhaps not over two fathoms in the deepest part, can yet easily overwhelm the wretched boats of the Enzelli and Parí bazár people. In fact, numbers of boats are lost every year, and others are driven over to the western shore, where there is nothing but a jungle full of wild beasts.

As soon as we issued from the Parí bazár river, we found ourselves surrounded on all sides by reeds and swamps, and we grounded more than once. It was a rare place for an ornithologist, for water-fowl in every conceivable variety were congregated in it. Not to speak of cormorants, divers, coots, wild duck, swans, geese, guillemots, gulls, snipes and cranes, there was a compact phalanx of at least 500 pelicans in front of us, looking like a regiment of soldiers. I gave my Enfield to the Consul, who was a capital shot, to fire at them, but it had been so long loaded, and was so damp, that it was some time before it would go off, and finally did so at a wrong moment, so that the shot went over the heads of the phalanx, but up they got, and up got with them ten thousand other great birds, making a noise like a charge of cavalry. I knocked over one of gigantic size, but it was evidently of an uneatable sort, and the wild duck and others that might have been made available for the cuisine would not come within range.

The northern shore of the Lagoon is for some three or four miles in the central part a narrow belt dividing the Lagoon from the Caspian Sea. In the centre of this belt is a passage, with ten feet water, connecting the Lagoon and the Caspian, and on the western shore of this passage are the village and fort of Enzelli, while on the eastern shore is the Imám-zádah, or shrine, of Káziyán, defended by another little fort. As the wind was tolerably fair, we reached Enzelli at 5 P.M., passing Kalamgondah, "Reed Island," the northern shore of which runs parallel to the village of Enzelli, and thus forms a channel where the water is always smooth. Here two Russian schuyts were lying at anchor, and about thirty smaller vessels. Quarters were given us in a house close to the Imárat or Palace of Sháhrukh Mirza, Governor of the district and Lord of the Marches. For an evening walk we strolled down to the Armenian church, a wooden shed on a foundation of brick. The *Kashish*, or Armenian priest, Ter Joannes Marcas, who had been several years in Calcutta, came out and talked with us in Hindústáni. He said the Mullas at Resht had prevented the church being built of brick, by pretending that it was to be used as a fort for the Russians: such are the absurd stories which find credence at Tehran. According to his account there are five Armenian families at Enzelli, and 300 in all India, of which 20 are at Madras, 12 at Bombay, 100 at Calcutta, 50 at Rangoon, 10 at Singapore, and 1 at Penang. At Ispahan, he said there were 1,000 families. We next walked to the fort, a mere shed, with one brass 32-pounder and one 12-pounder. There˘ is a similar fort at Káziyán. About thirty miserably dressed and awkward artillerymen formed to salute me. We then went some two miles along the shore of the Caspian, which appeared to be tideless. I tasted the water, and found it so far from salt as to be hardly brackish. There was no seaweed, but quantities of wood lined the beach, and among smaller fragments was one entire tree. The only shells were a few cockles, and the only things at all curious were some huge heads of the som fish, shaped like the head of the shark, but far more solid. The som is excessively voracious, and will seize a man or any animal in the water, and, had it but teeth, it would be the pest of the Caspian. Luckily it cannot bite off a limb, but it can drag an animal under water, and then mumble the flesh off the bones.

We were obliged to remain at Enzelli from the

1st to the 5th of April, waiting for the Russian
steamer to Ástarábád.   The day after my arrival I
received a visit from Sháhrukh Mirza, a handsome
youth, and to all appearance a smart soldier.   He is
an officer of artillery, and he talked much of his pro-
fession.   His pay was but 500 túmáns, about 240*l*.,
per annum; but a man in his position has great
opportunities, if he be corrupt, of enriching himself.
It is a far cry to Tehran, and he could levy what he
chose from the merchants at Enzelli.   Then there
are 200 *tufangchis* or matchlockmen under his command; that is, 200 names are on the roll, but fifty are
the names of men defunct, and fifty more those of
absentees, and if pay for all the 200, at 15 túmáns
per mensem, be drawn, there would be 1,500 túmáns
crying " Come eat me ! "   Further, there are on the
rolls 150 artillerymen, and but 100 present, and
Talish *tufangchis* twice ten times ten there should be,
but only echo answers when their names are called.
These things considered, I came to the conclusion
that a corrupt man would have *mudákhil*, or illicit
gains, per annum to the amount of 4,000 túmáns.
On the 3rd we rode four or five miles along the

Lagoon, taking our guns with us. We shot a few snipe, a partridge, and a hare. The number of waterfowl we saw defies description, but their very number prevented our killing any; for, wherever we appeared, they went off like a train of gunpowder, rising in thousands when one gave the signal. I landed repeatedly, but the reeds, taller than my head, prevented me from getting sight of the birds, though I heard them all about me, and kept exclaiming, like Prometheus—

Φεῦ, φεῦ, τί ποτ' αὖ κινάθισμα κλύω
Πέλας, οἰωνῶν; αἰθὴρ δ'ἐλαφραῖς
Πτερύγων ῥιπαῖς ὑποσυρίζει.

In some places, where the ground was more firm, it was torn up in every direction by wild hog, while in the swampy parts there were pools in which great, corpulent fish tumbled and tossed, ill at ease in the shallows, where some accident had stranded them. On the whole, I saw enough to convince me that during the winter the Lagoon of Enzelli would be a grand place for the naturalist and the sportsman, and a scientific man would probably discover some new varieties of plants, birds, and fish.

As to commercial matters, I found such a *tabula rasa*, and so much to fill it, that I could not get the subject out of my mind for a moment. " Heavens !" I mentally exclaimed, " if a Pierre I. were to arise in Persia, what a field he would have ! The first thing, of course, would be to abolish the *Via Scelerata* between Resht and Parí bazár, and make four miles of good macadamized road ; the next step would be to continue that road to the Lagoon of Enzelli, with a jetty, so that goods might be shipped right off on board a little steamer, to ply daily between the jetty and Enzelli. Another great improvement would be to admit the Russian steamers into the port at Enzelli, where they would be secure from storms, and where freight and passengers might be safely put on board or landed, instead of, as is now the case, being compelled to go a mile out to the steamers in little unseaworthy boats. Then there is the Enzelli lighthouse to be finished ; and last, not least, the neighbouring coal mines to be opened and worked. These plans carried out, the trade of Resht would soon be multiplied twenty-fold."

I may have been soliloquizing in this way on the

morning of the 5th of April, when my servant Taki rushed into the room, and said the smoke of a steamer was visible. We dressed in hot haste, and pulled off to the *Vodka*, a vessel of 350 tons, and 75-horse power, belonging to the Kavkas and Mercurei Company. The captain, a large languid man, with his jaws tied up on account of the toothache, received us on deck, and bowed, without saying anything. Presently a Mr. T——, an English engineer, came up, and telling us the captain spoke only Russian, volunteered to interpret for us, when the following colloquy took place:—

I. " Oh, thank you, will you please tell the captain that we are anxious to have a passage in his vessel to Ashurádah, as we want to return to Tehran by way of Astarábád."

T. " Captain says he thinks he is going back to Astara, he is not sure of going to Ashurádah ; he advises you not to embark with him."

I. " Oh! but tell him we have been waiting five days to go with him ; we cannot return any other way ; we really must ask him to give us a passage."

T. " Captain says he thinks he shall stop here

several days; you will be put to much inconvenience; his vessel is for freight, not for passengers; he would rather you went in some other vessel."

I. " Why, this is one of the vessels advertised to take passengers. I have got the printed notice in my pocket, in Russian. I can read Russian, though I cannot speak it : so I am sure I am right, and, with his permission, I shall stop."

T. " Captain says, very well, you can stop if you like, and take your chance ; you will have to pay so many roubles a day for yourselves, and so much for your servants."

With this somewhat inhospitable reception we were fain to be satisfied, and made such good use of our time, that before evening we were on most friendly terms, if not with our host, at all events with our hostess, the captain's wife, a sprightly Polonaise (*c'est tout dire*), who, with her two daughters, girls of six and seven years of age, followed her husband's fortunes on the yeasty wave. Nay, even the languid captain occasionally vouchsafed us a smile—with his eyes, with his lips he could not, for the handkerchief round his jaws hid them.

As for T——, his honest Northumbrian heart expanded at the sight of two countrymen in that outlandish region, and he squeezed my hand in his iron fist with such hearty good-will that he brought tears of sympathy into my eyes.

"Well, Mr. T——," I said, "I *am* surprised to see an Englishman here! It must surely be a dull life for you; so entirely among strangers."

"Well, yes, it is dull; but I am getting used to it. There are eight of us Englishmen in the Caspian, and since the day we came, we haven't seen a newspaper, nor had a letter. Maybe they want to keep us from corresponding with our friends, but that's silly of 'em, for if we were to leave, they couldn't work the vessels without us."

"And pray," said I, "though I see you speak Russian pretty well, do you not find it difficult to manage the men and explain things to them?"

"Well—yes, I do, rayther; that is, at first like I did. But now I manage 'em very well; for when aught's gotten to be done, I always knocks 'em doon first, and then explains it to 'em afterwards."

As we were not to sail till midnight on the 7th,

we went on an expedition to shoot wild hogs on
the 6th, but saw none, though their traces were
everywhere visible. On our return, a strong breeze
was blowing, and the native boatmen refused to go
off to the steamer, and T—— said there was some
danger, but we got on board nevertheless. There
was, however, quite enough sea on to be, as the
Yankees would say, "a caution," and we all agreed
that either the Russian vessels ought to be allowed
to enter the Lagoon, or the Shah ought to employ
a small steamer to carry out passengers and cargo
to them.

CHAPTER II.

Sturgeon-fishing in the White River—An hour with our Guns on
Land—Nautical Skill of the Russians—Aground on the Turkuman Coast—Ashurádah Harbour.

In spite of its having been settled that the *Vodka*
should leave Enzelli on the night of the 7th of April,
the morning of the 8th found us still at anchor,
but at half-past seven A.M. we started with a fair breeze
and a smooth sea. At eleven we touched on a sand-
bank, not shown in the wretched chart on which
the captain depended; but with a little scraping
we ran over it. Shortly afterwards a thick, cold
fog came on, and we anchored. As the land could
not be seen, and there was no chronometer on board,
nor, indeed, any other instrument, and as the log
was never hove, no one knew how far we had run.
In a little time the fog lifted, and we went on

23—2

again, and before 3 P.M. came to anchor a little to
the east of the mouth of the White River, which
discolours the sea to a considerable distance. As
soon as the anchor was down, Mr. T—— and myself
got into the ship's boat and went to where there
were about thirty boats, the crews of which were
engaged in catching sturgeon at the river's mouth.
The manner of fishing is curious. A number of
lines, each about 100 feet long, were stretched across
the river, which is very shallow, but rapid. From
these lines, at intervals of two feet, hung other lines
a yard or so long, with a number of sharp hooks of
a large size attached. The sturgeon, as they swim
down into the sea, hook themselves on these lines,
the water being so muddy that it is impossible to
see the hooks. The fish are great, heavy creatures,
from a yard to five feet long, and it is easy to see
when one is caught by the splashing. A boat is
instantly pulled to the spot and the fish is hauled
on board with a sort of gaff, and then knocked
on the head. The sturgeon has no teeth, and
lives by suction, and, of course, would not take
bait. We purchased one or two fish, and among

them a *som*, four and a half feet long, with an enormous stomach, out of which a fish of 7 lbs. weight was taken.

On getting back to the steamer, I picked up some information about the company to which it belonged. I found that the Kavkas Company originally worked the Caspian steamers, but failed, partly in consequence of some enormous frauds. The Mercurei Company, which also owns the river-steamers on the Volga, then took over the concern, and found itself in possession of the *Vodka* and *Kama*, English-built vessels of 70 horse-power, and 25,000 púds burden, and of the *Shah*, *Timáre*, *Caspe* and *Turkuman*, Swedish-built, of 70 horse-power, and 21,000 púds burden. They then commissioned from England two fast mail-boats, the *Constantine* and the *Bariatinski*, of 120 horse-power, and 5,000 púds burden, adapted to carry 250 passengers each. The fare from Astrakhan to Astarábád, that is, completely round the Caspian, is for the first-class passengers, seventy-five roubles; for the second-class, fifty roubles, and for the third-class, twenty-five roubles; and steamers leave Astrakhan on the

1st and 15th, and Astarabad on the 12th and 26th, except during the winter months.

On the 9th, Mr. T—— and myself taking the ship's boat and passing the mouth of the river, pulled to a small fishing-village, colonized by the Russians, who have the contract for the fisheries. It is about a mile up on the right bank of the river. We saw about forty boats fishing, and the take was very frequent. We saw two men wading, and one of them caught, with a gaff, a fish almost as big as himself, which would certainly have got the better of him, had not the other man come to his aid. The stream was so strong that our Russian boatmen could hardly stem it. When we got to the shore the mud was a yard deep, and we were carried from the boat pick-a-back on the shoulders of the Russian sailors in a most undignified fashion. The man who carried T—— sank to his knees, and remained fast for some time, though he made frantic efforts to disengage himself, having doubtless the dread of one of T——'s forcible explanations in view.

At the spot where we landed, the White River was from 250 to 300 yards broad, with a bank at least 15 feet higher than the water on the left side. There are about twenty houses in the village, neat, clean dwellings, and the dogs do not bark at Europeans. The store for sorting the fish is just at the landing-place. The isinglass is made from a long tape-like substance in the fish. This cartilage, or membrane, is about two inches broad, and not thicker than the cloth of a coat. It varies in length up to three feet. On passing the house of the Persian agent, he came out with a flushed face, looking very much as if he had been carousing, and presently the Russian agent came forth too, a great brawny, black-whiskered man, looking ditto. We took a tátar as guide, and set off about 9 A.M. to shoot. The coast is low, and covered with a thick jungle of thorns, long grass and reeds fifteen feet high, forming excellent cover for hog. Here and there are clumps of beautiful trees. About a mile from the village two pheasants got up, well within shot for T——, but he missed. We then came upon a tree, in the branches of which we descried the nest of an eagle. One of the sailors got up, and threw down two eaglets, which were killed by the fall, and a large fish partly eaten. Two miles further we put up five pheasants, and I killed one. There were traces of hog in all directions, and following these we came to a large pool filled with huge fish, floundering about in the shallows. Ducks and geese in hundreds hovered round, but would not come within shot. It now came on to rain heavily, so we returned, ransacking on our way three more eagles' nests, out of which we got several eggs as large as those of a duck, with three or four spots on them. With dogs the shooting would be excellent at this place, but the low jungle is so dense that nothing can be done without them. The people said panthers and tigers were to be found a little inland.

At 5 P.M. we left the Sufíd Rúd with smooth water, but a gloomy, rainy sky. Two vessels of about 150 tons each were riding at anchor at the river's mouth, and a flotilla of fishing-boats were busily plying their trade as we steamed away. Getting up at dawn on the 10th of April, I found a strong breeze blowing from the north-west. It rained, the sky was overcast, and the waves were rising fast.

The languid captain, it appeared, had never been on deck all night, though the weather was threatening. We were to stop at Mashed-i-sir, a seaport about 100 miles west of Ashurádah, to land the Russian consul, but the log had never been hove, and no attempt was made to ascertain our whereabouts, though the breeze kept freshening, and the weather was so thick that it was impossible to see more than two miles. As for me, I was interested in observing how the Caspian had changed from the gigantic, sleepy fish-pond it looked the first day I saw it, to a real sea, with waves of true ocean-colour —dark green, and crested with foam. But the captain was eating jujubes in his cabin, and waiting on Providence to show him where to anchor. Things went on thus till 4 P.M., when, lo! land was seen, and M. le Capitaine was summoned, and pronounced it to be Mashed-i-sir. T——, however, and the Persian boatswain declared that it was the coast near Ashurádah, and so it turned out, and consequently we had over-run our destination 100 miles, whereat the captain smiled languidly, and went down to eat more jujubes, and the little consul remained fuming

on deck, having a four days' journey by land inflicted
on him as a penalty for the jujubes already eaten by
the captain.

At 5.20 P.M. we sighted the island of Ashurádah,
and soon after saw a ship, which turned out to be
a Russian man-of-war, anchored off the Turkuman
coast, at the entrance of the channel, between that
coast and the island of Little Ashurádah, which leads
to Ashurádah harbour. It was now quite evident
that the vessel had been running ten knots during
the night, while the captain was sleeping peacefully,
and that though he had been thirty years in the
Caspian, he knew no more about the look of the
coast than I did, or any other stranger. At a
quarter-past six we came up with the Russian war-
steamer, and ran between her and a merchant vessel
which she was convoying for fear of the Turkuman
pirates. The wind was very fresh, and we were
fast overhauling the lights on the Turkuman coast.
I said to T——, "If we don't alter our course we
shall run ashore before long. We are steering south-
east, and our course ought to be south. We have
been on soundings since four o'clock, and I can see

the water is shoaling fast. Cannot you speak to
the captain, and tell him we shall strike directly
if he goes on in this way? At all events, get him
to take in sail and go half speed."

"Well," said T——, "it's no business of mine.
I've got to mind the engines. If he loses the ship,
it's his look-out; but I'll tell 'em to go half-speed."

It was well he did so. The man in the chains
was sounding with a stick, and calling out twelve
feet, eleven feet; presently he called ten feet. I
said to Fane, "Look out! we shall strike in a
minute." At this critical moment the captain actually
went down to his cabin, and directly afterwards—
thump, c-r-u-nch we went on to the sand. Then
all was confusion; showers of sparks were blowing
out of the funnel; sails were flapping with a loud
noise; men were running about in the dark, blundering against one another, and the waves broke heavily
over the vessel's stern, setting her deeper into the
sand. Fane and I loaded our revolvers, for there
were two large piratical Turkuman boats lying not
far off, and we could see many fires on the shore.
Luckily the bank we were on was soft, the water

shallow, and the vessel of strong English build, otherwise, T—— assured me, we should have gone to pieces and all on board would have perished, or been made prisoners by the Turkumans.

When the hubbub had a little subsided, I went to the cuddy, and played three games of chess with Madame —— the captain's wife, though it was rather difficult to keep the board steady from the lurching of the vessel and the thumping of the waves. After that, I went to sleep, as did every one on board, in spite of the Turkumans, who might easily have plundered the ship, as the Russians would not even load the cannon, though they knew very well that a number of their countrymen had been taken close to that very spot. But, with the exception of the English engineer and the Persian boatswain, there was no one who seemed to care what happened. Having to stop at Mashed-i-sir,' and to land the Russian consul there, we had run on blindly to Ashurádah, and in weather in which any landsman could have steered the vessel safely into port we had gone ashore, and done all that was possible to wreck the ship. As for the captain's wife, she was quite composed, and no wonder, for she was used to these little incidents. The voyage before, the steamer had run ashore at Salian, and her rudder, boats, and bulwarks had been swept away by the breakers. Even this, however, was nothing to what befel the Russian surveying vessel *Kouba*, commanded by Captain Poskotchen. This unfortunate ship, on the 15th of September, 1857, ran straight on to the rocks near Báku, and went down. The captain and twenty-four of the crew perished, and all the maps and surveys were lost, so that the only guide in the Caspian is a wretched map of 1826. It is only right, however, to say that Poskotchen, though he had clumsily lost the vessel, at least showed great courage in refusing to leave her while a man remained on board. He was only twenty-four years of age, and having been promoted out of his turn through interest, he was resolved to show that he was not altogether unworthy of the rank he had attained.

Before dawn on the 11th of April the Russians set to work to get the vessel off. The boats were lowered, and after several hours working she floated. Just then about thirty Turkuman fishing-boats came

out with seven or eight men in each. I could see
the piratical luggers very well with a glass, and they
seemed capable of holding from twenty to thirty
men each. At 7.30 we ran past the island of Little
Ashurádah, the eastern spit of which is about three
quarters of a mile from the Turkuman coast. A
shoal runs out some way beyond the spit, and there
were many pelicans upon it. I tried my Enfield
at them in vain, owing to the motion of the vessel.
At 9.30 A.M. we came to anchor at Gez Bandar, the
landing-place for the Persian village of Gez, which
is five miles inland. An hour afterwards we went
ashore, and passed on our way to the jetty a Russian
merchant vessel used for carrying cotton, that had
been captured by the Turkumans and retaken by
the Russians a few days before. The Turkumans
killed one of the cotton ship's crew, and would
doubtless have sold the rest at their convenience.

The Gez jetty is a miserable structure of planks,
but useful, nevertheless, as the water is too shallow
for a boat to run close in. The said jetty is scrupu-
lously removed in winter, lest it should aid the
enemies of Irán to land ! Gez Bandar can hardly be

called a village, as there are only four or five sheds belonging to the Russians, full of skins, the horns of deer, and cotton. The cotton was of a good kind, and sells at 11 kirans, or 10s. 1¼d. for the púd of 36 lbs., about 3½d. a pound. Among the skins I noticed those of the panther, the wild cat, and the martin. The Russians asked me 1l. 16s. for a panther skin, nine feet long from the snout to the tip of the tail. The wild-cat skins were 10d. each. All round the sheds was a dense jungle, which extends over the whole province of Astarábád, and swarms with wild beasts. The Russians at the sheds told me that a tiger had killed one of their horses two nights before. They were roused by the noise, and went out, when they saw the monster sitting on the carcase of the horse devouring it, whereupon they ran back into the sheds. I walked with T—— through the jungle to a large tree, called by the name of a certain Englishman, who is said to have passed the night in its hollow trunk, after a dinner with the Russians. There was a platform in it about twenty feet from the ground, where men sit to shoot wild beasts, and it is more likely that he climbed up there. T—— showed me

a spot, about 200 yards from the sheds, where he had
two shots at a panther, which went away wounded.
On my return I played chess with a young Russian
officer, who spoke very well and kindly of ——, but
said he should have died had —— stopped another
week, for he talked all day and read all night, with
two candles lit. " Often," he said, " I put out the
candles and then dozed off to sleep, but, whenever I
awoke, they had been lighted again, until they quite
haunted me, and I began to see them in my
dreams."

The morning of the 12th of April brought me a
polite invitation from Commodore Roudakoff. He
had sent a schooner for me, but as the *Vodka* was to
cross in the afternoon, I preferred going in her.
Meantime Fane, T ——, and myself paid a visit to
M. Fetsoff, commanding a schooner anchored close
by. This vessel, and four others of the same size,
about 100 tons, were painted white, and called the
White Squadron. They carried only four 6-pounders,
and two 3-pounder stern-chasers, and it was intended,
as larger vessels had arrived, to use them as hulks.
I examined and fired the rifle of one of the marines

on board M. Fetsoff's vessel, and it appeared to me as good as the Enfield. One of the officers on board produced a sketch map of the water communications which link the Caspian with the Baltic. There are three series of canals which run from the Caspian to Tver and Lake Ladoga, the Vyashnevolotskia, the Tikhvinskaya, and the Mariinskaya. By the last-named, T—— brought a steamer for use in the Volga river, and got 20*l.* for the trip, and an engagement to serve in the Caspian. By this route cotton (supposing the Russian Government to assent) might be brought from Ashurádah harbour, where it would cost 3½*d.* per pound, by water-carriage all the way to England, when, after paying freight and duty, it might be sold at a profit for a shilling per pound.

Soon after we returned to the *Vodka*, and about 1 P.M. she got up her anchor, and crossed to Ashurádah in one hour and a quarter, the distance being about eight miles. Fane and I landed immediately, and called on the commodore, an elderly man, with a noble expression of countenance. We found that he had served in all parts of the world, and had been attached to the Staff in the Caucasus.

and that his wife was sister to the renowned captain
of the *Vladimir*, Gregory Ivanovich Butakoff. After
our visit we walked over the island, which, with
careful stepping, I made to be about one mile and
640 paces long, and three quarters of a mile broad.
It was in 1841, that Hájí Mirza Aghassi, the prime
minister of Muhammad Sháh, permitted the Russians
to occupy this island, the importance of which was
then little understood. It was entirely uninhabited,
and the Turkumans used to resort there to divide
their booty after their piratical expeditions. Even so
late as 1859, eight Russians landing in the neighbouring promontory of Miyán Kálih, were attacked by
fourteen Turkumans, and obliged to retreat to their
boats, after one of the Turkumans had been killed.
The harbour of Ashurádah, which is large enough to
contain any number of ships, is formed by the promontory called Miyán Kálih, which runs out from
the main land near Ashraf, into the Caspian, curving
continually eastwards, and being some fifteen miles
in length. At its eastern extremity is a passage with
eight or ten feet of water about half a mile in width.
Then follows the island of Great Ashurádah, the

length of which has been stated as about one mile and one-third. There is then shoal water for half a mile, followed by the island of Little Ashurádah, two miles in length, then a shoal, and a narrow passage fast filling up with fifteen feet of water, and then a shoal for half a mile to the Turkuman coast.

The harbour of Ashurádah, therefore, is completely landlocked, having the Persian coast to the south and east, and Miyán Kálih, also Persian ground, and the two Ashurádahs, Russian territory, to the west and north. The whole extent of the harbour is twenty miles from west to east, and eight miles from north to south, and ships drawing twenty feet of water might anchor off Ashurádah. The western part of Great Ashurádah is being fast washed away. I noticed a cemetery there with six or seven tombs, which was being rapidly engulfed. Burials now take place in Miyán Kálih, and are forbidden in Ashurádah for sanitary reasons. On the other hand, the passage to the east of Little Ashurádah is filling so fast that it is thought it will be quite dry in twenty years. These changes, however, do not affect the value of the harbour, which is admitted to be the

only one worthy of the name in the Caspian. But it
is not only a good harbour, it is one in the right
place. To the east of it, almost parallel with
Astarábád, are passes into the table-land of Persia,
quite practicable at all seasons, so that a Russian
force collected at Ashurádah might first occupy
Astarábád, and then advance to Sháhrúd, and so
pass eastward to Herát, or westward to Tehrán, as
the occasion might require. Were such a move
contemplated, it is not to be doubted that the
Turkumans would assist the Russians, for one of
their chiefs, Kádir Khán, resides constantly at
Ashurádah, and every year adds to Russian influence
among the tribes. In the meantime, the greatest of
all the advantages which Russia possesses is, that the
failure of her ambitious designs in the Black Sea,
and her disasters in the Crimea, have lulled to rest
England's fears and suspicions regarding her. Hence
she can gradually mature her plans without risk of
attention being attracted to them, and the Caspian
can be swallowed in a moment, when the time for
opening her jaws arrives.

My walks about Ashurádah enabled me to judge

of the changes which the Russians have effected in
this once barren island : the reader shall walk with
me and see them. To begin at the western end :
there is first the residence of the commodore, with
two or three sitting-rooms, and several bedrooms.
The garden produces excellent peas, beans, lettuces,
and other vegetables. There is a fine fig-tree, only
five years old, with branches as thick as a man's leg,
for the rapid growth of vegetation here is quite surprising. There are also mulberry-trees, and plantations are to be seen in every direction. Observe also
a well of good water, and note that you have only
to stab the soil and it weeps. Stepping eastward
from the commodore's house, we come directly to a
plantation. Embosomed in it is the library, to which
the Grand Duke Constantine has subscribed 300
roubles. Beyond this is the church, which will hold
fifty persons, but is so full of paintings that one
might be pardoned for mistaking it for a picture-
gallery. The house of the priest is close by. He is
an Armenian, and comes from Báku, and his period
of service is but a year. Next to him lives the
doctor of the station; and the hospital, with two

wards for fifteen men each, is a little farther to the
eastward, and at the opposite side of what is now a
regular street of buildings.   This season there has
not been a single case of fever.   Facing the hospital
are twenty or thirty double huts for married sailors,
and then the *estaminet* and club, where I bought
86 lbs. of excellent flour for three roubles, about 9s.,
while the same quantity would have cost at Tehran,
when I left it, 3l. 5s.   I also bought sixteen fine wax
candles for two roubles, which would have cost five
times as much at Tehran.   We now come to four
barracks, each capable of holding fifty sailors.
Besides these, the hulks will accommodate another
100 men.

Having walked thus far, we may omit to visit a
number of scattered huts which occupy the rest of the
island, in order to pay a visit to the tent of the
Turkuman chief, Kádir Khán, who lives among the
Russians partly as an honoured guest, partly as
a hostage for the good behaviour of his countrymen,
the Yemút tribe, on the mainland.   It being the
festival of the Fitra Aid, the chief has gone to his
Obé, or encampment, but we shall enter his tent in

his absence. It is really a very handsome tent, made
of skins, sewn together, and set up over sticks, nicely
polished, and formed into a frame like the sides of a
straw hat with wider interstices. It is round, and
perhaps sixty feet in circumference. There are three
women inside, who care no more for showing their
faces than we do for seeing them, there being nothing
seductive in high cheek-bones, small twinkling eyes,
coarse features, and hands more fitted for making the
ear tingle, than for conveying the electric shock of
passion to the heart. A young child of the chief is
playing about. His name is Kurbán, "sacrifice," a
meaning which, in view of the gambols of the
interesting creature so designated, we prefer to
"gift." A male menial, likewise called Kurbán,
being able to converse in Persian, replies to our
questions. He tells us the tent would cost twenty-
five túmáns, 12*l.*, without the carpets and hangings,
and that it would load three camels.

Having seen all that is to be seen on the island,
we will next walk to the ships. There are eight war-
steamers, which could transport 4,000 men; five new
sloops that could convey 1,000 men; six merchant

steamers, in which 3,000 men could embark; and transports and other vessels capable of holding 2,000 more. In short, a force of 10,000 soldiers could be landed at any moment from Ashurádah on the Persian shore. Of these vessels, the nearest to the shore is the *Khaiva*, a screw steamer of 300 tons, with four 12-pounders, and seventy men. The engines were made at Nijni Novgorod. Observe that this steamer has three hermetically sealed compartments, so that she could hardly sink, no slight advantage, considering the specimens of Russian nautical skill given above. The Captain, M. Brulkine, was at Sebastopol, and served in one of the bastions. He has so many decorations that, like a well-known English officer, he might go by the name of "General Orders."

The next ship is the *Bucharest*, of the same size as the *Khaiva*, but with a crew of only sixty-one men. The captain is a Finn, Gorascherne by name. He tells me it cost him and his wife 300 roubles to come from Petersburg to this. He is not very encomiastic of the Russians, but complains of the dearness and dirt of the places through which he travelled, and still more of the thievish habits of the inhabitants. Having seen the *Khaira* and the *Bucharest*, we have a sufficient idea of the other war-steamers. We already know from the *Vodka* what the merchant steamers are. So here ends our peregrination.

Our time passed very pleasantly at Ashurádah. Nothing could exceed the hospitality and kindness of Commodore Roudakoff. On the 14th of April we dined again with him, and told him that we wished to go to Astarábád next day. He kindly promised to take us across to Gez Bandar in the *Bucharest*. As we were talking the evening gun was fired, with a most peculiar effect. Though only an 8-pounder, owing, I suppose, to the state of the atmosphere, the noise was prodigious and crashed like thunder among the hills, the reverberations continuing for several minutes.

Ladies are so scarce in the Caspian that the Russian officers are ready to worship them. On the 14th a grand serenade was got up in honour of Madame P——, which would probably have gone on indefinitely had it not been prorogued by a thunder-storm and a *borás* or tornado. Observing an elderly midshipman kiss a fair hand in a very fervid, im-

pressive manner, I attempted to quiz the lady, who
said very seriously, "M. So and So is so much in
love with me that it is quite embarrassing. My husband has reasoned with him and begged him to
conquer his feelings, but he says he can't, so he
comes every day—*to teach me algebra!*"

At 9.15 A.M. on the 15th of April we went on
board the *Bucharest,* which started immediately for
the Persian coast. The commodore asked me if I
would like to see the crew exercised, and on my
saying I should, the men were piped, or rather
bugled, to quarters. They loaded and fired the guns,
long 6-pounders, in one minute. We reached Gez
Bandar in sixty-five minutes. T—— said he had
often done it in the *Vodka* in three-quarters of an
hour, and this speech led to some sharp sparring
between him and the Russians, one of whom said,
"Ah, T——, if ever we have another war I shall
single you out." "Where's the use of waiting for
the next war?" said T——; "here are swords; let
us take down a couple, and see which is the best
man at once." This proposal for immediate hos-
tilities did not seem to gratify the Russian at all.

T—— was not more than five feet eight, but he was uncommonly thick-set and sinewy, and his look said "Close quarters" as clearly as though the words were written in a copy-book.

We had to wait an hour and a half for horses at Gez Bandar, when Fane, T——, and myself, with one or two Russian sailors and others, and our servants, started for Gez *en route* for Astar-ábád. It is said to be one farsakh to Gez, but we were an hour in riding it, the road leading through swamps and patches of cultivation surrounded by a tigerish jungle. Gez is a village consisting of about 120 houses. The roads near it were from two feet to a yard deep in mud. There is a dense jungle for from thirty to forty miles between it and the Obés of the Turkumans, and this, perhaps, saves the inhabitants from being carried off bodily for slaves. Zu'l-fikár Khán, the chief of the village, a pale, careworn man, of rather gentlemanly manners, came to see me. I asked him to dine with us. He sate at table and scarcely touched anything. After-wards he asked my servant to give him a dinner by himself, and begged a bottle of brandy, the greater

part of which he drank during the night, and moreover stole the tumbler, which we could ill spare. He
discoursed as if he were a Rustam in courage and a
Hátim in generosity, instead of being, as he really
was, a night-owl, worthy of the gloomy swamp in
which he dwelt. " Would the sáhib like to shoot?"
he said, and without waiting for a reply, but inter-
preting my look, he went on, " On my head and eyes
be it! I will send out my shikáris. They shall see
where the wild hog are; maybe, they will mark down
a tiger. The sáhib can sit in a tree and shoot him.
The Inglís shoot well. Mashallah! we had the
Inglís ——— here last year; he did nothing but
shoot. If his heart had not been merciful, he would
not have left a musquito in the jungle. The sáhib
will condescend to be my guest to-morrow. I will
accompany him when he goes to Astarábád. Whose
dogs are the Turkumans, that they should stop us?
By the sáhib's blessed head I swear I would defile
their fathers' graves were it not for the tongue of the
envious at Tehran. Wherever the fire of merit burns
they quench it with the water of calumny."

All this talk turned out, as I expected, mere *fan-*

faronnade. When I mounted at 8 A.M. on the 16th of April, Zu'l-fikár sent to excuse himself from going with me, on the ground that his horse was not ready. " He eats dirt!" muttered the Ghulám, Muhammad Beg, in reply. " He has not got a horse, and if he had one, he has taken so much of the forbidden liquor that he could no more sit up in his saddle than his soul could walk over Jehannum on the bridge of Sirát."

I rode out of Gez feverish and aching in every limb, and no wonder, for a more pestilential jungle-den could hardly be imagined than that village. The inhabitants admitted that with them the life of man was but two score and ten years, and the stagnant air choked by mountains to the south and a great forest all around bore witness to their words. We rode first for a mile due south through mud a yard deep; we then came to the Tehrán and Astarábád road running east and west. On this road occur at intervals patches of *sangfarsh*, or " pavement," being portions of the great *Via Strata* made for nearly 400 miles throughout the Caspian Provinces by Abbás the Great. For sixteen miles we progressed very pleasantly by this road, passing through a noble forest, in which the beech, oak, and elm, were recognized by us as old friends, among a multitude of trees with whose appearance we were not familiar. We then came to a place called Kurd Mahallah, where there is the shrine of an Imámzádah, with an ostrich egg suspended over the tomb. All around is a vast cemetery and the indistinct traces of a world-old city, where Kai Khusrau is said to have resided when he was blind, according to which legend the name of the place should be Kúr-Mahallah— " Blind-town "—but the Persians care no more for etymology than do the English.

We rode on for three farsakhs, or fourteen miles, more to another Imámzádah, called *Kafsh-girí* — " Place of leaving your slippers "—and a more appropriate name, I am bound to say, was never given. Here all semblance of a road vanished, and had we had slippers on, and been in our sober senses, we should have replaced them with the highest and thickest waterproof boots in our possession, or assuredly we should have left them deep in the most grasping, covetous slime that ever defrauded poor traveller of his foot-gear. Above and around us was a dense jungle, which closed behind us as we forced our way through. Below were pools of water, swamps more or less treacherous, and occasionally a brawling little stream that seemed to chafe as much as ourselves at not finding its way out of the wood. For seven weary miles this continued, and as our poor beasts had already come more than thirty, they would have given in, but for the spur and whip. As we drew near Astarábád a few large patches of cultivation appeared, but the solitude of the region as regards man may be imagined from the fact that at this short distance from one of the chief cities of the Persian empire, and, *pour ainsi dire*, on the high road to it, lay a huge wild boar, who barred the way with an indifference to our approach which showed that he had never been taught to respect the human face divine. T—— was so excited at the sight of the hog that he half jumped, half tumbled, over his horse's head, and discharged two barrels loaded with small shot at him. Fane and I also dismounted, and the monster, after looking for a moment as if he meant to charge, went off into the thickest part of the jungle, where we followed

him in vain. He was the very *beau idéal* of a wild
pig, with enormous tusks. We entered Astarábád at
7 P.M., having been eleven hours and twenty minutes
en route. One of the baggage horses, with my gun-
cases and other valuable articles, was left behind, and
it was to no purpose that I told four of our escort of
matchlockmen to go for it with a fresh horse. They
said, " We go, sir !" but they went not.

Meantime, no sooner had we entered the town
than the gates were shut, a precaution observed
everywhere in Persia, but doubly necessary at Astarábád, where the Turkuman hordes often carry off
prisoners from under, nay, sometimes from within,
the walls of the city. We rode through ruinous
heaps a quarter of a mile to the house of M. Goussif,
the Russian Consul, who hospitably received us. I
was so tired and ill that I was glad of a Turkish bath,
and no sooner was I out of it than I discovered that
no one had gone for the missing baggage, and,
further, that no one would go for fear of the Turkumans. On this I ordered my horse to be saddl·d.
and said I should go myself, when my servant Riza.
took heart of grace, and declared he would go, which

he accordingly did, with the ghulám of the Mission and four artillerymen. It was not a very pleasant expedition, for it was quite on the cards that they might be captured by the prowling Turkumans ; but they performed their duty very well, and found the tired-out baggage horse two miles from the city. As for the muleteers, they were not to be seen, and Riza hallooed for them for some time in vain. At last, recognizing his voice, they crept out of a deep thicket, in which they had ensconced themselves, and before midnight they were all safe in Astarábád.

CHAPTER III.

Astarábád—The Pile of Heads—Return to Gez Bandar—Ashraf—
Farahábád, the Deserted City—Tears of the Persians—Sárí—
Fírúzkúh—Return to Tehran.

We stopped four days in Astarábád, which deserves
a much longer stay, for on many accounts it is an
extremely interesting place.   Around the city goes on
a continual struggle between the nomade tribes of the
Turkumans and the more civilized settled Persian
race.   Not a day passes that some deed of blood is
not done, or some plundering foray or retributive
expedition undertaken.   Thus a country, which ought
to be a smiling garden, is made a vast jungle, in
which—

> Savage tigers watch their hapless prey,
> And savage men more murderous far than they.

Another point of interest is that Astarábád may be

called the cradle of the present dynasty of Persia. Agha Muhammad Sháh, the founder of the dynasty, drew his chief strength from this region, and the Ak Kalah, or "white castle" of the Kájárs, now ruined, is but three miles from Astarábád.

The appearance of the city, too, is very striking, and, in Persia at least, I have seen no such picturesque town. It is built on lofty ground, and commands a view over a vast plain, with a line of beautifully wooded hills to the south, overtopped by lofty mountains running from south-east to south-west, and, at the time of our visit, white with snow. A dense forest extends on the west to the sea, which glitters in the horizon, being about twenty miles off, as the crow flies, from the city wall. In this jungle, at regular intervals all the way to the sea, the Amír Nizam, the first prime-minister of the present Shah, caused towers to be built, and garrisoned, each by a detachment of fifty men. There was one in particular, called Kwájah Nafas, "Merchants' Rest," which was a great check on the marauders. But, when the Amír was put to death, all these places went to ruin; and of 6,000 túmáns which he sent to be expended in repairing the walls of Astarábád, all but 2,000 went into the capacious pockets of the governor.

From the eastern wall of the city, there is an enchanting view, first to the village of Muhammad-ábád, about four miles off, marked by a tall white tower, then on to several lakes, close to which appear the dark tents of the Turkumans. Further again, the river Gurgán, "wolf river," shines out at intervals ; and still further to the east is a vast sandy plain, extending to Khaivak. At the time of my visit, the whole landscape had a lovely purple hue from a flowering, but then leafless bush of that colour, forming excellent cover for pheasants, which may be killed close under the walls. The shape of the city is oblong. It has three gates : the Sháhrúd Gate to the east; that of Chihal Dukhtar, or "Forty Virgins," so called from a raid made by the Turkumans, in which forty maidens were captured, to the south ; and the Mazanderún Gate to the west, on which side, too, is a ridge running out for a quarter of a mile to an eminence about 200 feet high, which has once been fortified, and looks as if had been made for an acropolis. The wall is about a farsakh, or three miles and a half, in circuit. It is very dilapidated, and in many places the gaps are filled up with bushes. The ditch, forty feet deep, must have been once a formidable obstacle to assailants; but it is now full of bushes, and the descent is so gentle that any one could cross it. The Turkumans could at any time take Astarábád with the greatest ease. A place was pointed out to me where some of them, a short time before, had entered, and by which, after breaking into several houses and stealing a horse and other property, they retired with impunity.

On the 19th of April, I went all over the city. Once thriving and populous, I found it half deserted. The governor, the Mulk Ará, "ornament of the country," had just been deposed, and there was an interregnum until Muhammad Wali Khán Kájár Beglerbegi, the new governor, could arrive. Meantime affairs were administered by Mirza Muhammad Khán, the Foreign-office agent, called the Bályús, and I called on him just when his commission to act temporarily as governor arrived. Every one stood up, and the happy Bályús fluttered from his seat with a radiant countenance to receive the Shah's autograph, put it on his head, then on his eyes, and finally kissed it with great fervour. From the house of the Bályús, I went to that of the Kalántar, or mayor, a greybeard, who remembered Agha Muhammad Sháh, and who had been to Khaiva, Merv, and Bukhárá. He told me that half the Sháh's tribe of Kájárs was settled at Astarábád, and half at Merv. His residence, and that of the Bályús, were miserable places for men of rank, not so good as the houses of small tradesmen in England. The streets to them were paved with sharp, jagged stones, not at all agreeable to the feet of man or beast. It was a pleasure, however, to see in many places fine trees, under the delightful shade of which groups of men lounged and smoked. The trunks of two of these trees must have been more than twenty feet in circumference.

In paying these visits I had seen the bazars, wretched places indeed, situated about the centre of the city, where is also the principal mosque, a poor structure. I now rode to the south-eastern angle of the town, where stands the governor's palace. The

date over the door sets forth that it was built by
Agha Muhammad Shâh, in the year of the Hijrah,
1206, A.D. 1791, and the Kalántar could say that he
"minded the bigging o't." It must have been a very
pretty villa, with painted vestibules, and courts full
of orange-trees and fountains. It was when I saw
it the most disgraceful place for a governor's palace
that was, perhaps, ever seen. The artillerymen and
cavalry had stabled their horses in the best part of
the house, and had made a target of the Nakkárah
Khánah, or guard-room; only two rooms remained
habitable. In one the daughter of the Mulk Ará, wife
of Ismail Mirza, had lived, and in the other, in which
a splendid stained-glass window, and some other
decorations, still survived, the governor had held his
levées. The orange-trees had suffered from the
unusual severity of the winter, but one, upwards of
twenty feet high, was in full leaf.

The most curious thing we saw was the Ambár,
or "prison," a place about ten feet square, in which
Turkumans, when taken, are kept before execution.
In one corner of this den were piled forty-one human
heads stuffed with straw. After decapitation, the

scalp and skin of the face are taken off, stuffed
with straw, and dried in the sun. Only three were
heads of chiefs. One was the head of Altazar, chief
of about fifty families. This man used to trade with
the people of Astarábád, but, when he thought himself aggrieved, he was in the habit of forbidding his
tribe to deal, until his wrong was redressed. On one
occasion the governor of Astarábád, wishing to make
a display of prowess, chapáoed the village of Altazar,
and carried off all he had, to the value of 6,000
túmáns. Hereupon the neighbouring Turkuman
tribes made a grand foray into Persian territory, and
carried off twice as much as Altazar had lost. On
this the governor restored what he had taken, and got
back what had been taken from him, but he secretly
harboured a grudge against Altazar, and had him
waylaid as he was returning from a visit to the
Russian commodore at Ashurádah. Altazar was
seventy years old, but his age did not save him, and
indeed to look at the grizzled red locks one would
have supposed him much younger.

Another head was that of Kárá Khán, a celebrated
freebooter, whose fate was more deserved. Look-

ing at these ghastly relics, I said, "Is this Islám, not to bury the remains of the dead?" The keeper of the Ambár replied, "Other men's remains ought to be buried, but as for Turkumans, this is the proper fate for them." I said, "Not so, we are all the children of Adam. God makes no distinction between us." As I left the palace, I observed a cannon in one of the courts, and some one said that Turkumans were sometimes blown from it. This reminded me of the story in Holmes' *Shores of the Caspian*, in which the governor of Astarábád is represented as being amused at the playful insolence of his son, a boy of fourteen, one of whose youthful pranks was, without orders, to blow away a few Turkumans before his father had got out of bed.

I went next to the ruined fort of Muhammad Husain Khán Kájár, who was governor of Astarábád in the time of Nádir Sháh, and built a strong tower near the middle of the eastern wall of the city. Nádir, suspecting that he meant to revolt, wrote to him to say he had heard that the new fort had taken so many months to build, but that he would not give him as many days

to level it. Down it of course came, and I stepped
over its ruins, which extend about 200 yards in
length, with mounds in some places forty feet
high.

While I was riding about the town information
was brought to the authorities that a strong body of
Turkumans were out on a foray. Hereupon Sulaimán Khán Kájár, who commanded the artillery at
Astarábád, mounted and went out to reconnoitre,
with a couple of hundred horsemen. These de-
monstrations on the part of the Persians are generally useless, for the Turkumans have so many
friends in the town, that they are kept apprised of
every move. Thus some time before, when the
Zanjánah regiment came to Astarábád, the Mulk
Ará ordered them to surprise the village of the
Daus Turkumans ten miles off. The regiment was
furnished with guides, and a number of horsemen
joined it from the city; but the guides led the troops
out of the way, and made them march thirty-five
miles instead of ten, so that when they reached the
Gurgán river, they were disorganized with fatigue
and thirst. In that state they were charged by

seventy Turkuman horsemen, who cut down Ibrahím Khán, a really gallant officer, and two other men of note, and killed and wounded twenty soldiers, on which the rest took to flight, so that it may be truly said a thousand fled at the rebuke of ten.

The slave trade goes on briskly at Astarábád, and I was told that five hundred Kalpak girls had been sold there lately for from ten to forty túmáns each. Some of these unfortunates were brought to Tehran.

Our last evening at Astarábád was devoted to a visit to the hill outside the Mazandarún Gate. As this eminence is only a quarter of a mile from the wall of the city, it might seem no great exploit to walk there and drink a cup of tea. Nevertheless, such is the neighbourly feeling prevailing in these parts that the Russian Consul thought it necessary to turn out with every man he could muster, armed to the teeth. As a suitable diversion we set up a piece of paper and practised at it with our revolvers at thirty yards. Fane put one ball out of five right through the centre. I had only a single shot, which struck the paper ten inches from the centre; and the Russian did not hit the mark once.

At 3 P.M. on the 20th of April we left Astarábád
for Kafshgírí, which we reached at six o'clock, and
alighted at the new and neat house of Rahím Khán,
one of the richest landed proprietors in the province.
The family of the Khán were all at their Aylák, or
summer quarters, a beautiful spot in the mountains
three farsakhs off. Kafshgírí is a pretty village,
which can turn out a hundred horsemen. To the
north is an isolated pyramidal hill, very green and
beautiful, and also most useful as a look-out station.
A watchman is always on duty there, and a few days
before my arrival notice of a Turkuman raid having
been given, fifty of the Kafshgírí people mounted
and captured seven of the freebooters, who were lying
in durance close to where we were. Their scalps,
stuffed with straw, were probably added to the heap
in the *Ambár* at Astarábád. There were mulberry
plantations at Kafshgírí, and about 2,000 acres sown
with wheat, barley, and other grains.

We left Kafshgírí at 9 A.M. on the 21st of .April,
and reached Gez at 4.30 P.M., having been seven
hours and a half in getting over six farsakhs. We
were, however, unable to leave our baggage on ac-

count of the damage from Turkuman robbers, and the mud was so deep that we moved like snails. We saw many hawks and eagles on the road, and a wolf at which T—— shot and missed. Our ears were gladdened on this march by the blithe cry of the cuckoo, which we had not heard since we left England.

Zu-'l-fikár Khán breakfasted with us on the 22nd, with his usual air of cool, listless effrontery. He said a tiger had killed one of his cows two nights before, and that his *Mír i Shikár*, or chief huntsman, sate up for him, but he did not return to the carcase. He also mentioned that the Turkumans had just carried off six men from the coast near Ashraf. We mounted at 10 A.M., and rode briskly to Gez Bandar, where we went on board the *Vodka*, which steamed over to Ashurádah. We then bid adieu to Commodore Roudakoff and all our kind Russian friends, and, returning to Gez Bandar, landed at 5.15 P.M. While we were waiting for horses Fane's revolver was stolen, and, of course, every one accused everybody of the delinquency, as was only natural, where all were so capable of the theft. At 5.30 we set off at a sharp trot for Galukah, about two farsakhs, or

seven miles, distant. The path led at first through a
dense, tigerish jungle, with reeds twenty feet high,
the very place to expect in the dusk of the evening a
rush and a roar, which those who have heard it once
do not easily forget. After half a farsakh we reached
the small village of Naukhandah, and a farsakh and
a half more brought us to Galúkah, passing at three-
quarters of a farsakh Hastayah, and at one quarter
of a farsakh more the hamlet of Laiwan. The road
was astoundingly bad. In some places, indeed, there
was no road at all, but a series of swamps and rice-
fields, in which the horses sank to their knees. Had
we not had guides we never could have found our
way. We reached Galúkah at 7.30 P.M., and were
lodged in a comfortable cottage. In this day's journey
we passed from the province of Astarábád to the
more settled and cultivated one of Mazandarún.

I rose early on the 23rd, and wrote a Persian
letter to Zú'l-fikár Khán intimating that, if Fane's
pistol was not found, his shadow would be lessened
at Tehrán. I wrote also on the same subject to
Commodore Roudakoff and the Russian Consul at
Astarábád, who compelled Zú'l-fikár to find the

pistol, which, in fact, he did very easily, as he had it himself, having no doubt instructed his men to make a mistake about it on the first opportunity. As soon as the pistol was recovered it was sent to Tehrán by a Persian courier, who took it on to Resht, and it was not till October that I obtained it and restored it to Fane.

The Russian consul had eulogized to us the beauty of the women of Galúkah, but we were not fortunate in discovering any extraordinary charms. We started for Ashraf at 10.30 A.M. on the 23rd of April, and reached Ashraf, distant five farsakhs, at 3.30 P.M. The road for the greater part of the way was Sháh Abbás' causeway, once a noble work, but now ruined, and full of deep holes and ruts. In places the mud was a yard deep, but a magnificent road might easily be made on the foundation of the old causeway. The scenery was perfect of its kind. On the right was a plain, from ten to fifteen miles in breadth, covered with trees and rich verdure, interspersed with villages and cornfields. On the left, at two or three miles' distance, a succession of beautiful hills, wooded to the top, with here and there a hamlet crowning an eminence, ran parallel to the road. I observed one remarkably fine villa, belonging to Mirza Muhammad Khán Kulbádi. The fields we came tô were surrounded with hedges like those of England, ditched and staked. Men were ploughing and breaking clods in them, and a few women were also at work, while nightingales were singing in every thicket, and the cuckoo's note was heard in the distance. Our day's journey would have been a most agreeable one, had it not been spoiled by rain towards the close.

Ashraf is a ruined town, which in the time of Sháh Abbás the Great extended a mile farther than it now does to the east, to a bridge, near which are remains of a magnificent palace, called the Chashmah Imárat, or " Palace of Fountains." To the north-west is another palace of vast size, once united to the Chashmah Imárat by walls and a paved way, along which used to flow a clear stream, with tiny cascades at intervals over stone slabs curved to represent scales, so that there was a continual shimmer from the water as it fell. This palace is called the Chihal Situn, or " Forty Columns," and in it is a garden of eight acres planted with the most magnificent cypresses and orange-trees, and surrounded by a wall thirty feet high, and from four to six feet thick, which springs from a mound of earth also about thirty feet high. On the outer side of this mound grow many beautiful shrubs. At regular intervals in the wall are round bastions, in which soldiers and attendants were lodged. Adjoining this garden to the east is a smaller one of three acres, called the Bágh i Tappé, or " Garden of the Mound," planted with orange-trees, and having in the centre the Hammám, or warm baths. On the western side of the Chihal Sitún is the Bágh i Harím, or " Garden of the Seraglio." Here the royal ladies were lodged, in a building covering more than an acre, with very massive walls, but now so ruined that no idea can be formed of the plan. The seraglio again is connected with another palace to the north by a long line of garden, through which flowed a similar stream to that coming from the Chashmah Imárat. This northern palace is called the Sáhib i Zamán, or " Lord of the Age," and is a most tasteful building, of an oblong shape, three stories high, with arched

windows, and a very fine arched doorway facing the
seraglio.   It is now a ruin, and many shrubs grow
out of the walls.   Were the Chihal Sitún restored,
the Sáhib i Zamán ought to be kept in its present
most picturesque state, for, seen from the eastern wall
of the Chihal Sitún, nothing can be imagined more
beautiful.

Some miserable wretches, when we visited the
Sáhib i Zamán, had taken up their lodging in it, and
heaps of filth rendered the ascent to the upper stories
anything but pleasant.   At the four corners of the
second story are little boudoirs, about six feet square,
which are painted with love-scenes.   The pictures are
now blackened and defaced in such a manner that one
can but just make out that they were something in
the style of Greuze or Watteau.

The entrance to the large garden of the Chihal
Sitún is by a ruined arch opening into an oblong
enclosure of about two acres in extent, round which
guards were posted.   Over the arch was the Nakkárah
Khánah, " Kettle-drum or Guard Room."   In the
garden we observed many women digging up roots to
eat with their rice, for the famine was sore in the

land. The cypresses of the Chihal Sitún are more
than sixty feet high, and eight or nine feet in circumference, while the orange-trees are upwards of twenty-
five feet high and proportionately thick. The gardener
said all the trees were planted by Sháh Abbás, so that
they must be 250 years old. The palace in the
centre of the garden, built by Sháh Abbás, was burnt
down, and the present pavilion, which, in its turn, is
crumbling to decay, was built by Agha Muhammad,
or, according to others, by Nádir Sháh. There are
two wings two stories high, with four rooms in each,
and between these wings is a large room open at the
sides, and supported by twelve pillars. In front is a
tank from sixty to eighty feet square, filled now with
innumerable frogs, which chant the *Threnema* of
departed greatness with fifty-chorus power. It must
be admitted that the centre pavilion is quite unworthy
of the garden and the noble wall and towers that
surround it. A little care would render the garden a
real paradise, for nowhere in the world, perhaps, are
to be seen such cypresses and orange-trees, nowhere
is water of dazzling clearness more abundant, and on
no more level ground could an ever-verdant sward be

more easily maintained. As it is, huge weeds grow
everywhere in the garden, particularly one like the
lily-of-the-valley in leaf, which they call *tasigayá*,
and say is poisonous.   I was pleased, too, to shake
hands with my old English friends the nettle and
thistle, though they had rather a foreign look, and
introduced themselves under the names of *gazná* and
kardak.   Poisonous as some of the plants were, the
women who were digging for roots among them were
in no danger of being deceived.   The Persians are
very skilful in the use of simples, and I was often
struck with the numbers of people who resorted to
the Mission Garden at Tehran for herbs, and at the
facility with which they selected from among tufts of
weeds those with medicinal properties.

It was probably in the Palace of Forty Pillars that
the great Abbás, in 1627, received Sir Dodmore
Cotton, the English Ambassador, and feasted his
stomach with rich viands, and his eyes with dishes
and goblets of gold.   It was there, too, in all likeli-
hood, that that "most pragmatical pagan," the
Persian Minister, did woefully undo all the impression made on the King by the arrival of the English,

and by glozing words defraud the valorous Sir Robert Sherley of his due. Some of the interviews may, however, have taken place in the Chashmah Imárat, where the fountain, whence the palace is named, is clear as diamonds, and springs up naturally in inexhaustible abundance. In hot weather this place must have been a delicious retreat, though it could not save Sherley or Cotton from the miasma of Mazandarún, to which, in a few months after the interview with Abbás, they both fell victims.

After rambling over the palaces in the town, and admiring the beautiful woods on the hills, at the foot of which the ruins are situated — woods so near that the roar of the tiger and the panther is constantly heard from them at night by the palace-keepers — we set out by a well-made road for a palace on a height, at the distance of about half a mile from Ashraf. The palace is called Safiábád, from the grandson and successor of Abbás the Great, Sháh Safi, a sanguinary tyrant, who stabbed his favourite queen, and built this delightful place for his favourite daughter. The road gradually slopes up from Ashraf till it reaches the foot of a hill about

700 feet high, when the ascent becomes more severe. At the foot of the hill is the Nakkárah Khánah, and rooms for guards, all in ruins. From this the way up is paved, and for half the distance mounts at a gradient of 30°. The road then changes to a very narrow path, between banks ten feet high, and goes at a steep angle to the palace. The building stands north and south, and there is a two-storied house for the captain of the guard at the entrance of the court which leads to it. The site on which the palace is built is a square piece of ground of about two acres, with a gradual but rather steep slope to the north and west, and a precipice to the east. On the south the hill is connected by a narrow ridge with the mountains. There can be no doubt that, originally, the hill was much higher, and that the top has been cut down and levelled. The palace is square, and three stories high, with a grand centre hall, in which was a fountain. The building is massive, but the neglect of two centuries has ruined it, and the roof is gone. In front are some very fine cypresses, every one of which was notched and hacked. I complained of this wanton mischief, and was told that no one was

paid to protect the place, and, of course, no one cared what happened. For 10*l.* a year, they said, a saráidar might be engaged, who would prevent any further destruction. Water was originally brought from the mountains by an aqueduct, but this is broken and the supply cut off.

We sate for an hour at Safiábád, enjoying a panorama to which the world can supply few rivals. To the north, in front, extended a green level belt of country, about ten miles broad, from which curves forth the promontory of Miyán Kálih. This singular neck of land projects about fifteen miles into the Caspian, and is covered with jungle to the water's edge. There, are to be found innumerable beasts of prey—from the tiger to the wild cat—and game of all descriptions, so that, were a cordon of men and dogs to be formed across the peninsula where it leaves the mainland, and were the woods then beaten, there would be a battue that would astonish the most experienced sportsman. Beyond Miyán Kálih the sea sparkled in the distance, and to the right the harbour and shipping of Ashurádah were indistinctly visible. To the east a richly wooded country stretched far away to the forests of Astarábád, the town and palaces of Ashraf being the nearest objects in this direction. Behind us, on the south, were the mountains, and on the west a beautiful country, through which we were to pass on our homeward journey to Tehran. The sun had come out brightly after the showers of the morning, and the heat was that of an English summer, but tempered by a breeze that had kissed the snow on the lofty peaks to the south.

We lodged at Ashraf in a neat cottage, from which a bevy of fair women and girls were turned out to make room for us. In the centre of the largest room was an economical contrivance called a *Kursi*, which acts the part of an English fireplace. A cavity in the ground three feet deep is bricked round, and is covered by a square wooden seat. A charcoal fire is lighted below, and the family place themselves on the seat, and are toasted to a convenient warmth. In this cottage we received a visit from Ibrahím Khán, the temporary governor of Ashraf, a young fellow of twenty. He spoke much of the famine, and said the people were dying in great numbers, while others were selling their children. Wheat, he said, used to fetch, in Mazandarún, three kiráns a kharwár, or load, but it now sold for forty kiráns, and everything was dear in proportion. The Turkumans, too, were very troublesome, and had carried off five men in the last few days, and he was getting ready a *chapáo* to secure an equal number of Turkumans in order to effect an exchange. He said that after the death of Nádir Sháh, Ashraf was pillaged, and almost destroyed, by the Turkumans, and restored by Agha Muhammad Sháh, and again depopulated by the cholera. There were now only 1,200 families, and forty or fifty persons had died lately of the cholera. He spoke very contemptuously of the Russians, and declared they would not have a chance with the Persians, were the latter led by a good general like Nádir. "But now," he added, "there is no order, and the country is so depopulated that the wild beasts have become very troublesome. It is only a few days since two men were killed, and one wounded by tigers, who infest even the high roads." Yet this is the place to which Sháh Abbás moved a colony of seven thousand Armenians alone, to say nothing of Muhammadans.

At a quarter past one on the 24th of April, we were again *en route* for Nikah, a neat village belonging to Muhammad Khán Kulbádi, five farsakhs from Ashraf. Our horses this stage were the most miserable jades imaginable, and as the governor, Ibrahím Khán, pocketed the whole of the eight túmáns we payed as hire, the owners of the horses could neither feed their beasts nor themselves, and had we not had compassion on them, would have fainted by the way. We entered Nikah at 6 P.M., crossing, just before we reached the village, a river fifty yards broad, over which there is a good bridge.

From Nikah, at dawn on the 25th of April, we sent off our baggage south-west to Sárí, the capital of Mazandarún, and started ourselves in a north-westerly direction for Farahábád, interesting on account of a ruined palace in which Sháh Abbás the Great died in 1627 A.D. The poor villagers of Ashraf got those of Nikah to convey us on this stage, and themselves returned to their homes. This was a happy exchange for us, as we got capital horses, fresh and full of spirit. We left Nikah at 8 A.M., and got to Farahábád at 1 P.M. The road lay through

fields and swampy pastures, where there must be
wonderful duck and snipe shooting. We passed two
villages, and many herds and flocks. I found that
my horse jumped very well, and he went over a hedge
in a very creditable way, but the guide would go at a
rough trot, which exasperated Fane, though it did
not incommode me in the least. Presently the guide
lost his way in a seemingly interminable marshy
meadow, and we might have been unpleasantly "fixed,"
but that a native turned up, whom we immediately
pressed into our service, and carried on with us, till
we came to a broad deep river about twenty miles
from Nikah. The banks were perpendicular, and at
least thirty feet high, except at one place, where there
was a ferry. The boat, however, and the ferryman's
house were on the other side, and we had to bawl
long and sore before he heard us. At last he made
his appearance, and with him a dozen or so of
Kurdish children. Among these was a girl about
fourteen, a great beauty, and wonderfully well dressed
for such an outlandish place, in a white tunic and
veil and red trousers.

We crossed, one at a time, in the tiniest canoe

possible, which the least mismanagement would have upset. The water was about seven feet deep, and the current rapid ; the ferryman said a woman had been drowned in crossing a few days ago. Our horses swam over very well, and while they were being re-saddled, I took several shots at blue jays, which were very numerous at the place. The Persians have a superstition that this bird cannot be killed, and certainly, though I have often fired at them, I have never been able to kill one, which is annoying when one wants to confute a legend. From this stream Farahábád is three miles distant. It stands on a river about three miles from the Caspian. The first thing which meets the eye is a stone mosque with a low dome. North of this is an immense kárwánsarái and *rubát*, or monastery, enclosing what was once perhaps a garden, or court of three acres in extent. Beyond this are the huts of the fifty families which are now the entire population of this once flourishing place. Turning to the left, at the distance of a few hundred yards, is the palace in which the Great Abbás died. It very much resembles the Sáhib i Zamán at Ashraf, but is more massive. It stands in a walled enclosure, containing about six acres, at the entrance of which are the offices and baths. The building is now completely ruined, but there are some remains of painting, and some vaulted roofs which must have been very handsome.

After we had looked at the palace all the villagers assembled and besought us in the most piteous manner to represent their deplorable condition to the Sháh. They said that, two days before, the Turkumans had come up the river in three boats, with about twenty men in each boat, and had landed at 1 P.M., plundered and burnt a vessel, seized Yúsif, the Kadkhuda of the village, and nine others, and after binding them and notifying that they would accept túmáns 300 as ransom for the Kadkhuda, took them away. The Persians made no attempt at resistance as they were unarmed, and the Turku- mans had eight or ten matchlocks and as many swords. Ten days before that the Turkumans had landed, but did not carry off any prisoners. In all, however, they had taken one hundred captives from the coast. "Have pity on us," they added, "for the love of God, and inform the Sháh that unless

he send us aid we must fly to Astrakhan, or become
the property of the Turkumans." I said, "I will
represent your case to the Sháh, and I pity you from
my heart, but I am English, and I have no power
to aid you otherwise than by representing your mis-
fortunes to your own Government." "We will be
English subjects," they replied, "the subjects of any
one who will protect us. It is true the Sháh has
built a tower near this, but he has not put any
soldiers in it. Of what use, then, is the tower?"
I said what I could to soothe them and we then
turned our horses and rode towards Sárí. The road
crossed a grassy plain covered with bulrushes and
bushes, and very like an English common, and then
entered a most tigerish jungle, from which after six
miles it emerged at the village of Sháh Abbás
Khiyábán. We saw several jackals in this jungle.

We now again came upon the causeway of Abbás,
which ran as straight as a line to Sárí, the distance
being about six miles. The whole distance from
Nikah to Farahábád and thence to Sárí I should
reckon at from thirty-six to forty miles. Two miles
before reaching Sárí we entered a succession of pools

about a yard deep, which must be a serious obstacle after heavy rains. Tortoises were very numerous in these pools. The woods on either side were like those in Hertfordshire, only more swampy.

Súrí is conspicuous a long way off by a grove of magnificent cypresses. We were met as we entered the town by several farrashes, who took us to the Diwán Khánah, a neat building where the Governors hold their court. Sultán Husain Mirza, the eldest son of Mulk Ará, was there some time before our visit, and was succeeded by Ismail Mirza, his younger brother. At the time of our arrival there was an interregnum until the Shah's son, Masaud Mirza, the newly appointed Governor of Mazandarún, should arrive, with his deputy Mustafa Khán Afshar.

On the 26th of April we received a visit from Asadullah Mirza, a prince of the blood. He wore goggles and told me he was going to Ashurádah to consult the Russian doctor, as his sight was failing in consequence of ophthalmia. He seemed to be an intelligent man, and a great sportsman. He said he had often seen tigers when out shooting, and that Miyán Kálih was the place where they were most

numerous. He spoke of the famine, and told me
he recollected rice selling at three kiráns, less than
three shillings, the ass-load, and wheat at seven
kiráns, and that rice now fetched forty kiráns and
wheat one hundred kiráns the kharwár. After him
came the Kalántar, who was a man of few words,
and indeed said little but *Chashm,** *chashm,* "Eyes,
eyes," at the same time shutting his own, and grin-
ning sardonically. The last visitor was Abbás Kuli
Mirza, who struck me as one of the most intelligent
Persians I had ever met. He spoke of the mines of
Persia, and joined me in regretting that no effort was
made to work them. His brother, he said, when
Governor of Astarábád, had offered to the Persian
Government to work the coal-mines near Sháhrúd,
as the Russian commodore offered to buy all the coal
that could be raised. But the Persian Government
would not allow him to touch the mines, neither
would it work them itself. The Prince also said
that he had visited the silver, copper, and lead mines
at Kubad, in Mazandarún, with several scientific

---

* Short for " On my eyes be it ! " a polite form of assenting to
what is said.

officers, and that there could be no doubt of the importance of working those mines. He told me he had often used the bark of willow as a substitute for quinine with excellent effect.

In the evening I walked to the Bágh i Sháh, or royal garden, and the Jahán Numá, a ruined villa, built by Agha Muhammad Sháh. In the garden are rows of beautiful cypresses. Next day we returned the call of Abbás Kuli Mirza, whose mother is sister to the Sháh's mother, and whose father is also a near relative of the Sháh. This descendant and cousin of kings lives in a house like that of a well-to-do English labourer. He has, nevertheless, the courtesy of a prince, and when some friends came in, as he had not chairs to offer to them, he immediately descended from the chair on which he was sitting and sate on the ground. We went next to the house of Asadullah Mirza, which was more wretched still. This prince, however, knew how to behave, and showed not the slightest discomposure when Fane upset the fire of the pipe all over his best carpet. He said he had two places opened in his arms to relieve the weakness of his vision!

From the prince's we went to a sort of nursery
ground, where I bought five large orange-trees for
four kiráns, and ten smaller trees for three kiráns
each. After this we went over the Ark or Citadel,
in part of which we were living, and a ruinous part
it was. Two or three rooms only were habitable,
and there were the remains of a fine hall with a
handsome stained-glass window. In the courtyard
were four magnificent chenár trees, at least ninety
feet high, and the only date-tree I had seen in those
parts. The building stands about south-east and
north-west, and going in the former direction, and
passing from the garden to the right, is the Government House. First there is an arched summer-
room, dark and cool. Then comes a garden, with a
two-storied pavilion in the centre, and also a three-
storied tower, with stained-glass windows. In one
room are very pretty pictures of princes and ladies.
The tower, ninety feet high, commands a fine view
over a lovely country. All the roof is covered with
coloured tiles brought from Resht by Agha Muhammad Shāh, or the elder Mulk Ará, son of Fath Ali
Shāh. The ladies' apartments are well built, but

everything at the time of my visit was filthy and neglected.

Sárí is a modern town, built near the ruins of one of the oldest towns in Persia of the same name. To that place, says the legend, some 3,000 years before Christ, were brought all the nobles of Persia by Afrasiáb, and there they were detained as prisoners. Jonas Hanway speaks of four fire-temples, 120 feet high, which remained to his day, and must have been very ancient. At present Sárí is remarkable for nothing but frogs and fever. Short as our stay was, I had the tank in front of our room cleared of frogs, and they were taken out literally in bucketfuls.

We left Sárí at 8 A.M. on the 28th of April, and reached Aliábád, called four farsakhs from Sárí, at noon. The road runs west by north to Aliábád, and then turns south. About three miles from Sárí we came to a swamp, in which the Ghulám's mule fell down, and was dragged out with difficulty. Fane got through triumphantly, but I had to dismount, and got across with the help of two men, not without a wetting. This was the worst part of the journey,

27—2

but there was half a mile of deep swamp afterwards. The Khiyabán, or Causeway of Abbás, extends to past Aliábád, but is so villanously bad that it is much better to avoid it until within a mile of Aliá-bád, when it is as good as an English turnpike road. Aliábád is a village of fakirs, who live in wretched hovels, and assail you with the cry of " Hakk ! Hakk ! "   The only healthy place is at the cemetery, or Imámzádah, a building not inferior to and with very much the air of a country churchyard in England. All round are thickets of the box-tree, from ten to fifteen feet high, and the bright red flowers of the Judas-tree were very conspicuous.   The gateway of the cemetery is the place where travellers rest.   It is black with smoke, and filthy with the loitering vaga-bonds who house there day after day.   I disturbed from the steps some horrible mendicants who were roosting there.   They told us all sorts of lies about the road.   This place would never do to stop in at night, for, to say nothing of the filth, it is open at the sides, though roofed.

After leaving Aliábád, which we did at 2.40 P.M., the road becomes very beautiful, and at the third

mile enters a very remarkable green valley between
wooded hills so perpendicular that it seems as if the
hollow had originally been the bed of a river. We
reached Shírgáh, which is three farsakhs from Aliábád,
at 5.30 P.M. Towards Shírgáh, "Lion's Den," the
road begins to ascend, and crosses the Tálár River,
eighty feet broad, by a good bridge, after which it
mounts steep hills. The forest around is indescri-
bably beautiful. Apple, medlar, pear, mulberry,
cherry, and walnut trees grow wild, and the vine
everywhere clusters from tree to tree. The box-
tree rises to the height of thirty feet, and many
other evergreen shrubs fill up the intervals between
the ash, the tulip tree, and other giants of the forest.

Our things did not come up till 10 P.M., having
been fourteen hours *en route*, consequently we had
to be for six hours on the mud floor of a miserable
hovel, with little amusement but the fleas. It was
cold, too, and damp, for the rain had set in. I
passed the time in getting up the statistics of the
village. There were, I was told, ten families and
forty persons, including children, in Shírgáh. They
cultivated sixteen acres of rice, each acre yielding

eight kharwárs, and each kharwár bringing at the then famine prices twenty kiráns, but in ordinary seasons not more than five. The tax to government was 110 túmáns, but 40 túmáns in addition were taken from these unfortunate people, who represented themselves as ground down by the extortion of the officials. Indeed, the bare walls of the mud huts, the scanty clothing and thin faces of the inhabitants, confirmed their tale of distress, but they had riches which could not be taken from them : they were beautiful themselves, and the scenery around was beautiful. The young men were tall and well-made, and the girls, who were stamping out the rice and husking it, were prettier than many who are thought fair in Belgravia.

We started from Shírgáh at 10 A.M. on the 29th of April. Great were the rejoicings among the children of Tahmásp Kuli, the old Kadkhuda of the village, when I divided three kiráns among them. In return, Tahmásp gave me a caution as to mounting his horse, "which," said he, "has a trick of taking fright, when he sometimes casts his rider to the ground." The said horse was brought

alongside of a high terrace on which I was standing,
and I was on his back in a twinkling from that
convenient place. I had expected that he would
act according to what was told me of his delinquen-
cies, but he did nothing but tremble most violently.
After descending the lofty hill on which Shírgáh is
perched, we passed through a beautiful pasture-
ground, like a park, in which many horses were
feeding. Here my steed became troublesome,
neighing, fuming, and curvetting. Presently we
descended a very steep place, where I dismounted
and remounted without anything particular. A mile
or so farther on we began to get into rough ground.
At the end of a farsakh we entered on a series of
ascents and descents, with ruts a yard deep, great
stones piled confusedly together, and treacherous
beds of ooze and clay, often with a precipice of
from fifty to five hundred feet on the right, at the
bottom of which the turbid Tálár River swept furiously
along. What the meaning of Tálár applied to a
river may be I know not, but in general the word
signifies the high platform raised on poles, which
is the usual sleeping-place in this land of musquitoes.

For the whole of the stage from Shírgáh, and throughout the succeeding one, that is, for thirty miles, the
road passes up the valley of the Tálár, a valley which
seldom exceeds half a mile in breadth, and is shut in
by lofty mountains clothed with an unbroken forest.

After we had gone about two farsakhs, one of
our guides came up to me with an animated look,
caught my arm, and pointed off the road. Turning
my head, I saw a wild hog, about seventy yards off,
staring at me, with several of his brethren a little
farther off, indistinctly visible amongst the brush-
wood. I dismounted in a great hurry, and in my
excitement let off my rifle before I had brought it
to my shoulder. Off scampered immediately not
only the solitary "Ettrick Shepherd," but a dozen
or two of his friends, who broke cover at the sound.
By this time I had quite forgotten all about the
Kadkhuda's caution, and was going to mount as if
his horse was my oldest equine acquaintance, when
all of a sudden, with a tremendous kick and a bound,
he sent the man who was holding him sprawling,
and went off with me at speed standing with one
foot in the stirrup, and the other in the air. In

this graceful fashion I went for about fifty yards,
when, getting amongst the trees, and not being able
to get my leg over the saddle, which had a great
bundle tied to its croupe, I jumped down. My
steed was caught, but having once succeeded in
baffling me, he gave me infinite trouble, and such
a blow in the face with his obstinate head as almost
stunned me.

For the last two farsakhs to Zíráb, which is
about eighteen miles from Shírgáh, the road passes
beside rice-fields, the miasma from which is poisonous
in the extreme. Men were ploughing in mud up
to their thighs and the haunches of the animals,
and I saw a girl with bare legs treading the rice,
with the water reaching to her calves and a bitter
cold wind blowing. We reached Zíráb at 4.30 P.M.,
and found the post-house to be a vile, dirty hole,
like the place cursed by the Scotch laird, where
there was "neither man's meat, nor horse meat,
nor place to lie down." We had several times had
threatenings of fever, and how we escaped it in that
pestilential den I could not imagine. Were the
post-house built higher up from the swamp, things

would be better; but the cultivation of rice ought to be forbidden by law in Mazandarún, for from April to November there is scarcely an individual in the province who is not ill with fever; many die, and, were it not that numbers escape to the hills, the whole population would perish.

I rose, on the morning of the 30th of April, cold, aching, and miserable, with the prospect of a stage which the Russian Consul had described to us in his *Notes of the Way*, as " un chemin horriblement mauvais et- extremément dangereux ! " Still, Zíráb was not a place to linger in, and, however bad what lay before us, it was a comfort to leave that nest of filthy hovels at the brink of a fetid swamp. At 9.30 A.M. we mounted. My steed, the same who had plagued me the day before, was held by two men, but he plunged violently, gave me a great blow in the eye, and ran back twenty yards, till he was brought up by the wall. With this agreeable start, and a row with a mob of mendicants, whose importunities it was impossible to satisfy, we went on. It rained and thundered the whole day till we got to Surkh Rubát, which is five farsakhs from Zíráb. The road is

pithily described by the natives as *sar bálá, sar
páin,* "head up, head down," being a series of ascents
and descents, sometimes along a mere ledge of
slippery clay, with a precipice of 100 feet under your
nose. Our mules fell repeatedly, and my servant
Riza had a roll, which did not improve his clothing or
his temper; but no one was hurt. As for me, the
blow I had in my eye at starting was a caution not to
dismount, which I recollected better than the advice
of the old Kadkhuda.

About a farsakh before reaching Surkh Rubát, we
passed on our left some magnificent rocks, from 1,200
to 1,500 feet high, that frowned over the right bank
of the Tálár River, which here raged along puckered into
innumerable wrinkles, and looking more like whipped
syllabub than reasonable water. We had crossed
from the right bank to the left, about half way, by a
good bridge. We reached Surkh Rubát, "Red
Monastery," at 3 P.M. The place is but a small
hamlet, but the post-house is much better than that
at Zíráb, and was built by the postmaster at his own
expense, whereupon the Shahábu'l Mulk, the post-
master-general, put in another man, who resides at

Tehran, and sucks up all the profits. Tired and
feverish as I was, and dosed with calomel, I could
not help listening to the poor postmaster's complaints,
remembering always a speech that was made to me
by an old man at Tehran, who, after watching me for
an hour without saying a word, while I was being
victimized with the tedious, thousandth-time-repeated
story of the most notorious grievance-monger at the
Mission, said suddenly, "Mashállah! you are fit to
rule in Persia; you hear what men have to say!"

May's first morning dawned on me drinking
Epsom salts, and resolving on a halt, as we were now
clear of the forests of Mazandarún, and consequently
beyond the fever-region. After reading the *Edinburgh
Review*, I proposed a walk to Fane, and we set off on
the Fíruzkúh road, till we got to a ruined tower.
Into this we clambered, wondered at the strong
masonry, and decided that it was very ancient. The
only garrison that appeared was an enormous lizard.
About three farsakhs from this tower, in the direction
of Fírúzkúh, is a remarkable double peak, on which
are the remains of a fortress called the *Kalah i Dev i
Sufid*, "the Castle of the White Demon," being the

same white demon that Rustam, the Persian Hercules, slew somewhere in this district. I suppose that the Turkumans once held this country, and are the demons of the legend. Above Surkh Rubát is a very picturesque village, about half way up a mountain some 2,500 feet high. Fane and one of the French Mission went there on a sporting expedition, killed nothing, but were sorely discomfited by bugs. When out with their guns, the Frenchman would carry his at full cock, and Fane remonstrated, asking ironically, if he always carried his piece that way. "Mais certainement," said M. ——, "c'est la chasse !"

We left Surkh Rubát at 7 A.M. on the 2nd of May, and found the road stony at first, and then running by the edge of ravines. About three farsakhs from Surkh Rubát, we passed the Castle of the White Demon. There is a most romantic gorge in the mountains here, and as little appearance of a road as could well be imagined. Huge rocks approach to within twenty feet of one another, and between 'them flows a clear, rapid stream, about two feet deep. This is the road, and a most difficult one it must be, when fresh metal is laid on in the shape of a flood after heavy rains. About a mile beyond this we passed numbers of charcoal-burners, who, according to my theory, do as much injury to Persia as the Turkumans. In spite of the coal-mines which exist in every part of the Elburz, near Hamadán, and in many other places, the whole population of Persia warm their houses and cook their food with charcoal. Let any one, then, compute the amount of wood required to supply ten millions of people yearly with charcoal, and he will have an idea of the number of trees destroyed every year in Persia. My theory is that in former ages, in the time of Darius, for example, Persia was more wooded, and that the fall of rain was greater, and that as the destruction of the forests diminished the supply of rain, the decrease of vegetation and of atmospheric moisture went acting on one another in an increasing ratio, so that in many tracts neither trees are left, nor water. In a similar manner the woods on the Volga are being destroyed for fuel for the steamers, and, no doubt, this will produce a change in the climate of that region ere long.

At 9.45 we reached a ruined kárwánsarái, which

had once been a very fine building. Filth had accumulated in it to the depth of several feet. On the roof was a wretched donkey left to die of starvation. We had no corn to give it, and I could not make up my mind to shoot it. The crows came and perched near, waiting for the moment to pick out its eyes, and commence their horrid feast on the yet living animal. We went on again at 2.40 P.M., and got to Fírúzkúh, seven farsakhs from Surkh Rubát at 4.30 P.M. The road was a stony descent for nearly a farsakh, and then good and level, with turf in places to gallop on. Fírúzkúh, "Turquoise, or Fortunate Mountain," is a village with 100 houses, on the brink of a stream, over which frown perpendicular rocks 1,000 feet high. All the women turned out to look at us, and showed their faces very unconcernedly. Some were very good-looking, with rosy English complexions. I slept in a very good room built by Fath Ali Sháh, overlooking the stream. As we had been told to beware of the *shabgaz*, or poisonous bug, we kept candles burning all night. I bought two hill dogs for six kiráns each, large, powerful animals.

The 3rd of May was inaugurated by a grand row with the muleteers, who insisted on having the whole of their remaining hire to Tehran before starting, which I refused, and at length carried my point. While the wrangling was going on some of the poisonous bugs, which are in fact ticks, were brought to me. This kind differed from those at Miyáni, in that they had blood-red heads. We started at 8 A.M. with a very hot sun. Our road for about one hundred yards was up a stream, which when in flood must be troublesome. From Fírúzkúh onwards to Tehran we had constant views of Demavend, which I thought a less striking object than Ararat, but Fane assigned the first place to Demavend. The road was now a long stony descent. At six miles from Fírúzkúh we crossed the Kazanchai. Fane was the first to ride in, but soon came back and asked me to try. I made the attempt farther up the stream, where the water was shallower, but it, nevertheless, came to the horse's belly and in one place a little higher, and was very rapid. The water was very cold and killed my poor horse, who began to tremble and broke down entirely at a long hill we were

ascending. I dismounted and took the mule on
which Fane's servant was riding, while he led my
horse. So we passed a long succession of ascents
and descents to the village of Amínábád, a pretty
hamlet with six houses belonging to Farrukh Khán,
and thence to a filthy ruined kárwánsarái, which we
reached at 4 P.M. Here we stopped to drink, and the
fleas were so numerous that directly Fane set down
his cup three jumped into it. We had now to pass a
very rapid stream called the Dallachai, and Fane was
nearly swept away in crossing it. His horse was
all but down, and he lost his hunting-whip in the
water. I rode on a hundred yards and came to an
excellent bridge, of the existence of which our stupid
guide gave us no hint. Fane, too, now mounted a
mule, and, leaving my poor horse to die, we passed
along the edge of deep ravines to within two farsakhs
of our halting-place, where the road became good,
and we got to Saiyadábád at 7 P.M., having been
eleven hours in doing eight farsakhs. The place
we stopped at was a farmhouse, and the proprietor,
a Saiyid, said *shab-gaz*, "poisonous bugs," were found
in his house, but were not very dangerous. Our cook

had gone on to the next village, so we went supper-less to bed after a ride of upwards of thirty miles.

At 3.30 P.M. on the 4th of May we went on, and reached the fine village of Sarbandún in less than an hour, the distance being a farsakh. The village is situated on the brink of a clear stream which issues from a mountain gorge. At the distance of another farsakh we passed a still larger village, called Dahján, and at 6.15 P.M. we arrived at Ainah Barján, placed like all the villages in these parts on a stream issuing from the mountains. We put up in the Kadkhudá's house, which was very neat and clean. I particularly remarked the neatness of the ceilings of peeled sticks, as thick as a man's wrist, laid close together.

At 2.20 P.M., on the 5th of May, we left Ainah Barján, and not being able to procure fresh horses, we took on those we had for the preceding stage. The road was lined with dead mules. Six miles from Ainah Barján we passed the village of Jihád, with a fine stream, along which cultivation extends for miles. As my horse was a very good one, I left Fane, and galloped the rest of the way, about

eleven miles, to Bamáhan, where I arrived at
6.30 p.m. The greater part of the post-house had
fallen down, and had it rained we should have passed
an uncomfortable night.

We left Bamáhan at 4.30 a.m. on the 6th of
May. The first thing was to cross a very deep and
rapid torrent by a bridge so shaky that our journey
for the day was all but cut short at the commencement. On getting over this difficulty we found that,
with the exception of mine, scarcely a horse could
move. My steed was a strong galloway that had
just been brought in from grass, but was too puffed
up and conceited to gallop well. Every time I
attempted to canter I heard a cry of "Burnt father!"
behind me, and, looking back, saw poor Riza emerging from a cloud of dust, and apostrophizing his
wretched jade which had just come down with him.
In this way he fell six times, and as Fane's horse,
too, was utterly done, I left them, and went on by
myself, crossing at three and a half farsakhs, the
Jájrúd river, eighty yards broad, but shallow, by a
fine new bridge. The Sháh has a hunting-seat
near, but it is not visible from the road. At four

farsakhs the road descends a steep hill to the village
of Surkh Asár, "red marks," so called from the
colour of the soil. After another mile the road
turned from a westerly to a southerly direction, and
soon after the cultivation about Tehran came in
sight. I now found myself in a wilderness of crops,
and had to ask my way repeatedly. The city seemed
quite deserted, numbers of people having gone to
their own provinces on account of the famine, and
others having died. At 9.30 A.M. I reached the
Mission, having been exactly five hours in doing the
six farsakhs. Thus ended my expedition to the
Caspian provinces. It took me a fortnight to draw
up my various reports and translations from Russian,
and I had the satisfaction of reading some months
afterwards a despatch in which all I had done was
approved. The last line of that despatch remained
fixed in my memory. It was—"Mr. Eastwick,
whose judicious proceedings do him credit," being,
Fane said, the pithiest and most concise piece of
κῦδος he ever remembered.

Having been honoured by the Sháh with a
command for an account of my journey, I drew

out a brief narrative with suggestions for various
improvements, and sent it on the 13th of May, and
on the 21st Mr. Alison took me to an audience
at the Dáúdíyah Palace, when his Majesty asked
me many questions on the subject of the paper I
had drawn up, and orders were issued subsequently
for the execution of some of the things I had
suggested.

CHAPTER IV.

Dry Abstract of Events from May, 1861, to the Spring of 1862 (to
be skipped by the Reader)—Mr. Alison applies for Leave to
quit his Post—The Festival of the Nauroz at Tehran—The
Champion Wrestler—The Sháh's Palace and the Crown Jewels
of Persia—Arrival of Col. P. Stewart to construct the Electric
Telegraph—Renewed Negotiations and their Failure—Mr. Alison
postpones his Departure—Colonel Stewart and Mr. Dickson
leave Tehran—Advance of the Afgháns on Herát—The Author
applies to be transferred.

On my return from the Caspian Provinces I found
my work much increased, as I had now become the
medium through which all business was conducted,
and I had to go to Mr. Alison and from him to other
parties many times a day. It was thought, therefore, more convenient that I should leave the mud
Annexe pro. tem. and occupy the room which had
previously been the office, though I retained my
former quarters, furnished as before, and inhabited

by my servants, ready to be re-entered as soon as
I found fault with the new arrangement, which lasted
from the 13th of May to the 3rd of June, when
we went to our country quarters at Gulhek. There,
as all the houses were taken, and as my health would
not admit of my living in a tent, I occupied for the
season a room adjoining the Chancery. On the
18th of June Mr. Watson went away to England
on leave for six months, and did not return till
the 6th of February, 1862. On the 22nd of July, as
cholera was very severe, not only in Tehran, but
also in the villages round Gulhek, we moved up
into the mountains near Demavend, to seek a more
salubrious atmosphere at an altitude of 7,000 feet
above the sea. On the 31st of July a report I
had been long preparing on the commerce of Persia
was sent off to Government. It is dated July the 5th
in the reports of Her Majesty's Secretaries of Embassy and Legation presented to Parliament in 1862.
We now made a short but extremely interesting tour
in the mountains, and I laid down a map of our
journeys which may some day see the light. On
the 10th of August we returned to Gulhek.

The Mashíru 'd daulah, late Ambassador from the Sháh to the English Government, having now returned to Persia, the important question of the construction of an electric telegraph through Persia, as a means of communication between England and India, was busily discussed. Long negotiations took place, which all ended in absolute failure. Mr. Alison, of course, often conferred with me on the subject, and I told him very frankly my views, which were not adopted, but, as will be seen hereafter, turned out to be correct. Another important case was a question of compensation to Mír Ali Naki Khán, a Persian nobleman, of the highest rank, under the protection of the British Government, whose house had been robbed to the alleged amount of 50,000l. This case was the opprobrium of the Mission, and had been going on for years, without the slightest approach towards settlement.

. On the 6th of October we returned to Tehran. I again chose the room I had occupied from the 13th of May to the 3rd of June. It was convenient for business, though not so comfortable as my own quarters, and the sun fell directly upon it, which was well enough in extremely cold weather, but at other times highly disagreeable. The winter of 1861–1862 passed more pleasantly as regards public affairs than that of 1860. Food was comparatively cheap, and there was no rioting. But in other respects I was less agreeably situated. Circumstances occurred which made me very anxious to get away, but I could not, for on the 15th of January, 1862, Mr. Alison sent for me, and said he was going to apply for leave, and that I should be left in charge of the Mission, and accordingly, on the 5th of February, Mr. Alison's application for permission to quit Tehran went to Lord Russell and was granted. Dr. Dickson also applied about the same time for leave, with the intention of going home with Mr. Alison, and Mr. W. Dickson and Mr. Glen were also preparing to go to England. It was, therefore, entirely out of the question that I could leave Persia.

Time hobbled on, it does not roll in Persia, and beautiful spring, with her bosom full of flies and a few flowers, was advancing. The ancient Persians taught, beside the three things that Byron has im-

mortalized, that the New Year begins, not in the
depth of winter when Nature herself is dead, but
at the vernal equinox when she revives—and I think
they were right. But in the year of the dog (see
Calendar of the Turks), corresponding with 1862 of the
Faringís, Ramazán, the month of fasting, fell right
athwart the Festival of the Nauroz, and as the sons of
Adam cannot rejoice, like Jins and such like higher
beings, with an empty stomach, it was decided to put
off the Feast of the New Year to the 1st of April,
coincident with the 1st of Shawwál, on which the
fasting of Ramazán ends, and the Bairám begins.

"It was ten of April morn" by the time that we
had donned our uniforms, and were waiting for our
chief, who made his appearance at one hour to noon.
Then we mounted and filed in a long cavalcade to the
palace. The great square was full of citizens and
soldiers, and there was a goodly uproar, which made
our horses walk sideways, with an occasional frisk
that disarranged our cocked hats, to the great delight
of the populace.

At the " Sublime Porte " we all dismounted, and
walked into the waiting-room of the palace, a very

plain apartment, with no prospect but the passage
by which we entered, and the heads of a few scores
of staring servants. The Russian Minister had
already arrived, a thin man with an emaciated, intelligent countenance, in a gay uniform with many
orders, and so had the Turkish Envoy, stout and
broad-shouldered, with a handsome Jewish face.
The Ishikchí Aghássi, or Persian master of the
ceremonies, with his aide, were making reiterated
inquiries as to the state of the brain of their European visitors, and handsomely dressed servants kept
perpetually bringing in tea, coffee, and pipes, pipes,
coffee, and tea. In another quarter of an hour the
Comte de G——, true representative of polite, loqua-
cious, egotistic Gaul, made his appearance, and
shortly afterwards Yahya Khán (a name which, interpreted literally, is equivalent to Lord John), a confidential attendant of the Shâh, summoned us to
the royal presence. As soon as we had stepped
into the inner quadrangle of the palace we were
joined by the Minister of Foreign Affairs, dressed
in scarlet stockings and that becoming turban one
so much admires in the engravings to Lane's *Arabian*

Nights. We now walked along among the rosebeds till we came within fifty feet of the audience chamber, when we all slipped off our goloshes and bowed, the Sháh looking at us imperturbably from the window. After another twenty paces we bowed again, then ascended a flight of steps and passed under a curtain into the room where the Sháh was.

Násiru'd dín Sháh, the present ruler of Persia, is thirty-two years of age, five feet six inches high, well and rather strongly made, with black and long moustaches, but no beard, hazel eyes, and a mild, good-humoured expression. He stood to receive the foreign envoys. Round his neck were six strings of pearls and emeralds, each gem of which might have been an earl's ransom, and he wore a diamond aigrette in his lamb-skin cap that would have been a dowry for an empress. The scabbard of his sword was studded so thickly with diamonds from hilt to point, that a ray of light could not have entered between them, and was worth, they said, a quarter of a million sterling. In face of that blaze of jewels our policemen's coats and gold lace looked utterly mean. The Russian Minister, who was our *doyen,*

now said a few words in French by way of congratu-
lation to the Sháh, and the Russian head dragoman,
whose name appropriately signifies " sturgeon," interpreted them. In return, the Sháh asked each of the
foreign envoys, *ahwál i shumá khub ast*, " are you
well ? " and then inquired of the Russian Minister why
he did not learn Persian. The Russian answered that
there was time yet to learn it, which, considering that
he was sixty years of age, and had been half his life
in Persia, seemed a rather pleasant statement.

We now went to see the Salám, or " general
salute," in the outer quadrangle of the palace, which
has an area of between one and two acres, and was
entirely surrounded by three regiments of soldiers
drawn up in single line, with their backs to the wall.
In the building that faces down this quadrangle, the
Sháh's throne was placed, a throne which was brought
from the golden halls of Sháhjehánábád. We all went
into a small room on the left hand of that in which the
enthronization was to be, but in a story above it, and
as none but the Sháh must be seen sitting on this
solemn occasion, the windows were shut upon us ; but
the mercurial Gaul broke out some panes to see the

ceremony more distinctly. On the tops of the walls, and on the roof of the palace, hundreds of people were clustered, while the great court below them was filled by a multitude of the higher officials of the kingdom, standing in richly-dressed groups, according to their rank, from the Ministers downwards. In the centre of these a small knot of European officers, the instructors of the Sháh's troops, were conspicuous, and among them England was well represented by Colonel Dolmage, formerly of the 23rd Royal Welsh Fusiliers, a handsome man six feet and an inch high, looking more than a match for any Saracen in the assembly.

It would be vain, without the aid of the Muse who indited Homer's catalogue of ships, to attempt a description of all the dresses that glittered, like beds of flowers, under our eyes that day. On the left of the throne stood the Sipáh Sálár, or Commander-in-Chief, a big, broad, heavy man, blazing in gold and diamonds. On the right were the great civil officers of State, with those tall graceful Arabian turbans. Lower down were rows of Mustaufis, or secretaries, and below them were Afgháns and

Sistánis, the latter remarkable for their vast turbans of snowy white. Two dresses surpassed all the rest in magnificence, that of the Ainu 'l Mulk, the "Eye of the State," who is the king's brother-in-law, and that of the Sháh's son-in-law, the son of the Sipáh Sálár. The former was such a dress as Nero might have worn when he presided at the Olympic games, or as might have glittered on Elagabalus as priest of the Syrian sun-god. At the distance at which we were, I could not distinguish the material, but it sent forth purple and golden flashes at every movement its wearer made.

The Sháh's approach to the throne-room was announced by salvoes of artillery, and then a clear, sonorous voice called like a clarion, *Gittir*, "he has passed!" When the Sháh had taken his seat, all bowed the graceful Persian bow, by stooping the body, with the palms of the hands slightly resting on the knees. The Ainu 'l Mulk, now walking backwards from the Sháh, moved down the assembly, giving handfuls of silver coins to all from a splendid golden salver. Inferior officers distributed sherbet from priceless vessels of gold studded with gems, and the most costly china. A Mulá, or doctor of Islám, then stood forth and uttered, in a loud and melodious voice, the *Khutbah*, or prayer for the sovereign. After this the Poet Laureate recited an ode, and with this the ceremony ended.

As a wind-up we went to see the wrestling and other games, which were to take place in the great Maidán, or plain of the Ark. We sate in the Tehran and Tabríz telegraph-office, in front of which a place for the lists was cleared and watered. About 2 P.M. a crowd of wrestlers, jugglers, and mountebanks dressed as devils, of fighting rams and dancing monkeys, suddenly inundated the arena. This plan of serving up all the entertainment at once is very absurd, for the eye and the attention are so distracted by the multiplicity of objects that no one spectacle is thoroughly enjoyed. For my part, I was most taken up with the wrestlers, who were really very skilful, and one or two of whom exhibited prodigies of strength. In particular a gigantic athlete from Yezd attracted all eyes. With shaven head and bare feet, he measured over six feet six inches, and from the waist upward was magnificently made. His chest was vast, and the ribs came remarkably low down, while his arms resembled the trunks of trees, rather than the limbs of a man. Only his legs were not worthy of the superb upper structure. He first exhibited his skill in the use of the clubs, producing several pairs of an enormous size, which he used with wonderful dexterity, and finished by throwing them *under his legs* for twenty or thirty feet up into the air, and catching them again.

When the giant had ended this display, several men advanced towards him, and challenged him to wrestle. One by one they grappled with their tremendous antagonist, and one after another they were lifted from the ground and thrown, sometimes with such force that we expected them never to rise again. They were fine, powerful men in general, from five feet nine to six feet high, but they had no chance with the Yezd champion. In the meantime the crowd had been gradually encroaching on the arena, and it was evident that, unless something was done, the games would be interrupted. In particular a body of matchlockmen made themselves very obnoxious by pushing in amongst the performers, and the Sháh's farrashes, who were keeping the ring, were obliged to make a combined onslaught on the intruders. With their long white sticks they raised a merry clatter on the heads of the matchlockmen, and drove them back many yards, when they re-formed, and in turn charged the farrashes, and a sharp *melée* ensued. But the farrashes were supported by the consciousness of being in authority, and plied their staves with still greater vigour, so that they at last chased the rebels completely off the ground, amid a roar of applause from the multitude. While this was going on, the Yezdi had been wrestling with his last opponent, who next to himself seemed to be the most powerful man present, not tall, but prodigiously broad and muscular, with a bull neck and loins of iron. The struggle had been a prolonged one, and occasionally the short athlete seemed to gain the advantage, though I suspect the Yezdi allowed the spectators to think his strength was failing in order to add to the piquancy of the contest. At last when expectation had been well wound up, the Yezdi seemed to make an immense effort, the muscles on his arms stood out like cordage, he drew his opponent in towards him, and then slipping his right arm down from the short man's shoulder to the small of his back, bent him in, and sweeping his legs from under him, laid him flat on the ground. This ended the show, and the giant was led off in triumph amid a crowd of admirers, to receive a dress of honour, and a reward from some official, who doubtless got the better of him in a wrestle for *mudákhil.**

A fortnight after this, I went with the Turkish minister, an Italian, and a Russian lady to see the Sháh's jewels, which are certainly the greatest sight in their way the world can show. We presented ourselves at the palace at 3 P.M., and were received by Yahya Khán, who took us out of the second and inner great court of the palace, into a small quadrangle not far from the sacred precincts of the Harím. We then went up a steep stair to a small room about 20 feet by 14, where jewels to the value of six or seven millions were laid out on carpets, at the far end of the room, while near the

---

* Fees.

door, fruits, coffee, and sweetmeats were placed for us.
The first thing that struck me was the smallness of
the door, and the steepness of the stairs. It was not
a nice place to escape from, if one had tried to make
off with a crown or two. Several men stood at the
door, and others by the sweetmeats, and near the
jewels on a chair sate the Mustaufiu'l Mamálik, or
Persian Chancellor of the Exchequer, a very fit man
to be the keeper of the jewels, enormously rich,
close, reserved, bigoted. Being a Saiyíd, he wore
the sacred colour, and was so full of sanctity and
haughtiness, that the very atmosphere around him
seemed to breathe "Noli me tangere." It was
thought a singular proof of Sir H. Rawlinson's
wonderful popularity and influence in Persia that this
man came to call upon him ; to no other infidel has
such a favour been vouchsafed.

In such a show of gems as seemed to realize the
wonders of Aladdin's lamp, the eye was too much
dazzled and the memory too confused for description
to be possible. But I remember that at the back of all
was the Kaianian crown, and on either side of it two
Persian lambskin caps adorned with splendid aigrettes

of diamonds. The crown itself was shaped like a flower-pot, with the small end open, and the other closed. On the top of the crown was an uncut ruby, apparently without flaw, as big as a hen's egg. In front of the crown were dresses covered with diamonds and pearls, trays with necklaces of pearls, rubies and emeralds, and some hundreds of diamond, ruby, and turquoise rings. In front of these again were gauntlets and belts covered with pearls and diamonds, and conspicuous among them the Kaianian belt, about a foot deep, weighing perhaps eighteen pounds, and one complete mass of pearls, diamonds, emeralds, and rubies. Still nearer to us stood a drinking bowl completely studded with enormous jewels, a tray full of foreign orders set in brilliants, and in front of all lay a dozen swords, one or two of which are worth a quarter of a million each. Along with these were epaulettes covered with diamonds, and armlets so contrived that the brilliants revolved and kept up a continual shimmer.

It was difficult among so many to single out particular gems. Perhaps, however, the first place ought to be assigned to the famous Daryá i Núr, or

"Sea of Light," the sister diamond to our Panjáb trophy, the Kúh i Núr, or "Mountain of Light." It is an inch and a half long, an inch broad, and three-eighths of an inch thick. It has the name of Fath Ali Sháh on one side, and the inscribing this name reduced the value of the diamond, so, at least, said Yahya Khán, "deux millions—mais deux millions de quoi—de piastres, de francs—que sais-je?" I was not prodigiously impressed with this jewel. It is a monstrous diamond, but not very brilliant. I could pardon a rustic who should mistake it for glass. Nevertheless it has a wondrous history. The Persians say—and, to copy the Jowettian expression, I partly agree with them—that the Sea of Light and the Mountain of Light were jewels in the sword of Afrásiáb, who lived 3,000 years B.C. Rustam took them from Afrásiáb, and they continued in the crown of Persia till they were carried away by Tímúr, from whom they descended to Muhammad Sháh, King of Delhi, and Nádír brought them from India; but when he was slain, Ahmed Sháh Abdalli carried off the Kúh i Núr, which descended to Sháh Shuja, and was taken from him by Ranjít Singh. The Daryá i Núr remained in Persia with the greater part of the other gems that Nádir brought from India.

Among the rings is one in which is set the famous Pitt diamond, sent by George IV. to Fath Ali Sháh. Sir H. Sutherland used to tell how he was present when a Persian nobleman arrived from Tehran to stop Sir H. Jones from going to the capital, French influence being then paramount. After Sir Harford had exhausted every argument to show that he ought to be received, without making any impression on the Persian Khán, he said, " Well! if it must be so, I shall return, and abandon all hope of making my countenance white in the presence of the Sháh. I go, and this must return with me !" So saying, he took from his waistcoat pocket the beautiful diamond ring which had been sent for the Sháh. But the sparkle of the gem produced a magical effect ; the Khán no sooner beheld it than he lost his balance and fell back from his seat quite out of breath ; then recovering himself, he shouted, " Stop, stop ! Elchí! may your *lutf*, your condescending kindness, go on increasing! This alters the matter. I will send off an express to the heaven-resembling threshold of the

Asylum of the World. I swear by your head you will
be received with all honour. Masháliah! it is not
every one that has diamonds like the Inglís." He
was as good as his word; the express courier was
despatched, and Sir Harford entered the city of
Tehran by one gate, while General Gardanne was
packed off by the other.

Another very large diamond is the Táj i Humá,
or " Diadem of the Phœnix." It seemed to me as
big as the top of a man's thumb. There is also the
finest turquoise in the world, three or four inches
long, and without a flaw, and I remarked a smaller
one of unique beauty, three-quarters of an inch
long, and three-eighths of an inch broad; the colour
was lovely, and almost as refreshing to the eyes
as Persian poets pretend. There are also many
sapphires, as big as marbles, and rubies and pearls
the size of nuts; and I am certain that I counted
nearly a hundred emeralds, from half an inch square
to an inch and three-quarters long and an inch broad.
In the sword-scabbard, which is covered with diamonds,
there is not, perhaps, a single stone smaller than
the nail of a man's little finger. Lastly, there is

an emerald as big as a walnut, covered with the names of kings who had possessed it.

We had coffee and tea, and then walked through courts filled with orange-trees and roses, and watered by clear streams from a reservoir, half an acre in extent, where the water sprang up, as from a natural fountain, to the height of several feet. We then inspected a room hung with Gobelin tapestry, and next entered the library filled with priceless MSS. Of all the calligraphers Mír seems to be the most famous, and his writing is valued at two túmáns a line. At this rate the MSS. by him in the Sháh's possession must be worth hundreds of thousands of pounds. The armoury is small and inferior to many European collections. In a room overlooking the Great Tank, are some pictures, one of the Virgin and Child, and another of Judith and Holofernes. In another apartment is an immense collection of knick-knacks, and among them some splendid China bowls presented by the East India Company.

Mais revenons à nos moutons—on the 20th of May a new impetus was given to the negotiations for the telegraph by the arrival of Lieut.-Colonel Patrick

Stewart. This distinguished officer had constructed and superintended the telegraph in Havelock's glorious advance from Bengal to Lucknow. Since then he had had great experience in the laying of various electric lines, and he was now sent by the Viceroy of India to superintend the line, which the British Government was anxious should be constructed from Khanikain, on the frontier of the Pashalik of Baghdad, to Tehran, and from Tehran to Bushire, or to Bandar Abbás. Colonel Stewart was accompanied by Captain Champain, of the Bengal Engineers, who rode in from Kúm on the 22nd of May. Both officers were temporarily attached to the Tehran Mission, and exerted themselves to supply such information as might assist Mr. Alison in his negotiation, and the Persian Government in coming to a conclusion. But there is no place in the world where the *quo modo* is more important than in Persia. The negotiations were not successful. Of course, after I had once stated my notion of the way the question ought to be dealt with, my duty was simply to obey my directions, and many a wearisome hour I passed in profitless interviews and discussions. My first meeting with the Mashíru'd daulah, the Persian ambassador, who had mooted the question with Sir C. Wood, was the drollest thing possible, but somewhat wearisome nevertheless. I and the Mashír had never met before, and when I was introduced to him, being as deaf as some other pillars of the State I could mention, he mistook my name Eastwick for Stevens, pronounced by the Orientals, *Istevens.* Now Stevens is a name well known in Persia and Turkey, as there are several brothers so called, who are, or have been, consuls in both countries. The old Mashír, therefore, hearing the familiar sound, thought I was a brother of the consul at Trebizonde, and feeling himself at home with a member of that family, and being weary of the world and all things in it, squatted himself down beside me and laid his head on my knees.

" Good heavens ! " said I to myself, " what a situation ! Did ' ever one hear of a negotiation carried on in this fashion ? and I a perfect stranger, too ! How horribly undignified ! What on earth will the servants think ! Suppose he goes to sleep ; what is to be done ? "

Hereupon I began to address a number of questions to the old man, and endeavoured, without being rude, to get rid of the encumbrance of his head. But all he would do was to rouse himself for a moment, still keeping his great hand on my knee, and with a mournful shake of the head, ejaculate—" Balí ! balí ! Yes—yes, I know, I know. What is the use of all this? I told them —they will not believe."

At last, suspecting he mistook me for somebody else, I said,—" Janáb, excellency! did you see my brother at the India Office ? "

" Yes, yes ; I know. I saw your brother at Trebizonde — your brother that was at Tehran. Where is he now ? And George Sáhib, where is he?"

It was not till after endless blunderings of this kind and mystifications, that I at last conveyed to the poor old man's mind that I was a stranger, and no Stevens at all. But when once he was aware of his mistake he drew back immediately, and apologized, and though afterwards we became the greatest friends, he never went the length of reposing his weary head on my knee again.

Meantime, Mr. Alison had given up his intention of going to England, and on the 30th of April told me he should remain. As soon as I was made aware of this fact, and that there was no imperative necessity for my staying at Tehran, I determined —owing to particular circumstances — to use my best endeavours to get away, and proposed that I should immediately go to Tabríz to take charge of the consulate general there, as when Mr. Abbott some time before applied for leave, Mr. Alison had said he wished I would undertake the duties of consul-general. Now, however, Mr. Alison was unwilling to part with me, and on telegraphing to Mr. Abbott to know when he could leave, that gentleman informed me that he did not mean to go before September. All I could do, therefore, was to write to my friends in England to get me another post, and in the meantime, on the 7th May, I left the room I had occupied during the winter of 1861–62, and during the time I expected Mr. Alison's immediate departure, and returned to my original quarters in the mud *annexe*, which Mr. Alison had for some time permitted a Major Young, of the

Sháh's service, to occupy. The major, however, had gone to Ispahán *en route* for India, and Fane had accompanied him, but was recalled by Mr. Alison on the 17th of April. Indeed, we could ill spare hands, as, though Mr. Watson had returned from Europe, Mr. W. Dickson had proceeded thither on the 29th of April, and Mr. Glen was about to follow him.

On the 6th of June we moved up to Gulhek, where I, Fane, and Watson, took up our lodgings in the house of Ismail Khán, for the use of which we made the Khán a handsome present in lieu of rent. As Mr. Alison had taken up his lodgings in the Chancellerie, the office also was moved to our house.

On the 19th of June, as all hope of success in the negotiation for the telegraph was at an end, Colonel Patrick Stewart left us for England, a step which was also required by his health. Captain Champain was directed by Mr. Alison to proceed immediately to Baghdád, but obtained permission to remain until the dreadful heat of July, August and September was past. As to the danger of travelling during these months, I myself can now testify, as events had arisen at the time referred to, which induced the Government to send me on a journey even more trying than that from Tehrán to Baghdád. On the 28th of June we received intelligence from Meshed that Dost Muhammad Khán, the Amír of Kábul, had reached Kandahár with three regiments of infantry, 2,000 horse, and five guns, and that the rest of his disposable forces were following him. The same day Mr. Alison was sent for by the Sháh to an audience at which I interpreted. The Sháh stated that he had received intelligence that Muhammad Amír Khán * and Muhammad Sharíf Khán had invested Farah, which for its strength and importance may be called Little Herát, with a powerful army. His Majesty further expressed his belief that Farah would fall, and that the Dost would not be satisfied until he got possession of Herát also. In this belief I fully coincided. Without pausing, however, to state here the grounds on which my opinion was founded, I shall briefly mention that Farah did surrender on the 8th of July to the Amír, and that he marched the same day for Herát, which is 140

---

* Sons of Dost Muhammad.

miles due north of Farah, as the crow flies, but considerably more by the road. On the 22nd of July the Dost took Sabzáwar, on the road from Farah to Herát, and seventy-five miles south of the latter town; on the 26th his cavalry defeated that of Herát and killed the two principal commanders, Sardárs Akram Khán and Yúsif Khán, Achakzyes, and on the 27th Herát itself was invested by the Dost with 16,000 men and thirty-two guns. The arrival of so large an Afghán army, commanded by a leader so famous as the Amír, Dost Muhammad Khán, on the Persian frontier, naturally caused deep anxiety to the Sháh, and his Majesty was anxious that a commission, composed of a member of the British Legation and a Persian officer of high rank, should be sent to the camp of the Amír to arrange the differences between him and his nephew, the ruler of Herát. This proposal was submitted to the British Government, and Mr. Alison suggested that I should be sent to Khúrásán to keep the Government informed through Mr. Alison of the state of affairs, and to be on the spot should negotiations with the Amír be thought necessary.

On the 2nd of August I was compelled* by circumstances over which I had no control, to apply to Lord Russell to transfer me to some other appointment, and the Secretaryship at Athens being then vacant, I applied especially for that. Mr. Alison, I have subsequently learned, opposed this transfer, but he did so on grounds very flattering to myself. He stated to Lord Russell that I was "an able and conscientious officer, and that my removal from Tehran would be an irreparable loss to the public service." † The reader, when he comes to the end of this narrative, will, if I mistake not, pardon what may here appear egotism in my repeating expressions so encomiastic of myself.

On the 5th of August Mr. Ronald Thomson, recently promoted to be Oriental Secretary, arrived at Gulhek from an absence of two years in Europe. On the following day I set out on my lonely and painful journey to the scene of trouble in Khúrásán.

---

* Certain representations were made to me by parties, who afterwards equivocated to such a degree as to render their statements worthless.

† I have been further informed that Mr. Alison wrote to his friend Mr. Layard regarding me, in terms of unqualified commendation.

CHAPTER V.

Delicate Nature of the Mission entrusted to me in Khúrásán—Departure from Gulhek—Interview with the Amínu 'd daulah—His Character and Fitness for the Office of Grand Vazír—From Tehran to Khátunábád—Aiwán i Kaif—Ancient Fort and Mound of the Fire-Worshippers—Defile of Sardárí or Caspian Straits—Aradun—The Persian Opera—Dih Namak—Lasjird—Semnún—Ahúán—Gúchah—Damghán, or Hecatompylos.

THE inhabitants of Meshed are, perhaps, the most fanatical people in the world, and their hatred of infidels was stimulated at the time of my departure for Khúrásán, by reports that Dost Muhammad was merely the paid servant of the English, and was doing the work of the English Government in besieging Herát. Moreover, the investment of that place touched the Meshedís to the quick, for it put a stop to a lucrative trade between them and the Herátís, and encouraged the Turkumans to commit increasing ravages in Khúrásán. Owing

to these circumstances, so menacing was the aspect
of affairs at Meshed as regards British protégés in
August, 1862, that the agent of the Mission in
that city wrote to say he considered himself in
danger, in consequence of the reports that British
officers were in the camp of the Dost, and that he
should be glad to know what was intended, in order
that he might provide for his safety. It is true
that there was an idea abroad, especially among
the high officials, that I was going to Herát to
turn back the Amír, but I could expect nothing but
an increase of exasperation when that hope was
disappointed, as it was destined to be.

On the whole, therefore, I had little to rely
upon, but the consciousness of my own earnest wish
to promote the cause of peace, and a hearty desire
for the welfare of Persia. Orientals in general,
and especially the Persians, are singularly acute in
reading character, and they prize ·sincerity and
truthfulness all the higher because they themselves
are rather deficient in those qualities. Not that
the Persians at all deserve the absurd attacks that
have been made upon them by some European

writers. When they have to deal with a doubtful character, they will do their best to circumvent him, and, as they are infinitely sharper than any European, they are tolerably sure to succeed against the clumsier knavery of the West. But with the true they will be true, and, acting on that belief, I have had the good fortune to succeed in all my dealings with them. My parting interview with Farrukh Khán, the Amínu 'd daulah, who holds the office of home secretary in Persia, was quite corroborative of what has just been said of the influence obtainable in Persia by an honest exhibition of friendly sentiments.

I left Gulhek about 3 P.M. on the 6th of August, and rode down to Tehran in heat like that of a furnace. I was extremely unwell, and on reaching the Mission, was obliged to send an excuse to Farrukh Khán, on whom I had promised to call that night. At 7 A.M. on the 7th, I rode to his Excellency's house, and was received by him, on account of the heat, in a shady spot in one of the courts, where the air was less oppressive than in a room. On my applying for the necessary letters, he ordered his secretaries to write them in the strongest terms to the officials on the line of my march, enjoining the commanders of troops furnishing escorts to mount and attend me themselves, as it was the Sháh's wish that I should be treated with the greatest honour possible. He further informed me that the Sháh had been pleased to express entire confidence in me, and he added that as for himself he would write with his own hand to the prince-governor of Khúrásán, to say that I was his personal friend, and that he hoped I should be on equally friendly terms with the prince. Lastly, he offered me one of his confidential servants as an attendant; a kindness which, of course, I declined, but not from any dread of the man acting as a spy, for I had nothing to conceal.

Farrukh Khán, on whom the Sháh has conferred the title of Amínu 'd daulah, equivalent to our "lord president," is a native of Káshán, and served in the royal household from his childhood. He is upwards of six feet high, and has been extremely handsome. His manners are most courtly, and to hear him speak Persian is a real pleasure to all who know and like the language. That which raised him to his present

high position was his success as ambassador in
negotiating the Treaty of Paris, which put an end
to the war between Persia and England. For that
service the Sháh bestowed on him, among other
things, a jewelled girdle, worth 10,000*l*. As no
man in Persia better understands the value of the
English alliance, or has seen so much of Europe
and European courts, the office of Sadr Azim, or
Grand Vazír, could nowhere be so well conferred as
on Farrukh Khán, more especially as he is a sincere
and devoted servant of the Sháh, and most zealous
for the honour and welfare of his country.

I started from Tehran at 8 P.M. on the 8th of
August. Had I been superstitious I might have
imagined a bad omen in a kick I received from a
vicious horse as I rode out of the city. The beast
was standing some way off, but he ran back and
delivered both his heels with such hearty good-will
that had they struck my leg instead of my stirrup-
iron, I should have been lamed for life. As it was,
the jar stung my foot most painfully.

I arrived at the filthy hamlet of Khátunábád,
"the lady's village," at 2.15 A.M. There are about

fifty hovels in the place, and so numerous are the
musquitoes, that the lady after whom it is called
must have a skin like the hide of a buffalo, if she
can close her eyes in it. I could not, and awoke
with my face all over bumps. I passed the morning
of the 9th in walking up and down in my miserable
den, an arched dog-hole, with a formidable crack
in the roof. Sit still I could not, for the prongs
of the musquitoes and sand-flies, and I have no
doubt my incessant tramping must have amused a
girl, who kept staring at me in a most exasperating
manner out of an aperture in an adjacent dog-
hole.

I left Khátunábád at 5.40 P.M., with the sun still
intensely hot. M. Ferrier complained of being mad-
dened by the heat in this district in May: what
would he have said had he been with me in August,
when the snow has all vanished from the mountains,
and the wind seems laden with fire! Three miles to
the north of Khátunábád is Hisár Amír, under the
hills, which beyond it are beautifully striated. The
view of Demavend is particularly fine from this point.
After about three miles I passed on the left Kabúd

Gumbad, "Blue dome," where there are a mud tower
and· a post-station. Three miles further I passed
Karkarábád, where are deep watercourses and all the
signs of great floods in winter, the earth over great
spaces having been washed away, leaving nothing
but stones. I reached Aiwán i Kaif at 3 A.M. on
the 10th, the distance being about twenty-eight
miles.

Aiwán i Kaif signifies "Palace of pleasure," but
the name is properly Aiwán i Kai, "Palace of the
Kaianians," from a fortress about two miles off, long
since ruined. Had I the naming of the place, however, I should call it Aiwán i Kaik, "Palace of
fleas," for I was quite unable to sleep in consequence
of the punctures of these insects. The village is
sadly decayed, but there were still about 200 families.
A Táziyah, or musical performance, in honour of the
sons of Ali, was going on in the mud-fort. The man
in whose house I was lodging told me he purchased
his property for túmáns 100 = 50*l.* It consisted of
a large mansion with a *birúni*, "outside premises,"
for the men, and an *andarúni*, "inner house," for the
women, and a large garden, and must have cost five

times what Ali Akbar, my host, gave for it. But its
value, and that of all the other houses, were reduced
by a piece of injustice very common in Persia. The
Khán of Demavend, who lives near the source of
the *Kanáts*, "watercourses," on which Aiwán i Kaif
depends, had built five new villages higher up the
stream, and cut it off for the benefit of his own
tenants. In England the remedy would be an action
for easements, in Persia the aggrieved inhabitants
migrate.

At 5 A.M. on the 11th I rode to the ruins from
which Aiwán i Kaif has its name. They lie about
two miles south-south-west of the village and between
it and a range of hills which supply Tehran with salt.
The salt is got by blasting, and is pure, without
admixture of earth. The supply is exhaustless. In
the hills are numbers of deer, who are very fond of
the saline springs. On the way to the ancient ruins
I passed a saráï of the time of Abbás, and a fort
which was destroyed by the Afghán before the reign
of Nádir. A mile and a half from this are the ruins
of a square fort, 115 yards long by 100 yards broad.
The foundations are of great strength, being built

of burnt brick and mortar of so fine a quality that
it is carried off by the people of the surrounding
villages to be used again. The walls, ten feet thick,
were probably faced with burnt bricks, or, at least,
pilastered with them in the *ták numá* style, but the
pilasters have been dug out and carried away. At
the entrance of the fort there has been a large
Istalkh or artificial reservoir, to which many watercourses lead. These are so ancient that the mounds
near their shafts have sunk almost level with the
ground. In the centre of the fort there has been
a tower of burnt bricks. To the south is a smaller
fort, and a quarter of a mile to the east is a Fire-
worshippers' mound, about the size of the large fort
and now not more than thirty feet high. On the
top are the remains of a temple. The smaller fort,
is called *Chihal Dukhtar*, and the legend is, that a
princess lived there, who, with thirty-nine other
maidens, dressed as men, and went forth so attired
to the chase and to war. The plain for a mile or two
around is covered with bricks and pottery. The
village of Aiwán is assigned to the Sháh's master
of the horse, and pays 200 túmáns in cash, 250 khar-

wars of wheat, and 300 of straw. The ruins in the vicinity are, no doubt, of the time of the Parthians.

I left Aiwán at 6.30 P.M. for Aradun, which is eight farsakhs off. M. Ferrier, in his *Caravan Journeys*, p. 56, of the English translation, speaking of Aiwán, which he calls Haivanak, a name strangely like Khavarnak, the palace of King Bahrám in Babylonia, says that a mountain-gorge is passed about two hours from it, where the vultures are in myriads and would destroy any animal that entered it. This is evidently an idle story of the natives. Vultures do not meet in myriads to compare the length of one another's beaks, they only congregate where there are dead animals, and dead animals are not to be found where there is no traffic.

For the first eight miles from Aiwán the road is like that of the preceding stage, level and good, with several watercourses crossing it. Then begins the Sardárí Pass, which I agree with M. Ferrier in regarding as the famous Caspian Straits, the distance being just what it should be from Rhages. I differ with him entirely, however, as to the length of the pass, which he reckons at two miles and

four-fifths of a mile, whereas I should call it four
miles at least. At the western extremity are two old
castles, and in the centre is a curious old tower,
the architecture of which resembles that of the
stone Saráí of Núshírván, in the pass of Ahúán.
It is probably from 1,500 to 2,000 years old. The
breadth of the pass varies from 50 to 300 yards,
with rocks of about 500 feet high on either side.
The hills are salt, and there is a brackish stream
flowing through the pass, the eastern opening of
which is so narrow that it might easily be missed,
when one would have to make a détour for some
miles to the south, where there is no water.

On issuing from the pass, the fertile district of
Khar is entered. I reached the large village of
Kishlák, " winter quarters," at 1 A.M. on the
12th. There was extensive cultivation around it.
At 4.30 A.M. I arrived at Aradun, a village,
where the peasants are proprietors. The cultivation
is very extensive around it, and produces 2,500
kharwárs of wheat. There are miles of cotton and
chiltuk ground, though there are only about 100
families in the village, who get, among other things,

15 kharwárs of wheat each for their own share. I alighted at Aradun, in the *táziyah khánah,* "place where the lamentations for the family of Ali are performed." I use the last word advisedly, for it is indeed a theatrical performance, and may be called the Persian Opera. I witnessed at Aradun one of these operas, the story of which had little to do with the sons of Ali. It was by Jauharí, and was called Zechariah, and the subject was the life and martyrdom of a prophet so named. The actors chaunted their parts from MSS., and the audience, chiefly women, wept incessantly. The tyrant, or executioner, I could not make out which, was a monstrous time in putting Zechariah to death, throwing him down half-a-dozen times, and sawing at his neck with a knife, and then with a sword. In spite of all this, the martyr rose to his feet again and recited a plaintive ditty descriptive of his sufferings, during which the tyrant sharpened his sword with a knife. At last quite tired out, as indeed so was I, at the length of his victim's declamation, he shouted, "Thou must die," and then threw him down for the last time. But even here there was a further

delay, while a large bowl was brought in to receive the imaginary blood, in order that the carpet might not be spoiled. The sawing at the neck was then repeated for the sixth time, and the prophet was carried out, after which a pasteboard head, with a face of ghastly whiteness, and without any hair, was brought in and exhibited to the spectators, who sobbed aloud as they looked at it. In the last scene the tyrant sawed away at a tree, and on my asking why, my servant Taki, a gigantic man with a most lugubrious countenance, said the devil had got into the tree, whereupon I remained in a state of great mystification. Meantime the sun set, and the audience scampered off as fast as possible, most likely to dinner.

I was very nearly being stung by a scorpion at Aradun. It was close to me when I noticed it. It was about five inches long, yellow, and very thick. The castle at this place is worth a visit. It stands on a mound 60 feet high, and on the steepest side the parapet at the top is, perhaps, 130 feet from the ground. From this there is a fine view over an immense plain. To the east are seen the white walls of the fort and station of Dih Namak, "village of salt;" to the south other villages are seen, and to the north are the mountains which, with the Elburz, form a continuous chain along this frontier of Persia. The walls of the castle are immensely thick, and the legend ascribes its construction to the Dívs.

I left Aradun at 9 P.M., and on my journey to Dih Namak, the next station, encountered hundreds of pilgrims returning from Meshed, and going to Karbalah. They were singing hymns, and usually asked us to what shrine we were bound. One Arab pursued us a long way with his prayers in hope of a present. He was riding a mare worth 100 túmáns, but begged furiously, calling out, " The benedictions of Karbalah, of Najaf, of Mecca be upon you! In the name of Muhammad and all his family bestow somewhat on me!" My servant Riza, who was almoner-in-chief, would give him nothing, and he was equally obdurate with some Mulás, who begged of me at Aradun, though he admitted they were not hypocrites.

I reached Dih Namak, four farsakhs, at 2 A.M. on the 13th of August, and found a small, but tolerably clean post-station, which, however, must be a bad lodging in winter, as there is no fireplace. The ceiling, too, was bent inwards more than a foot, and was evidently in a dangerous state. The water at Dih Namak is quite brackish, and smells like stale fish. Towards the south large tracts of soil have a glistening white appearance. I was told they were salt-marshes, and that people are sometimes swallowed up in attempting to cross them. The heat at this place was dreadful; nevertheless, I walked a little way to see an old earthen fort, said, as usual, to have been built by the Divs. I found it full of gipsy-looking people from Semnún.

At 6.20 P.M. on the 13th, I started for Lasjird, and after riding about a mile came up with seven *Khabk i darri,* or " mountain partridges," five hens and two cocks, feeding near the road. This was the first time I had seen that shy and beautiful bird, which is nearly the size of the small bustard, and stands fifteen inches high. I followed them a very long way without being able to get a shot. For about two miles before arriving at Lasjird, the road passes through what cannot be better described than as a gigantic rut between rocks. In some places it is not more than five feet broad, and of about the same depth. In this stage, too, I met many *zauwárs*, or pilgrims. There is a remarkable circular fort at Lasjird, built of earth, and eighty feet high.* The door is a huge stone, weighing, perhaps, a ton. This turns on a pivot, and is closed by a bar as thick as a man's thigh. The walls are eight or ten feet thick, so that the people inside have only to roll to their stone and ascend to the rooms which run round the interior of the fort in a sort of galleries, and they are safe. About forty-five feet from the ground there is a balcony, and all filth is thrown thence, so that in the course of years a rampart has been formed, which the hardiest soldier would hesitate to cross. How it is that the people inside do not die of the plague, or of typhus, is really surprising, for the odour is insupportable. The galleries inside are as populous as a rabbit-warren, with six or seven persons in each room. There was no hiding of faces, and some of the females were handsome.

---

* M. Ferrier says twenty-four feet.

I left Lasjird at 4.30 P.M. on the 14th of August, and at 7 reached the fine village of Surkhah, where there are 500 families. The cultivation around is extensive, and there are several other villages near. I rode to the fort, which is quite ruined, but must have been strong, and capable of holding 2,000 men. The walls are twelve feet thick. The guide said that this stronghold had been built against the Turkumans, whose ravages had now ceased for forty years. The jackals here were very numerous.

Surkhah produces about 1,400 kharwárs of wheat, of which it pays 200 to the shrine at Meshed. I found the cotton-plants at this place in flower, and made inquiries as to the method of cultivation. The plants are kept without water for a month, and are then irrigated every twelve days. They were too thickly sown, and the fields were not properly weeded, whence the plants were stunted. The people, however, told me that a jireb, or acre, would produce 90 mans, about 500 lbs. of cotton.

I reached Semnún at 1 A.M. on the 15th of August, and was two hours before I could find the post-house, which is a little outside the walls. It has a clean upper room, but one so small that the sun heats it like a furnace. Though extremely unwell, I mounted at 5.30, and went into the town to see the principal buildings. I rode first to the chief mosque, and there luckily met the farráshbáshí of the Governor, Husain Khán, a son of the Sipáh Sálár. This official volunteered to escort me round the town, and as he was with me, no objection was offered to my mounting the gigantic pillar, or minaret, from the top of which the Azán, or summons to prayer, is made. There are ninety-nine steps to the top of the pillar, which is of burnt brick, and not very unlike the Buddhist pillars in India. It tapers to the capital, and is, I should think, about 100 feet high. From the top there is a fine view over the truly Oriental and picturesque city of Semnún. Some twenty feet from it, in the very centre of the town, is the chief mosque, the front of which is covered with beautiful Kufik inscriptions in blue, on a white ground. An old ákhund told me that the mosque and minaret were a thousand years old, and that it was four centuries since the minaret had been repaired. To the west appeared another minaret, or isolated pillar, and the Ark, or Government house, very neat-looking, and apparently in good preservation. To the south-east is a fine mosque built by Fath Ali Sháh. Close to this mosque stands a *madrisah*, or college, with 100 students, and a school for children. South of this, and not many hundred yards off, are three remarkable castles, two of them built of earth, and the other faced with brick. In plan they resemble somewhat our baronial residences, and have an imposing appearance. Originally they must have been a hundred feet high, but they are now broken down and ruined. In the ground floor of one there was a deep pit, a dungeon, or well, down which a stone took some seconds to fall.

On descending from the minaret I went to the Sháh's mosque, and the people made no objection to my walking through it. I also examined the castles, and some fields of tobacco close by. The plants in there were two feet high. An acre will yield 50 lbs. weight of the best sort of tobacco, called the *sih barg,* or ,, three leaves," being the leaves at the top of the plant. The planting begins about the 1st of July.

Semnún owes much of its beauty to its trees. Every house seems to have its garden, and water flows through every street. There are many *chenárs* of great size, and I remarked one in particular, the girth of which must have been thirty feet. Round these trees terraces are built, and seats placed, where the weary repose and newsmongers congregate.

I spent the morning of the 16th of August in examining the methods of cleaning cotton, and in making inquiries about its cultivation. Such information as I gleaned will be found in my second Commercial Report, at page 266 of the Reports of H.M.'s Secretaries of Embassy, presented to Parliament in 1863.

I left Semnún at 5.30 P.M., and, after travelling five miles, came to where the plain begins to shelve up to the mountains on the north: Here the ground was thickly studded with tufts of rough grass and prickly shrubs. After going three miles farther I felt very ill and exhausted, and stopped to take tea. My servants soon kindled a fire, which raged and crackled among the bushes, stimulated by a tempestuous wind that had arisen. Soon after this we entered the hills, and it being dark, and the ground extremely rough, I dismounted, and walked, falling repeatedly, though supported by Rizá. Meantime, the wind increased to a hurricane, and was so cold that I was fain to put on a very thick cloak. I reached Ahúwán, about twenty-four miles from Semnún, at 3 A.M. on the 17th of August. I was here attacked with such violent rheumatism from the biting wind of the night that I was obliged to halt for a day. Several of my servants, too, were laid up. Indeed the cold at Ahúwán and in the passes leading to it is so intense that people are often frozen to death in winter, and caravans are detained for many days together by the snow. Hájí Mirza Aghássi built a fort at Ahúwán, and settled many families in it; but all in vain—no one would stop. The fort is ruined, but there is a large brick saráí, built by Sháh Abbás, and one much more remarkable, of stone, which is ascribed to Núshírván. Near this my servant pointed out four foxes sitting. It seems that no one shoots at Ahúwán, as wild animals at the place are sacred, in consequence of an absurd legend, that Ali met here a deer that complained to him of a huntsman who had carried off her fawn. Ali, says the story, restored the fawn to its dam.

I rose on the 18th, better, but very weak. The silence and solitude of the place were quite oppressive. I left Ahúwán at 3 P.M. For about six miles the road passed over moderate hills, and then entering a plain became as good as any turnpike road in England. I noticed that the mountains in the north were here much higher than any I had seen since I left Tehran. They appeared to be 10,000 feet high. Here I saw a second covey of the *khabk i darri*, but could not get a shot at them. Several hundreds of travellers and pilgrims passed me. I reached Gushah or Kushak at 9.15 P.M.

I awoke on the morning of the 19th of August with a very cold wind blowing over my head, and rose up racked with neuralgic pains. I left Gushah, which is but a small hamlet, with a tolerable post-house and sarái, at 2 P.M. After riding three farsakhs, I came to a group of villages, of which the principal one is Daulatábád, to the south of the road, while to the north are Ismaílábád and others stretching right away to the foot of the mountains. After passing

this extensively cultivated district the road leads
through a barren plain, with here and there low
ridges, not ill adapted for concealing marauders. I
reached Damghán at 9 P.M., and alighted at the post-
house, which is pleasantly situated at a few hundred
yards' distance from the town, beside a rivulet with a
few rows of trees near it. The poisonous bug is very
common at Damghán, and is to be found at the two
next stations beyond it towards the desert.

As I was very desirous of examining the roads
which communicate between Damghán and Mazandarún, of which M. Ferrier says, reducing them to a
single one, " The road which descends from the
mountains of Mazanderan by the gorge through
which runs the river of Damghán is very difficult and
very little frequented," I determined to halt and
explore them. The heat being quite terrific, I
remained at the post-station during the 21st, and
waited till night for my expedition. Meantime, I
employed the morning in visiting Damghán itself, to
see if I could discover any antiquities which would
justify the belief that it is the ancient Hecatompylos.
I went first to the fort, which is 300 yards to the

north-east of the post-house. It is of earth, and
ruined, but there are some curious traceries on the
walls, which I have not remarked on other fortresses
built of earth. In the centre are the rooms formerly
occupied by the Governor, faced with burnt brick,
with what has been a fountain in front. South of
this are two remarkable minarets of burnt brick, with
Kufik inscriptions. One is shattered at the top. The
other, more perfect, adjoins a mosque, with the date
A.H. 1119=A.D. 1707; the mosque, of course, being
a modern adjunct to the minaret, or perhaps built on
the ruins of a more ancient edifice. In this mosque
is a *madrisah* with twenty pupils, which I entered,
and found the mulá snoring outrageously. I took the
liberty of awaking this metaphorical pillar of the
church, in order to make some inquiries as to the
pillar of brick which overlooked his abode, but ‘he
could not give me any information. I then ascended
the minaret, and found there were 106 steps, the
height being probably 100 feet. By seizing a bar at
the top a man who was with me was able to make the
minaret rock perceptibly. The inscription resembles
that on the tower at Rhages.

The broken minaret adjoins a very old and curious building, which is the only place I could discover that might possibly be a relic of Hecatompylos. Here a mosque, now quite ruined, but probably not more than six centuries old, has been built over a far more ancient structure, round which the débris of buildings have accumulated to such a degree that it appears to be subterraneous. The pillars of this ancient palace or temple are huge, short, and massive, like the pillars of a crypt. All around are ruins, and at no great distance is an ancient tomb of some Muhammadan saint, who was, an old man informed me, the brother of Imám Riza. This assertion my servant Riza indignantly denied, thinking foul scorn, no doubt, that the Imám of the golden shrine should have a brother interred in such a beggarly fashion and in a place so obscure. There are now only 500 families in Damghán, but ruins extend for miles around. Here on the 2nd of October, 1729, Nádir won his first great victory and totally defeated the Afghán leader Ashraf with his army of 30,000 men. Here, as the whirligig of time brought its revenges, the ferocious Zakí Khán Zand planted a garden with

Persians, head downwards, and in 1796 the no less ferocious Agha Muhammad destroyed Sháh Rukh, the grandson of Nádir, by pouring molten lead into a crown of paste put upon his temples.

CHAPTER VI.

Chashmah i Alí—Mountain of the Wind—Roads to Mazandarún—
Dih Mulá—Sháhrúd—The Shuffler detected—Hájí Mutallib
Khán Afshár—Illness of the Author—Mai a Mai—Caravan-
travelling across the Desert—Hills of the Robbers—Turkuman
Preserves—The Gurkhar—Miyán Dasht—Al Aják—Abbásábád
— Sadrábád — In extremis — Mazínún.—Mihr— Sabzáwar —
Rubát Zafarúní—The Turquoise Mines—A Night's Wander-
ings—Naishapur—The Friend in Need.

I ROSE at midnight, and when thirty minutes of the
21st of August had slipped from the rosary of the
year, I mounted what the cunning postmaster mag-
niloquently called "the Arabian horse" of his stable.
But fine words butter no parsnips, nor will a garran
renew his youth, call him how you will. My aged
animal, after a small make-believe canter, subsided
to a paralytic hobble with a stumble at every fifth
step. Rizá, my servant, was still worse mounted,
and, his jade having fallen four times in the first

mile, he transferred him then and there to the guide, who had slily appropriated the only good horse of the lot. We rode on in darkness and silence for two miles, when we reached some low hills, and gradually ascending for six miles farther we found ourselves in the mountains, and crossed a fine rapid stream, which is the river of Damghán, and has its source at the Chashmah i Alí. At 4.30 A.M. we passed under a huge rock about 1,500 feet high, on the top of which the guide said there were a ruined castle and a reservoir. In half an hour more we reached the pretty village of Astánah, " the threshold." Here we met a quaint old villager riding a good nag, which we endeavoured to hire in exchange for one of our wretched animals. The fellow kept us in play till he was close to his own house, when he galloped off, leaving us half angry, half amused. A dialogue something after this fashion had taken place between him and the mission ghulám :—

Ghulám.—"We are going to the Chashmah i Bâd, and want four horses, as ours are tired. Will you lend us yours? we will pay you well."

Quaint Villager.—" Going to Chashmah i Bád— No! what for?"

G.—"For the *tamáshah*, just to see the sight."

Q. V.—"Going for the *tamáshah*? Egad, you are right. There's a deal to be seen—it's monstrous pretty. There's first of all——"

G.—"Ay, ay, but about your horse?"

Q. V.—"Horse—why, you have four of your own, and very good ones, at least I should think so."

G.—"Yes, they might be worse. But anyhow they are tired. Will you let us have yours? We will pay you well."

Q. V.—"Ay, ay, no doubt. But you will find no difficulty about horses. There are plenty, bless you, in Astánah. There's Rashíd has a good one, and Ibrahím Beg and twenty others."

G.—"Yes—but will you lend us yours?"

Q. V. (who has got near home.)—"Why, no, I won't. I won't lend him at any price, so *khudá háfiz*, 'good-by.' "

At Astánah no one would aid us, or even show us the way, until after a *fracas* between our guide and one of the villagers, when a great dirty good-humoured fellow said he would go. From Astánah to Chashmah i Ali is only a mile, by an excellent road, but one which has several branches. The spring is in the centre of a valley, surrounded by mountains, which, by their arid look, enhance the beauty of the grove and rich verdure in which the fountain is embosomed. The water gushes copiously from a rock, and is as clear, to use my servant's poetical expression, as the water of the eye. It flows into an oblong tank, about 600 feet long by 80 feet broad, shaded on all sides by fine *chenárs*, poplars, and other trees, planted probably in Agha Muhammad Sháh's time. Bridging the middle of the tank is a pavilion, built by the present Sháh, while one erected by his grandfather stands at the eastern extremity of the water. Close to the spring is the Ziyárat gáh, or place of pilgrimage, with a stone marked by the fossil of some animal, which the Muhammadans say is an indentation made by the hoof of Ali's horse. All around were crowds of Mazandaruní pilgrims, the girls and young women smartly dressed, and all gay as rustics at an English fair. The water literally swarmed with fish, not unlike the tench, the largest weighing, perhaps, two pounds. To feed them the pilgrims had polluted the water, which otherwise would be as pure as diamonds, with heaps of the entrails of sheep. While my breakfast was being prepared, I talked to the keeper of the pavilion, who said there was an excellent road to Sárí, in Mazandarún, and that thousands of pilgrims came every summer to visit the paradise, as he termed it. He added that in winter the place was shut in by snow.

After an hour's rest, I mounted and rode on six miles through a swampy green valley shut in by mountains, where I put up three *khabk i darrí*, "mountain partridges," to the picturesque village of Chahárdah Kalah, which is close to the Chashmah i Bád. Here I rested for an hour in an upper room, not badly built, but of which the owners must have been poor indeed. The furniture consisted of two coarse rugs, a pillow, a spinning machine, and a cloth spread out and full of clover, of which Rizá told me the gudewife, a frightened lassie of fifteen, was about to make soup. "Clover soup!" thought I. "Well, I have heard of living in clover, but I have never realized the idea before." After half an hour's rest I went on to the Chashmah i Bád. The sun was now intensely powerful, but, the elevation being great, the breeze was cool. After going half a mile, I came to a rugged hill about fifty feet high, the top of which was walled round. Going into the enclosure, I found a great pit, with very steep sides, at the bottom of which was a mineral spring of greenish water, about a yard in diameter. With some difficulty, I scrambled down and got a little of it in a cup. It was very cold, and intensely acrid, so much so that I could not get the nauseous taste out of my mouth for hours. The legend is, that if any filth is thrown into this spring, the sky immediately becomes overcast, and a terrible storm arises, whence the name Chashmah i Bád, or "Fountain of the Wind." I would not encourage the superstition by making any experiment, well knowing that, whatever the result, the belief of the ignorant people about would remain unaltered. Not far from this spring was a very good road, which they said led to Mazandarún. We now rode south for a mile and a half across a plain with a salt stream, and another of sweet water, with several large gardens, but scarce a cottage to be seen. We then entered a road in the

hills, and ascended continually for two miles, meeting
from time to time parties of muleteers and others
going to Mazandarún.   We now came to a broad road,
which descended continually to the plain country
round Damghán.   On either side were mountains,
from 1,000 to 2,000 feet high, bare of trees, but not
destitute of water and grass.   A very strong breeze,
almost a gale, blew up from the low country, and but
for it the sun would have been quite intolerable, for
there was not a cloud in the sky.   My horse being
quite done up, I walked all the way to the plain, six
or eight miles, as indeed did the servants and the
ghulám.   The guide alone stuck to the saddle until
we came to a deep watercourse, when his poor tired
beast fell headlong in, and was with difficulty saved
from drowning, being dragged out by the tail.

On reaching the plain, the breeze dropped, and the
heat was so terrific that I was fain to throw myself on
the ground, and put my head under the shade of a rock
not more than six feet high, while my servant and the
ghulám tried to shield me from the sun by holding up
a cloak.   After a time I went on again, suffering as
well from a tormenting thirst, as from a sun like that

of Bengal. Nevertheless, as Rizá sagely observed, *Chárahi nist,* "there was no remedy," and, with great suffering and difficulty, we succeeded in reaching Damghán by 5.30 P.M., having been sixteen hours in the saddle or walking, and having accomplished between forty and fifty miles. In this expedition I obtained convincing proof that M. Ferrier was wrongly informed as to the communication between Damghán and Mazandarún. I saw myself two good roads, by one of which Sárí is reached in three stages, and I have no doubt there are others at no very great distance; and the number of pilgrims I met at Chashmah i Ali showed that the roads are much frequented.

Exhausted as I was, I started again after an hour's rest from Damghán for Dih Mulá, seven farsakhs, which I reached at 3 A.M. on the 22nd of August. Dih Mulá is fortified, and contains perhaps 200 families. The post-house is just outside the walls. The village belongs to the Zuhíru 'd daulah, the Sháh's chamberlain, and it pays to him 2,000 túmáns a year, and 500 kharwárs of grain. I noticed at this place, as I was dressing, two little incidents very characteristic of Persia. A boy about six years

32—2

old, a very Cupidon for beauty, came from the village
dressed in a ragged blue coat, which did not cover his
hips. He carried a little sack, and began to collect
dung from the road, which he took up with his pretty
little hands, and stuffed into the sack. When it was
full, he went to a filthy pool, in which I had just
seen several nasty people washing themselves, lay
down on his little stomach, and drank his fill. After
that he went back to his bag, shouldered it, and went
off quite happy, and laden, as might be truly said,
with filth outside and in. I observed another boy, a
good deal older, but dressed after the same absurd
fashion, all coat and no trousers, who was idling
about, amusing himself. All of a sudden, an idea
struck him; he went into the middle of the street,
put his hand to his mouth to increase the sound, and
shouted, not some ribaldry, or buffoon's cry, as in ten
cases to one would have happened with a *gamin* of
Europe, but *Allâhu Akbar*, "God is great!"

At 5 P.M. on the 22nd, I left Dih Mulá, "the
Mulá's village," and had not gone far before, as I
was riding after a fine covey of partridges, I spied a
Jafari mar, or copper-bellied viper, about four feet

long, which my servant killed. The bite of this snake is said to cause death in an hour. From Dih Mulá, the chain of mountains running continuously from the spur of the Elburz, near Tehran, appears to come to an end just at Sháhrúd, whence a vast plain stretches without a break to the horizon. In point of fact, the mountains turn northwards, almost at a right angle, and after some thirty miles begin again to run due east.

I reached Sháhrúd at 9 P.M. The post-house is large and commodious, but infected with the venomous bug. Here one of my servants, who had been seized with fever at Dih Mulá, became so ill, that I was obliged to give the post-master a small sum of money to take care of him, and to pay for his funeral, should he die, as it seemed he would.

As an agent of the Russian Kavkaz and Mercurei Company had been for some time established at Sháhrúd, I determined to visit him, to collect, if possible, commercial information. Accordingly I sent to say I would, if convenient, pay him a visit, to which he replied that it was his duty to call upon me, and that he would do so at 2 P.M. At that hour, instead of the agent, came his Persian Mirza, with an apology, saying that his master had been suddenly summoned to Astarábád, on most important business, but that he hoped to see me on my return from Khúrásán. The Mirza was a solemn-looking man, but I thought I detected a momentary twinkle in his eye as he made this not very plausible excuse. However, I asked him to sit down, gave him tea, and obtained from him some information I wanted. In the evening I rode through the bázár, and, passing the Russian agency, a small, but neat store, thought I would ask for some things I required for my journey. The servants, who knew nothing of the excuse that had been sent to me, were just about to show me into a room, where sate my friend who had been called away on such urgent business, when, taking pity on him, I said I had changed my mind, and left him to manage his excuses better another time.

In consequence of the Amínu 'd daulah's letters to the authorities to show me attention, Ján Muhammad Khán, brother of the Zuhíru 'd daulah, and Governor of Sháhrúd Bustám, called on me. He said

his province extended 200 miles, till it touched that
of Turshíz, and that it contained 300 villages.
Damghán, he said, before Nádir destroyed it, was a
great city, and could, in earlier times, supply 60,000
horsemen. In Sháhrúd Bustám, he added, there was
nothing remarkable but a shaking minaret at Bustám,
which appropriately dates from the time of Shekh
Baiazíd, who lived in the ninth century. The road
from Sháhrúd to Astarábád, he said, was practicable
for camels, but there was some danger from the
Turkumans. The Russians had a summer retreat at
Ratkar, twenty-eight miles from Sháhrúd, where game
was in abundance. The transactions of the Russian
company in that quarter amounted to about 50,000
túmáns a year.

With the Governor came Hají Muhammad Khán
Afshár, the commandant of the troops stationed at
Sháhrúd for escorting travellers over the desert. He
said that the danger of the next four stages was
owing to there being as many as fifty passes through
the mountains, at this part of the range, from the
Turkuman country into Persia. The plunderers were
Takis of Girdkalah, not related to those of Merv.

Twenty years back they had swords and bows, but
now they had plenty of double-barrelled guns.   The
Háji said that some ten years ago a thousand of these
Takis made a chapáo as far as Damghán.

During the whole of the 24th of August bands of
pilgrims came pouring in to Sháhrúd, to take advantage of the strong escort which it was known would
be sent with me.   All day long resounded their
hymns in praise of Imám Rizá.   At 3.15 P.M. I
started from Sháhrúd in a sick litter, for I had been
seized with fever, and was quite unable to ride.   In
an hour and a half we reached the ruined village of
Badasht, and halted in the saráí till Háji Mutallib
Khán and the escort should come up.   My illness
increased apace, and I would gladly have stopped
where I was, but the escort and the hundreds of
pilgrims could not be detained.   At length, about
6 P.M., the rumbling of a gun was heard, and a horseman came to say the escort was ready.   We then
started, and soon got into the thick of a caravan of
about 700 people.   A little after 7 P.M. we reached
Khairábád, a second ruined village, where we halted
and formed, and then set forward into the dark night

and the desert, with a stage of forty miles before us. By this time I was in strong fever, and too ill to know what happened till we reached the next stage, Mai a Mai, at 8.15 A.M. on the 25th of August. The danger from marauders in this march is not so great as in the three following stages. Mai a Mai is a fine village, with about 300 houses, a tolerable saráí, and good water.

We started again at 3 A.M. on the 26th in pitch darkness, and at 5.30 came to the famous *Dahanah i Zaidah*, " Gorge of Zaidah," where many and many a luckless traveller has been carried off into hopeless slavery. There Mutallib Khán, like an intelligent commander, halted his men, and marshalled the whole caravan. I was still very ill, but I got out of the litter, and mounted one of my horses, and beheld what was really a very pretty spectacle. The country all around was a weird heath, with here and there ridges of from 50 to 100 feet high, behind which any number of robbers might hide. At some distance were tall hills, on which, the Háji said, there were ruins that show there had once been a thriving population in these now desolate regions. The arms of our escort flashed in the rising sun, and must have been visible at an immense distance in this vast desert, where everything else was of a sombre hue. In front was the cannon, a brass six-pounder, with twelve or fifteen artillerymen, and a handsome young officer. Then came the silk-covered litters of a number of ladies of rank, and behind them thirty or forty servants, escorted by fifty shamkhálchís, soldiers with long matchlocks fired from rests. These warriors rode on asses, but were by no means to be despised, as having weapons that would admit of deadly aim at 800 yards. After these rode a body of eighty of the Sháh's cavalry, with a standard-bearer. These horsemen threw out vedettes on their flanks very skilfully. Then followed the Zawwár, or pilgrims, about 500 men and women. The majority of the men were armed with matchlocks. In rear of all rode a few of the cavalry. As for myself, when I had done watching the pageant, I took up my position beside Mutallib Khán just in rear of the gun. The country all about swarmed with game, as we soon saw proved, for the horsemen shot several partridges close to the roadside, and one man killed a hare very cleverly, firing from his saddle at the animal as it ran. Thus we passed, disposed in the best order possible for resisting an attack, two other places, well known as localities in which the Turkumans used to waylay caravans. At the second of these the scouts galloped in, reporting clouds of dust on the right flank. Hereupon the Khán ordered a halt, and we rode to an eminence to reconnoitre. After gazing a little, we discovered that it was a large herd of wild asses, that, alarmed at our approach, were going off farther into the desert.

We reached Miyán dasht, the second halting-place in the desert, at noon on the 26th of August. Exposure to the fierce sun had brought on another violent attack of fever, and I could hardly crawl to bed. Nevertheless at 5.30 A.M. on the 27th of August the caravan mustered and went on, and I with them in my litter. As we passed the gate of the fort the Khán told me to look up. Over the gate was a thing resembling a huge horn of masonry, in which a number of Turkuman heads were stuck. The horn was fractured in the middle, and I was told that this was done by the pilgrims, who invariably pelted the heads with stones as they passed the gate. On my saying some words of disapprobation the Khán laughed and said, "How can any mercy be shown to these ruffians? The Inglís are magnanimous, but they do not know the truth as regards the Turkumans. These men destroy our villages, slay the old and feeble, and carry off the young and beautiful. The prisoners are often dragged along, and, if unable to keep up, are pricked with spears, and when quite exhausted barbarously butchered. Arrived in the Turkuman country mothers are separated from their children, husbands from wives. The wretched captives are exposed naked to the examination of Khaivak and Bukhára slave-dealers, and are sold into hopeless bondage. Nay, it sometimes happens, where resistance has been made, that the most shocking indignities are offered to innocent Persian females before the eyes of their male relatives. And shall we not burn the fathers of these miscreants when they fall into our power? I tell you, Sáhib, that the only mercy I would show them is to let them slaughter one another. Such dogs' sons should be their own executioners."

I was too ill to argue, or, indeed, to take much note of anything. At 9.30 A.M. we reached a little fort called Al Aják, where some fifty militiamen are kept by the Sháh to protect the road. Before reaching this the Hájí pointed out the spot where an Afghán chief of the reigning Bárakzye family, Alim Khán, son of Mehr dil Khán of Kandahár, met his fate. This nobleman was on his way to Herát, in the belief that the Persian Government would confer the sovereignty of that place upon him. But Sultán Ahmed Khán, the more favoured candidate, passed him on the road, and was received at Herát as ruler. Alim Khán started back to Tehrán to remonstrate, attended only by a single servant, and was here attacked by the Turkumans and died sword in hand fighting gallantly to the last. His servant was carried off to slavery. In this case, too, time has brought its revenges, and Sultán Ahmed has perished with most of his family in the city he was so proud to gain.

Not far from our next halting-place, Abbásábád, which we reached at noon, Mutallib Khán showed me the place where he had waylaid a party of fifty

Turkumans and destroyed them nearly to a man.
They were returning from sacking a village, each
man with a fair maiden or a boy before him on his
saddle, and money and valuables besides. The Khán,
who had been three days in pursuit of them, lay hid
with some thirty picked horsemen behind a ridge,
whence as the Turkumans approached he came out
on them at the gallop. Before they could get clear
of their prisoners he was upon them and had cut
down eight or ten. The rest fled and the Persians
followed, hewing them down one after another until
out of the fifty forty-two were cut to pieces. Even
the eight who got away from pursuit most likely
perished of thirst in the desert, so that the vengeance was complete.

The Khán also showed me at a little distance
from the road a copper mine, the working of which
had been suspended, owing to the attacks of the
Turkumans. The ore, I had been already informed
at Sháhrúd, was found near the surface, and contained
sixty per cent. of copper. As soon as I got into
Abbásábád I lay down, and asked for some rice
congee to quench the thirst that tormented me.

How I longed and panted for the beverage, and
when it came I drank the tumbler nearly all off,
without pausing an instant. Then I discovered that
the cook had half filled the glass with salt! Such
is the nursing that sick men find in Persia. I was
now too ill to eat anything, and I was further
weakened by constant fever; but it was impossible
to stop, so I was up before daylight on the 28th,
preparing for the fourth stage through the desert
to Mazinún. I know not if it was owing to my
illness, but the wind seemed to me poisonously
cold. As I looked out from my room on the lurid
mist that enveloped the outskirts of Abbásábád, I
thought I had never seen a more truly infernal
place. The soil is black and calcined, and one would
imagine that all the cinders in the world had been
shot at that spot.

We started at 5.30 A.M., and reached the Pul
i Abríshm, or "Bridge of Silk," a little before nine.
This is the frontier of Khúrásán, and a farsakh
beyond it lies Sadrábád, a village founded by the
late Sadr Azim, but only half finished. We arrived
there at 10 A.M., the distance being four farsakhs.

Just there I met a Shâh's messenger carrying
despatches, and with them a letter for me from
Colonel Dolmage, superintendent of the arsenal at
Meshed. This I read and sent on to Mr. Alison.
The artillery escort now left me, and it was 11 A.M.
before we went on for Mazínún, and consequently
the sun was in its full power—the flaming sun of
the desert, veiled by no cloud, stopped by no friendly
branches, but aided and reflected by a soil in part
rocky, in part sandy, or glittering with salt. I had
not gone two miles of the twelve remaining to
Mazínún, when I was seized with severe shivering
fits and a convulsive twitching of the face and jaws,
together with excruciating pains in the back. At
the same time my mouth, which was parched with
thirst, filled with a sort of crust, which seemed
to choke me. With the little voice I had left, I
besought the Khán to give me water, but there was
none to be had, and then to put me down in the
litter to die. Of course, instead of listening to me,
he urged on the muleteers, who were leading my
litter, and used all sorts of promises and threats
to them, being apprehensive that I should expire on

the road. At last we came to an old ruined Imámzádah, and there, exerting all the little strength I
had left, I threw myself from the litter, and, declaring
I could go no further, besought the Khán, if he
had any bowels of compassion, to carry me into
the building. This was done, and I remained four
hours in a sort of swoon, stretched on the mud floor.
The Khán, however, wisely sent on some one to
Mazínún to bring water, and as soon as it arrived
he made tea, of which I drank quantities. So about
4 P.M. I was able to get upon my feet, and mount
a good fresh horse which had been brought for me,
and letting him go at top speed, and merely holding
on as best I could, I succeeded in reaching Mazínún
more dead than alive. There the Khán and the
escort left me. I gave the escort twenty-five gold
túmáns, and the Khán said, "I will ask the pilgrims
to pray for you. You will not die, Insháliah! if
it please God! I shall escort you back, when you
return from Herát. You are going on a good errand
—on an errand of peace, and peace be with you!"

I passed the 29th of August and the 30th till
6 P.M. at Mazínún, suffering as much as can be

suffered without death. The small upper room of
the post-house was heated by the flaming sun of
Khúrásán like an oven. The water, brought from
an ambár, or tank, was full of insects, and had a
filthy smell and nauseous taste. It is no exaggeration to say I should have been suffocated, had
not my servants fanned me incessantly, and kept
wet towels continually to my head. Indeed, but for
the kind care of my servants, and particularly of
Ríza, who was never weary of watching, I should
have died in that miserable den, burnt up with
fever and tormented by swarms of flies, which in the
East sometimes fill the mouth of a dying man as he
lies gasping for breath. Nor were flies the only pest
there, for under the clothes in which I lay my
servant killed a large scorpion. Enough! an Eastern
kárwánsaráí is a sorry place for a sick chamber.
I knew that my only chance of life was to go forward,
and about sunset on the 30th of August I was
lifted into the litter and continued my journey.
Luckily a strong breeze sprang up, which seemed to
have come from some spot cooled by a thunder-
storm, for cool and refreshing it was, and I felt

revived. At 1 A.M. on the 31st we reached Sadgar, a fine village with many gardens, and an hour afterwards we arrived at Mihr, twenty-four miles from Mazínún, and at a much higher elevation. There I halted for the night, and sent on the Mission Ghulám to Meshed to Colonel Dolmage, with an account of my illness, and a request that he would come out to meet me to Naishapúr. At 6.30 P.M. I went on again to Sabzáwar, a weary march of forty miles, and arrived at sunrise.

The miserable little upper room in the post-house was only less hot than that at Mazínún, but the longest and most painful day must have an end, and when sunset came, I started for Rubát Zafarúni, " the yellow monastery," twenty-four miles distant, and reached it at 2.30 A.M. on the 2nd of September. The post-house lies midway between the fort, in which a few families of peasants reside, and the ancient Rubát, beside which is a vast kárwánsaráí, built by Abbás. The Rubát has been a building of immense strength, with foundations of solid masonry, and walls eight feet thick. The bricks have curious yellow spangles in them, which scintillate like

particles of gold, and hence the Rubát has its name.
The legend is that an immensely rich merchant was
preparing to build the Rubát, and out of charity
purchased three camel-loads of saffron of a poor man,
who had tried in vain to dispose of them elsewhere.
Not wanting the saffron, and being loath to mortify
the poor vendor by returning it, the founder of the
Rubát caused it to be mixed with the bricks, when to
stamp approval on the charitable act, the saffron was
all changed to gold dust, and is still seen in the
bricks.

Rubát Zafarúní is the nearest stage to the famous
turquoise mines of Khúrásán. The way to them
lies through the mountains four miles north of
Rubát, and the whole distance to be travelled is
about six farsakhs to the mines, and six farsakhs
back, or eight farsakhs to Naishapúr, supposing the
traveller to be going to Meshed. These mines used
to be taxed at 1,000 túmáns a year, but the Government now receives more from them, besides the
contract money, which is included in the general
farming licence for all the mines in Khúrásán. As
some three miles of the hill in which the mines are

have been already worked, and are encumbered with
rubbish, the expense of working increases every year.
The rubbish, however, is sifted, and sometimes an
outlay of five túmáns will bring in forty times that
sum. The two principal mines are called Abdu 'r
Rizák and Shaddád. In some places the works are
stopped by water, and the stones procured from near
those spots are of inferior colour. The *tund,* or
dark blue, is the hue preferred. The inferior stones
are made into rings with inscriptions, and are taken
by the pilgrims going to Mecca, who again find a
ready sale for them among the Arabs. The more
valuable stones are bought by the Persian grandees,
or are taken to Europe by the Resht and Astrakhán
route.

Rubát Zafarúní lies in a vast plain covered with
low bushes and rough grass, which requires only
man's care, and a supply of water, that could easily
be brought from the hills, to be clothed with smiling
crops. This plain is divided from that of Naishapúr
by a chain of mountains fifteen miles broad. The
road through them ascends continually, Naishapúr
being from 1,500 to 2,000 feet above Rubát. The

whole stage from Rubát to Naishapúr is forty miles,
and I thought if I could but accomplish it I might
shake off the fever, as I should get on higher ground,
and into a cooler climate. Although, therefore, my
teeth were chattering with ague all day on the 3rd
of September, and I was dreadfully reduced, I got
myself placed in the litter, and at 5.30 P.M. set out
from Rubát. After travelling eight miles south-east
through the plain, the road turned more to the east,
and entered the hills to the left near a most remarkable rock, which looks exactly like a huge pipkin
cracked down the middle. A mile on from this is a
ruined saráí, where I found a crowd of people
encamped. Here we got a guide, and entered a low
tamarisk jungle full of streams. It was now dark,
and before long the miserable guide took us off the
road, and with every step the ground grew rougher,
and the jungle thicker, till I began to think I had
never, in all my wanderings, not even in Astarábád,
encountered such a road. The unhappy mules that
carried the litter slipped, floundered, and plunged
through dense thickets, up gulleys and down
dells, till they finally came to a dead stop, and

the wretched guide, crying out, "Amán! amán! mercy! mercy!" acknowledged he had lost his way. It was a pleasant position for a man half dead with ague and fever to be left in, and but for the exertions of my servant Riza, I should assuredly have remained all night in that wild jungle. By his help, however, we at last regained the road, and, passing along under beetling rocks and through many small streams, we arrived at 1 A.M. on the 4th of September at Shora, the half-way village to Naishapúr. Here my servant lighted a fire, and gave me some tea, and after the mules had been fed we proceeded, and at sunrise had got out of the hills to the plain of Naishapúr. As in my then state I could not have endured the sun, I now mounted my Kárábághi horse and let him go as fast as he could carry me. The gallant little animal, though he had already come twenty-eight miles, started off and took me at full gallop to Naishapúr, where I arrived in about an hour, though there were many deep watercourses, at each of which I was delayed a little.

I was so ill when my horse brought me to the

door of the little post-house outside the city gate of Naishapúr, that I was unable to dismount, and was lifted off my horse, and helped up to the room where Colonel Dolmage was waiting to receive me. This gentleman, having formerly been the surgeon of one of her Majesty's regiments, soon understood my case, and by his care and skill saved my life. With that generous kindness for which he is so justly esteemed, he had left his important avocations at Meshed, and had ridden 120 miles, in heat which would render most people unwilling to leave their houses, to come to my assistance, though I had no claim whatever upon him, further than that I was an Englishman dangerously ill. It must be remembered, too, that journeys in Persia are very expensive, but Colonel Dolmage was not the man to grudge expense where a sick fellow-countryman was concerned.

CHAPTER VII.

Departure from Naishapúr — Durúd — Jahgark — Tabáshír and
Gulistán—Entry into Meshed—Pleasures of an Istikbál—My
Lodgings with the jovial Daroghah—Grandees of Meshed—
Flight of Khúrásání Chiefs—The Powder Factory at Meshed—
Arrival of Káfilah from Sístán—Letter to Dost Muhammad
Khán—Khwájah Rabiyah—Graves of Sálár and his Followers—
Legend of Imám Riza—Religious Terrors of a Muhammadan
Saint—The City of Meshed, and a Ride round it—The first
Step of Winter—The Imám Jumah and his Son—Why there
are no Heretics in Meshed—Herát News and Letter from Dost
Muhammad—The Imám's Kitchen.

During the 4th and 5th of September, and till the
evening of the 6th, I lay ill, and unable to move, at
Naishapúr. The post-house being too hot for a
sick man, Colonel Dolmage had kindly conveyed
me to the pleasant garden of Imám Verdi Khán,
which is about a quarter of a mile from the city
walls, is shaded by many trees and cooled by rivulets.
Here in an upper room I escaped from that terrible

sun, whose scorching rays had afflicted me for so many
days—days, like those of the fourth vial, when I
could have gnawed my tongue for anguish. It was
not one instant earlier than was necessary to save
life that I thus reached shelter and came under
skilful care. The paroxysms of fever gave way only
to such quantities of quinine as I dare not mention,
and strong doses of laudanum alone quieted the
violent heart palpitations that shook me.

About 5 P.M. on the 6th I was able again to
mount my horse, and continue my journey to Meshed.
In passing through Naishapúr I returned the call
of Sultán Husain Mirza, son of the governor, Parwíz
Mirza, and but a boy, yet acting governor. We
found the young prince, who is a very Adonis,
attended by three gaunt and solemn Mujtáhids with
white turbans of formidable dimensions. There
was also there a Persian physician, who talked glibly
of Moscow and other foreign parts, and among other
things said, " *Sar i shumá*, by your head, the
climate of Naishapúr is the climate of Teflís over
again." I thought this odd, but it was explained
when Dolmage whispered to me: "Don't mind him.

He has never been out of Khúrásán. It's a way
he has." Talking of Naishapúr, one of the Mujtáhids
said that the old city was to the south-east of the
present one, that there were three accounts of the
manner in which it was destroyed. Some said it
was by an earthquake, others by a fall of snow,
while others maintained it was ruined by the Turkumans. This, no doubt, is the true story. Old
Naishapúr was a very great city, and one of the
most ancient in the world, having been founded by
Tahmuras, one of the Píshdádyan kings, the fourth
from Adam or Noah. The modern town contains
13,000 inhabitants. I was told that the great
mosque was larger than that at Meshed, but I did
not see it, and suspect an exaggeration.

We reached Durúd, a village in the hills, six
farsakhs from Naishapúr, about midnight. Two miles
before getting to this village the road enters a *darrah*,
or pass, of low hills, with a fine stream on the right.
Durúd itself is a beautiful spot with plentiful vine-
yards and orchards, watered by the stream just
mentioned. We had now reached a cool atmosphere
and were to mount still higher. On the 7th of

September, at 2 P.M., we left Durúd. The road
led under trees by the side of a clear stream for
about three miles, with high mountains on either
side. After this we began to ascend, and the ascent
soon became steep and the trees less numerous, till
they almost ceased. About 4 P.M. we overtook our
own baggage and many parties of pilgrims, and at
five o'clock we came to a low dirty saráí, where there
was a large encampment of people going to Meshed.
Soon after this we came to the difficulty of the
whole stage, a very steep bit of road which takes a
horse fifteen minutes to climb. The last part is
rather dangerous, as a stumble might send a horse
sheer down 800 feet. The view at the top is very
magnificent. Unhappily we were prevented by the
haze from seeing Meshed. At 6 P.M. we reached
a kárwánsaráí on the Meshed side of the pass, four
farsakhs from Durúd, and whence it is called three
farsakhs to Jahgark. To me, however, the distance
seemed fifteen miles, for on and on we rode in a
valley a quarter of a mile broad, with hills from
500 to 1,000 feet high on either side, and veined
by a clear stream arched over by trees. This stream

we had continually to cross, and we did not get to
Jahgark till 11 P.M. It is a village of about 500
houses, to which the people of Meshed come for
change of air, and to enjoy the shade and cool
breezes of the delicious valley through which I had
just passed. Must it also be said that music, love,
and the forbidden juice are here indulged in with
greater freedom than near the shrine of the Imám?
This also is to some an inducement to visit
Jahgark.

We left Jahgark at sunrise on the 8th, and rode
through a pretty, shady valley, four miles to the
beautiful village of Tabáshír. High on a mountain
on the right is the fort, where the villagers take
refuge when an enemy appears in their lovely valley.
The Hisámu's Saltanah, in the rebellion of Khúrásán,
besieged it, and with great difficulty brought up guns
against it, but failed to take it. From this it is
about four miles to the village of Gulistán, where
there is a picturesque fort, which was taken by
Jafir Kuli Mirza, one of the Hisámu's Saltanah's
officers. The approach to Gulistán is by an avenue
of mulberry-trees a mile and a quarter long, planted

by a devout Meshedí for the benefit of the pilgrims. I was now quite exhausted, and was truly glad to find the luxurious English carriage of the Mashíru'd daulah, with six horses, waiting for me. The Mashír had recently been appointed guardian of the Shrine of the Imám Riza, an office worth 20,000*l*. a year, and as he had not forgotten our acquaintance in Tehrán, he sent his carriage for me with many kind messages. From 9.30 to 11 A.M. the carriage rolled along a road which would have extracted some hard sayings from the mouth of an English coachman. But the springs were good, and we were almost out of the mountains when I was met by the British vakíl at Meshed, Hájí Muhammad Kábulí, a wily individual, who, to use a homely expression, knows not only on which side his bread is buttered, but also how a little of his neighbour's butter could be rubbed off. A mile further on, my Istikbál was waiting for me, about four miles from the city. It consisted of one hundred picked Khúrásání horsemen, commanded by Hasan Khán, the senior sarhang in Meshed. With him were the Kalántar, or mayor of the city, and the chief Mirza of the Vazír, who made me a flowery speech, to which I replied with such weeds as then grew in my poor exhausted mental garden.

At 1.30 P.M. we reached the city by the Bálá Khiyábán Gate, and after driving along for a quarter of a mile, I had to mount, as the streets were too narrow for a carriage. There was a great concourse of people, and, as usually happens with Istikbáls, every one rushed frantically to get first at the narrowest places. At one of these a man carrying under his horse's belly a chafing-dish with burning charcoal for lighting pipes, passed so close to Dolmage's led horse, a fiery chestnut, that he lashed out and broke the leg of Dolmage's head servant in three places, and not content with that, distributed several other kicks to the horses round him. I was grieved to see the poor servant stretched bleeding on the ground, and Dolmage was still more distressed, as the man was a most faithful and valuable attendant. Happily, however, under Dolmage's skilful management, he, after several weeks' suffering, recovered.

My lodging at Meshed was the harím of the Daroghah, or chief magistrate, of the city. There were the outer rooms in which my servants were, and the sanctum for myself. It consisted of an upper room, from which, if I were so minded, I could peep into a large court where there were a number of ladies, and in sager moods look over the north-eastern part of the city; of a kitchen attached to the said upper room, and of a large bedroom. In the niches of my upper room there were pictures of Persian fashionables receiving wine-cups from fair ones with flushed, not to say flustered, countenances, the whole tableau having a decidedly Oriental Cremorne look. On the ceiling parrots and cockatoos in the stiffest possible attitudes were thrusting bunches of flowers under the noses of sprawling females, while birds and flowers of some unknown country ornamented the interstices of the niches. This room, being about eighteen feet long, had two doors and six windows, the windows all in a row on one side, and both windows and doors being shut in the usual Persian fashion with folding shutters, each shutter two feet broad with a chain above and below, which hooked into a ring in the wall just above the shutters. Close these shutters and you gasp for breath, open them and you admit swarms of flies by day and legions of cats by night. In this room, then, I lay down exhausted, while the magnates of my Istikbál squatted down on carpets and cushions, drank tea and smoked, and finally, hoping that my arrival might be fortunate, took leave.

As soon as I became aware that I was living in the apartments of the wives of the Daroghah I began to ponder what had become of the fair ones, and of the Daroghah himself. But the hubbub of my coming was scarcely over when I was enlightened on these points. On the other side of my southern wall there arose female voices, sometimes in mirthful, but not seldom in shrill angry tones, and with them a solitary male voice, which as night came on waxed loud and jovial, and expended itself in ditties, which drew forth answering music, and melodies about love and wine, and finally (for as illness made me wakeful I heard it at all hours) grew maudlin and quarrelsome, and cursed and was cursed in turn by shriller tongues. So I soon learned where the fair occupants of my chamber had betaken themselves, and what manner of man the Daroghah was, and how the gaseous particles of his establishment, being compressed in too narrow space by my intrusion, did suffer frequent combustion and explosion.   In truth mine host lived fast, and, at times, when wine got the mastery, would put off the magistrate *in toto*, and descend into the streets with his myrmidons and discharge pistols at a venture into the darkness of the night, and play other merry tricks more pleasant to the ludificator than the ludibrium.

Howbeit, as to these vagaries I kept silence when I called on the grandees of Meshed and received their calls.   Chief among these authorities were the Governor, Asadullah Mirza, and the Mutawali, or Guardian of Imám Rizá's shrine, my old friend the Mashír.   Asadullah Mirza is a prince of the blood, very handsome and courteous, six feet high, inclining to be stout, intelligent, good-natured, and humane. He was Governor of Turbat, but acting for Sultán Murád Mirza, the Hisámu's Saltanah, as Governor of Meshed, when I reached that city; Sultán Murád Mirza being, with an army of 15,000 men, three stages on the road to Herát.   Asadullah Mirza is well disposed to the English, and he spoke to me

in very friendly terms of Captain Jones, Resident
at Bushire, from whom he had received kindness.
He was living in the Ark, and, when I called there
upon him, a place was pointed out where a short
time before eighty Turkuman marauders had been
executed. I was told that all of them displayed
that indifference to death which springs from a life
in the open air, early habituation to danger, and
ignorance of man's responsibility. Some of them,
however, offered to purchase their lives, but the
executioners only replied with a stab, and, indeed,
one or two of the prisoners were already dying from
these blows before they were stripped and placed in
a row to have their throats cut. At my third visit
to the Prince I passed a room on my right hand as
I went in quite full of Turkumans just taken. Those
I saw were rather good-looking young fellows with
hazel eyes. They seemed unconcerned though death
was at their elbow.

The Mashír was, or had been, more than six feet
high, but he stooped from old age. His features
were large, and his look solemn and sad, or rather
weary. He had been educated at Woolwich, and

his great bony hands and large frame showed what
a strong man he had been. But the Káim Makám,
Prime Minister in 1832, had a spite against him,
and sent for him by express from Fárs, and as soon
as he arrived in Tehrán, packed him off to Khúrásán,
without so much as a change of raiment. In this
miserable plight he had to serve with Abbás Mirza,
and his constitution never recovered the hardships
he went through. He spoke English very well once,
but had forgotten it a little, when I knew him, and
used to make queer mistakes. Thus, one day talking
of a certain diplomate, he said, " He is very clever, but
he goes too much behind the ladies," meaning, "he
runs after the ladies." The Mashír was, I believe,
a true lover of his country and a sincere man, and,
moreover, he was so deaf that one could hardly have
concocted any mischief with him without its being
known. He was an enthusiast about Lord Palmerston, but when he spoke of others he would
shake his head in a way more expressive than
Burleigh's nod, and his expression became almost
ludicrously dismal.   .

The third person in importance at Meshed was

Muhammad Husain Khán, the Vazír of Khúrásán, a
conscientious, good man. His wife was, I was told, a
pious, charitable woman—religious according to her
light; and his daughter a beautiful, amiable girl. In
short, his was a family I should have been glad to
have known, had it been possible. Though not
nearly so rich as the Mashír, he lived magnificently,
and I have seldom seen anything more beautiful than
his coffee cups, or rather the stands for them, of
gold, set with the finest turquoises.

The first thing of importance that happened after
my arrival at Meshed was the flight of several chiefs
of Khúrásán to Dost Muhammad. The first of them
was Imám Verdi Beg, governor of Jám. The Amír
of Kábul received him politely, but sent him on to
Kandahár, that his presence at Herát might not
occasion disputes with the Persian Government.
After him Sulaimán Khán Tímúrí, late governor of
Kháf, escaped to the Amír, and was followed by
Bahádur Khán, the Beglerbegí of Derajez, and by
Ali Kuli Khán Tímúrí, and two Hazárah chiefs,
Bábá Khán, and a kinsman of his. Each of these
noblemen had a few horsemen with him. The Persian

Government ordered the houses of the refugees in
Meshed to be razed to the ground, and, though disaffection was thought to be rife, I did not hear of any
other escapes to the enemy.

Meantime, the Prince-Governor of Khúrásán was
at Kalandarábád, three stages on the road to Herát,
with a powerful force of from fifteen to twenty
thousand men, and his presence kept down discontent in the province, and awed the Turkumans, who,
nevertheless, made several inroads, and plundered
Turbat, among other places. The arsenal at Meshed
was, of course, busily at work supplying stores to the
Persian camp, and one of my first rides was to the
powder factory, where Colonel Dolmage was making
gunpowder equal to the best manufactured in England.
The factory was about ten miles to the west of the city;
and I found that the machinery was very simple. A
large wheel, turned by water, set in motion twenty
pestles, each about six feet long, and shaped like the
handle of a hunting whip. These came down on
mortars, built in the floor, in which the charcoal was
first put, then the saltpetre, and then the sulphur.
In spite of the care taken, an accident happened just

when I arrived, by which three or four men were killed and several wounded.

The three days' wonder about the accident had scarcely subsided when a large Káfilah came in from Sístán, and I took the opportunity to make inquiries as to the state of that province, which Persia claims on the ground of ancient possession, colonization, and the willing obedience of the Sístánis themselves. The population is partly Persian and Shiah, inclining, of course, to the Sháh's rule, and partly Bilúchí and Sunní, better affected to the Afgháns. But the chiefs of both sects are in the pay of Persia, and the flag of the Sháh waves over the principal fortress. In the interests of civilization it is surely better that a wild country like Sístán should be under the rule of a responsible government like that of Persia, than under independent chiefs, who are merely highway robbers and murderers on a grand scale.

On the 25th of September I put myself in communication with Dost Muhammad Khán. Personally, I was most anxious to see him. During the Kábul war I had been in charge of Shikárpúr, and Dost Muhammad's name was with me a household word.

I could have reached his camp in six days, and, perhaps, might have been useful in healing the breach between Persians and Afgháns. Sultán Ahmed Khán, of course, looked to my coming as the' drowning man does to a straw. It was his only chance of life, and, though he deserved little at our hands, for he looked on at the murder of Sir W. Macnaghten, if he did not take an active part in it, yet, still, we had recognized him as ruler of Herát, and had spoken him fair, and it would have been a magnanimous act to have saved his life. On his part, the Dost was anxious to see me, but the fall of Herát and the death of Sultán Ahmed were both registered in the book of fate, and no message of mercy was sent.

Meantime, under the kind care of Colonel Dolmage, I was gradually regaining strength, and, though at first so weak that I was obliged to crawl upstairs on all-fours, I was now able to ride about and examine the famous city of Meshed and its environs. One of my rides was to the shrine of Khwájah Rabiyah, on the north-west of the city. I rode to the Nauzun Gate, and there got into the Mashír's carriage, which pitched and rolled like a ship in a storm along the rough road. After a drive of two miles, I reached the clump of trees and garden in which the shrine is. The building is beautifully faced with richly-coloured tiles or Káshís. It is a square, with a rotunda dome in the centre. Within, in the centre of the building, is the wooden tomb of Khwájah Rabiyah, a saint of the time of Ali; and on the left is the grave of Fath Khán Kájár, who was obliged by Nádir Sháh to level his fort at Astarábád, and was afterwards slain by the tyrant. Outside are still more interesting monuments. Three piles of bricks and stones mark the spot where Muhammad Hasan Khán Kájár, the favourite son of the Asifu'd daulah, Prince-Governor of Khúrásán, in the time of M. Ferrier, is buried with his son and nephew. Hasan Khán was surnamed Sálár, or commander-in-chief, by Fath Ali Sháh, and was cousin to Muhammad Sháh. In 1848 he raised a rebellion in Khúrásán, and held out in Meshed for nearly two years, but was at last taken and strangled. Opposite are the graves of about forty officers who joined the rebellion, and were all put to death. It is said that Arslán Khán, the Sálár's son, was a man of

Herculean strength, and, though unarmed, he made a desperate resistance when the order for his execution arrived, and was only overpowered by the united efforts of ten powerful men.

While I was surveying these sad mementos of ambition that o'erleapt itself, I was accosted by a most agreeable man, Akhund Mulá Sádik, a Mulá of Meshed, with whom I entered into a long conversation. Among other things he dilated much on the miracles of Imám Rizá, and on his cruel murder by the Khalif Maimún. "The Imám," said he, "had the gift of omnipresence, and once when a native of China came to test his power, and asked what a friend of his was doing in China, he made answer, 'Look into my hand.' When the man looked he beheld his home in China, and his friend walking in the garden with another person whose back was towards him. At last, when the stranger turned his face, what was the astonishment of the Chinese to behold the countenance of the Imám, who thus solved the great question as to the possibility of being in two places at the same instant." "But tell me," I said, "has the Imám

left no worthy successor? Who are your holy men
now?" "At present," said the Mulá, "the garden
of holiness is dried up, and the most flourishing
plant in it is but lately dead, the famous teacher
and priest, on whom be peace, Hájí Mujtáhid."·
I asked if the Hájí's sanctity preserved him from
the terrors of death, and how he had acquitted himself at the last. "The Hájí," said the Mulá, "was,
I know not why, always in fear about death, and
he would be constantly perplexing himself as to
what he should answer to the angels Munkir and
Nakír, who examine the defunct. I reminded him
that he was as safe as in Paradise itself, for his
body would lie close to that of the blessed Imám.
But it was all to no purpose, and he died in the
odour of sanctity, but as much afraid as the most
unclean criminal."

Another day I rode completely round the city,
starting from and returning to the northern or
Idgáh Gate. Outside this gate are two or three fine
gardens, and particularly one belonging to the
Hisámu's Saltanah, which produced peaches much
larger than any I have seen in England, delicious

grapes and figs, and enormous quinces of an ex-
quisite perfume. Here, too, is probably the weakest
part of the town, and where an attack would succeed
most easily. After a quarter of a mile, there is a
branch road to the right, which goes round the city,
while the main road goes on straight to two curious
rocky hills, which form the end of a spur from the
line of mountains on the north. These hills are
about a mile and a half in a direct line to the
north-east of the Ark of Meshed. They are called
Kúhsang, and there is a ruined shrine at the foot
of one of them, in which lives a fakír, who would
probably be carried off by the Turkumans, were
he worth taking. The road continues past the
hermitage, and goes into the mountains to villages
safe from marauders by the difficulty of access to
them.

To return now to my ride. Taking the branch
from the road just described, I came after a few
hundred yards to the Ark Gate of the city. The
ground here is very rough, and the ditch broad,
and forty feet deep, and it could be filled with
water from a reservoir and watercourses further on.

About a hundred yards from the Ark Gate the northern wall of the city ends, and the eastern begins at right angles to it. At this angle is the Ark, and the wall is well built up to the height of twenty-five feet. The eastern wall zigzags out to the east, and after a few hundred yards passes a reservoir and an excellent spring of water called Saráb, and here, at a quarter of a mile from the north-eastern angle of the city wall, is the Saráb Gate. A little further on the wall begins to turn towards the west, and after another quarter of a mile the southern wall may be said to begin. Following this for a mile, I came to the Bálá Khiyábán Gate, opposite to the entrance into the Mosque of Imám Rizá. The ground is very rough all along this part, and the rifle-pits are still to be seen from which the citizens used to fire when they were besieged by the Hisámu's Saltanah. In half a mile more the Naugun Gate is reached, and a little before this the western wall begins and runs on for three quarters of a mile, after which the northern wall begins and continues for three quarters of a mile to the Páin Khiyábán Gate, and thence a quarter of a mile to the gate of Idgáh. On the whole, therefore, the circuit of the city is about four miles, but I was unable to take any measurements or exact bearings by compass, owing to the extreme jealousy of the people, and my description may not, therefore, be very accurate. The population of Meshed may be reckoned at from 80,000 to 100,000 persons,~ and there is sufficient garden and arable ground within the city to produce corn enough to support them for a long time. In case of siege, probably fifteen thousand men would be found to bear arms in defence of the city.

During the latter half of September, the great heat had been gradually lessening, but winter came on the 4th of October with a sudden stride indeed. The effect on my health was remarkable. I had gone to bed determining to be up early and to take a long ride, saying to myself that, emaciated and ill as I was, I would have a struggle for life, and see what exercise would do for me. At dawn on the 4th Riza came to me and said : "*Bád i tund ast, va abr, va hawá khailí mukhtalif ast*—There is a violent wind, the sky is cloudy, and the weather is

very contrary to health." To this I replied, somewhat to his surprise, "Bring the horses; this is
just the day for me." When I got outside the
city the cold was so intense that I could hardly
hold the reins, and the watercourses were all frozen
over with ice, which I could not break with the
blow of a pebble. This frost lasted but for two days.

On the 5th of October I went to call upon the
Imám Jumah, a personage of great sanctity, as being
a true Saiyid, or descendant of the Prophet, an aged
man, and high priest of the most bigoted population
in the world. His house is in the Saráb quarter,
and his fine garden is watered by canals from the
springs of Salsabíl, the Shekh, and the Mosque.
He is very rich, possesses large estates, and is said
to marry a fair damsel every month, whom he
shortly afterwards divorces. His eldest son, however,
is a thorn in his side, and he has passed him over,
and takes as his deputy his third son, whose name is
Hidáyatullah, but who is surnamed Masumu'l aïmah,
the "Innocent of the Imáms," or "Pope Innocent."
On arriving, a servant came to tell me that the
high priest was at prayers, on which I amused

myself by walking in the garden with the Vakíl. After a decorous interval we were informed that the holy man would see us.

"But," said the agent, "he is at prayers."

"Never mind," replied the messenger, "he bids you enter."

Accordingly we stepped into a room about thirty feet square, in which, among other things, was a clock, out of which jumped a little bird, which hopped and squeaked while the hour was being struck. There was also a large chair in which they bade me seat myself, and a stove of a common kind, such as one sees in a low-class steamer. In the centre of the room was the high priest, who must have been handsome in his youth, for his features were good, and his blue eyes were still bright and his arm plump, praying on his prayer-carpet, on which were a book, the Hidáya, in a cover of rose-coloured silk, a comb for the beard, and several other articles.

"'Talk,'" said the Imám Jumah; "do not mind me." I said I had rather not talk while prayers were going on. He said, "Oh! I thought your heart would

be dull! that's why I told you to talk." I said,
"Excuse me, I shall not be dull. I would rather
not talk till you have done praying." So he went
on praying, bowing, and prostrating himself, also
coughing and spitting, and combing his beard, and
occasionally saying "How d'ye do?" to persons
who came into the room. This lasted for more
than half an hour, after which he went out of the
room, then returned, sat on his bed, and talked.
He said he liked the English; that they were of
better caste than the Russians; that he had been
pleased with an English minister he met with
Muhammad Shâh; that our consul at Baghdad
(Sir H. Rawlinson) had been kind to him, and had
lent him a house with an inscription to Alí in it,
at which he marvelled, seeing he was among Turks
and Sunnís. During this talk he incessantly called
for his spittoons, of which he had quite an assort-
ment, and interrupted himself to ask his doctor to
feel his pulse, and to complain of a pain in his nose,
which organ he kept squeezing with his fingers in
a most whimsical fashion. All of a sudden he
asked me how old he was. Taken a little off my

guard, I said I had heard he was eighty. He is in fact eighty-five. This answer might have cost me his good-will. He sputtered out with great energy, " It is false ! " and then turning to his doctor, he said, " I am sixty-eight, am I not ? "

" By your blessed head ! " said the doctor, " I did not know you were so much. Praise be to God, you have all the vigour of a young man. If your holiness says you are sixty-eight, it must be so; but I can hardly believe it."

I saw the rogue's eye twinkle as the old man turned to me triumphantly and said, " It is true. I am sixty, and a year or two more."

To change the subject I asked if his family had been long in Khúrásán. He said, " My family is the family of the decapitated ones " (meaning of Ali), " but my ancestors went first to Egypt, then to Syria, and then to Ispahán, and lastly, to Khúrásán, where they have been for six generations." At parting he called me his friend, patted me on the chest, and asked me to come again soon—civilities which I received with due *empressement*, for I knew he was the most influential man in Khúrásán after the Prince-Governor.

Some days after I called on the Imám Jumah's son, the Masúmu 'l Aïmah, who leads the prayers in the Great Mosque. As his lodgings were within the sacred precincts, where no infidel is allowed to tread, he received me at another place. He, however, lent me a telescope to look at the beautiful carving on the minarets of the mosque. Several mulás were present, and we had a long conversation on religion, at the end of which the Imám's son exclaimed, " *Chandán ikhtiláf níst*—there is no great difference," between Islám and Christianity. He seemed puzzled about the doctrine of the Trinity, and said the Catholics believed there were three gods, of whom the Virgin Mary was one. I told him the story of the German knight who robbed the vendor of indulgences, having previously obtained from him an indulgence for so doing, and he laughed immoderately at it. On my asking him if there were any sects in Meshed, he said, "No, there are none. There were some Jews, but they are now all Muhammadans; in fact, we kill those who are not of the orthodox faith, consequently there are no heretics."

Meantime, the Ghulám Ghafár Beg, conveying

35—2

my letter to Dost Muhammad, had reached Herút,
received his answer, and returned. It was 3 A.M. on
the 11th of October when he arrived. The letter from
the Amír declared, in the usual Oriental style, that
all that he had was mine, his house my house, I had
only to come. The Ghulám said that when he
crossed the frontier, thirty Afgháns joined him as
escort, but a tremendous storm arose which blew
down all the tents in the Dost's camp, and when he
got there, only five of the horsemen remained with
him. He reckoned the Amír's troops at 32,000 men,
with twenty-nine guns, and the Herátís at 8,000.
Sultán Ahmed had had six batteries outside the
town, but one of these had been captured by the
Dost, recaptured and again retaken, with a loss to
the Amír of 46 men killed and wounded, and to the
Herátís of 180 killed and 80 taken prisoners. The
Dost had four camps, one on each side of the city,
1,000 men under Mír Alam Khán at Ghorian, and
600 at Kohístán, under Táj Muhammad.

Some days after, the Mashír begged me to call
and talk over the aspect of affairs. Afterwards he
took me to see the public kitchen, supported by the

revenues of the Imám's shrine. This kitchen is in the avenue of Bálá Khiyábán, which runs up to the western gate of the Imám's mosque. Eight hundred persons are fed at this kitchen daily. I saw the dinner served up—there was a goodly mess for every two persons, that is, four breads, four chops, and a platter of rice. Any stranger may dine for twenty days. Thence I went to the new hospital, built by the Mashír for eighty sick persons. It is in a fine large garden, and the Mashír told me he intended to endow it with funds.

CHAPTER VIII.

Novel Cure for the Bite of a Bug—Alarming State of Meshed—
Arrest of an Artilleryman, and gallant Act of Colonel Dolmage
—The Mashír leads the Author into imminent Peril—Defile-
ment of the Mosque—Ferment amongst the Mulás—Departure
from Meshed—Sang-bast—Farímon—Death of the Charger
—Istikbal at Kalandarábád—First Interview with Sultán Murád
Mirza — The Vazír of Herát—Intense Cold — Underground
Lodgings — Second Interview and Conversation with Sultán
Murád Mirza.

TWENTY-ONE days after I had left my servant Takí
apparently dying at Sháhrúd he rejoined me. I had
advanced him the money for his funeral expenses,
and he met me with rather a sheepish look, as if he
felt it might be thought he had not acted quite
honourably in expending the amount in rejoining me,
instead of dying as he said he should. The poor
fellow was so weak that he could scarcely crawl, and
he would not believe that his was a case of simple
fever, but insisted that he had been bitten by the

poisonous bug at Dih Mulá. Impressed with this
notion, he resolved on going through the regular cure
prescribed at Meshed for such a bite. After a day
or two, seeing him come tottering in, looking more
like a corpse than a living being, I inquired what
remedies he was taking, and was not a little surprised
to hear their nature. It seems that those who are
bitten, or think they are bitten, by the Argas Persicus, go to a house at Meshed, where bowls of curds
are served out to them. After they have drunk the
contents, they sit down in a seat suspended from
ropes, which is then spun violently round, till it
acquires a motion like a top. The effect of this
movement acting on the curds is to produce vomiting to such an extent that sea-sickness is a pleasant
pastime in comparison. Of course the patient is so
weakened that no more life remains in him, and he
faints. Poor Takí, a huge man in his palmy days,
became weaker than an infant, so much so that one
day, after the remedy, he fell headlong and gave himself a deep wound in his head. But Persian constitutions are strong, and at the end of a fortnight's
retching, my invalid was really cured, and went to

thank Imám Riza for his recovery. Meantime, however, he had been a trouble rather than an assistance
to me; and as my cook, too, was lying at the point
of death with typhus, Riza had to cook and do the
work of four men, which he accomplished with
that imperturbable good humour which characterizes
the Persian servant.

The normal state of Khúrásán is war. Petty
plunderings, murders, brigandage, small insurrec-
tions, executions of five, ten, or twenty robbers take
place weekly, and cavalry engagements, sieges of
fortresses or towns annually, with a considerable war
every five or ten years. The siege of Herát, the
pretensions and intrigues of Dost Muhammad, the
elation of the Turkumans consequent on the destruction of Hamza Mirza's army of 30,000 men at Merv,
had, when I was at Meshed, greatly intensified the
evils of a state of affairs always bad. Bodies of
Turkuman horse were continually on the move, and
some of them passed on their cruel errands close to
the city. On the other hand, parties of Khúrásání
free lances were no less often mustered for the work
of retaliation. In the city itself daily fights and

murders took place, and the general tableau was one of bloodshed, audacious plots, and ruthless executions.

To exemplify this state of things more particularly let us mark down a few of the events which happened from the 13th of September inclusive. On that day from twenty to thirty cavalry officers were placed in arrest under suspicion of a design to join Dost Muhammad, and a sortie from Herát, with severe fighting and heavy loss on both sides, was reported.

On the 14th, it was ascertained that several chiefs of rank had actually escaped from Meshed, and had gone off with parties of their adherents to join the Amír, or the Turkumans. On the 16th, news came of an attack by Alí Kulí Khán and some thousand Turkumans on Derajez. On the 20th, 400 Turkumans were heard of, plundering on the Herát frontier, and Nauroz Mirza, with a body of Persian cavalry, went in pursuit of them. On the 25th the Farrásh báshí of the Prince-Governor, with a strong body of riflemen, marched through Meshed to attack the Turkumans who were wasting the district of Derajez with fire and sword. Another sortie of the Herátís was reported on the 1st of October and on the 7th

a third, which ended in 400 Herátis being taken
prisoners. On the 10th there was a very serious disturbance in Meshed between a body of Kurds under
Amír Husain Khán and the soldiers of the Khalaj
regiment. The Kurds attacked the guard-house and
wounded several soldiers, when the police of the city
attacked them in turn and drove them off, taking
several prisoners, who were bastinadoed and had their
ears cut off. On this, the Kurdish chief assembled
his men to plunder the city, and the garrison were
kept under arms and on the alert, until the Prince-
Governor prevailed on the Kurd to come to his camp.

On the 14th of October the Daroghah called on
me and said he had been at a murderous fight in the
city, and showed me a wound he had received in it.
The same day one of the Vazír's farrashes was killed
in a riot, and another man was literally cut to pieces
by some drunken artillerymen, and eight Turkumans,
two heads, and eleven horses were brought in by
a party of forty Khurásánís who had been out on a
chapáo. Next day the Governor of Meshed told me
he had just received news that a strong body of
Turkúmans had plundered Turbat and carried off

many captives and much spoil. The same night there was a large incendiary fire so near my lodging that I could see to read by the light of it.

On the 16th, another fight at Herát was reported, in which Alam Khán, the nephew of Sultán Ahmed Khán, was killed, and many others, and next day several hundreds of Jamshídís went over to the Dost. The same day, at 2 P.M., as I was sitting in my room, two pistol-shots were fired close under the wall of my lodging, in a place where I could not have seen what was going on even had I looked ; but having heard so many shots about the city, I did not take the trouble to rise from my book. An hour or two afterwards Riza, my servant, came and reported what had occurred. He and Farjullah Beg, one of the Mission Ghuláms, a very powerful Kurd, about six feet high, were standing at the door of my house, just as Shír Ali, a servant of Colonel Dolmage, passed them, walking with the owner of Dolmage's house. Presently a gigantic artilleryman came out from a disorderly house drunk, and began to abuse them, no doubt as being servants of a Káfir. They retorted, on which the artilleryman drew out his pistols and fired them at Dolmage's landlord, and then cut down Shír Ali with his kámah, a sort of short sword like the old Roman, dividing the collar-bone, and all but severing the sub-clavicle artery. Had that artery been cut the man would have died on the spot. Dolmage, hearing the disturbance, rushed out with a heavy hunting-whip, calling on some farráshes of the Vazír to follow him. They refused, saying they should be killed; but Riza and Farjullah joined Dolmage in pursuit of the assassin, came up with him near the city wall, knocked the kámah out of his hand, and took him prisoner. The difficulty now was to convey the huge, brawny ruffian—a fellow six feet three inches high—all through the city to the Vazír without a rescue, for his brother artillerymen, the *topchis*, as soon as they heard what had happened, assembled to the number of two hundred, and posted themselves in the way they thought Dolmage would come. On the other hand, a lot of determined fellows came down from the arsenal to assist Dolmage, who was their chief, and things looked very promising indeed for a general fight. There was, however, a roundabout way to the Vazír's house little known, by which Dolmage managed to convey his prisoner to the Vazír without encountering the *topchís*.

. It was, perhaps, lucky that I had not seen this disturbance nor been seen in it, for I am not at all sure that my presence would not have made matters much worse, and caused my own and Colonel Dolmage's death. In fact, I was at that very moment in the greatest danger, owing to an extraordinary piece of imprudence on the part of the Mashíru 'd daulah, who, wishing to show me a civility, almost occasioned my being murdered. On the 16th, about 11 A.M., the Mashír sent a confidential servant to me to say he wished me to call on him, and that he would show me the *Haram* or Sanctuary. Of course, I supposed he meant to do as the Imám Jumah's son had done, let me see the mosque at a distance, for I well knew the jealous fury of the Meshedís as regards the shrine of the Imám. This is so great that they will not allow any one but a true believer to come even within the outer precincts of the mosque, and those precincts are *bast,* or sanctuary, and no criminal, or debtor, could be taken from them. It so happened that the road from my lodging to the house of the

British Vakíl at Meshed, Hájí Muhammad Kábulí, led for a few steps through these precincts, and I was obliged to make a long circuit not to offend the people. The Vakíl himself told me that if I attempted to set foot in any part of the *bast*, there would be a disturbance, and my life would be in danger. This being the case, it never entered my head that the Mashír would expose me and himself to the imminent risk of being torn to pieces by taking me into the sacred enclosure.

In perfect ignorance, then, of what the Mashír intended, I went to his house about three hours before sunset. We had a very long conversation, and I told him that in consequence of several pressing invitations from the Hisámu's Saltanah to visit him, I was going to join his camp on the Monday following. The Mashír said, " You will not require any horsemen to escort you. The road is quite safe." I said, " Very well," though I knew that a few miles outside the walls of the city there was no such thing as safety from the Turkumans. He then turned to several Persians who were seated near him, and repeated that no horsemen were necessary. One of them replied in a bland way: "What your Eminence says must be right. Still, there are foolish rumours abroad. The Turkumans are dogs; they run hither and thither; who can tell where those children of unclean mothers may be found? The Prince has ordered the Hazárah horse, who were going to camp to-day, to halt, and go with the English Mustashár." The Mashír shook his head and murmured, "It will give him the idea that Khúrásán is disturbed." The other answered, "Yes! Better that, than that the Mustashár should be taken and our Government have to pay 10,000 túmáns ransom, as it did for the French photographer!"

The conversation then changed to other subjects, and speaking of ——, the Mashír said, "He is not very clever, though he writes better than he speaks. He does not converse at all : he only looks."

Talking on in this way it grew dark, and I kept wondering whether the old man had forgotten all about the mosque. I thought he, perhaps, wished me to see the illuminations from some window, for this was Thursday night, or, according to Eastern reckoning, Friday, the Sunday of the Muhammadans. At last the Mashír rose up and said, "We will go now." On descending the stairs, I found a crowd of servants and others, about two hundred people in all. We went out of the courtyard, and through a number of passages, and then ascended some stairs, and entered a suite of rooms which had been very handsomely decorated. Here he paused for a moment, and I observed a whispering amongst the servants, and several of them seemed very much flustered and confused. Riza, especially, who was a brave man, but rather a zealot, turned quite pale. Suddenly the Mashír went on again, a curtain was drawn aside, and I saw a blaze of light which quite dazzled me, coming, as I did, out of dark passages. In a second or two I was exclaiming to myself, "Good Heavens! can it be possible? — we are going right into the Great Mosque!"

It was, indeed, so. We were entering a sort of alcove, about ten feet from the ground, in the quadrangle of the mosque, which had been magnificently illuminated by the special order of the Mashír. The quadrangle was filled with people, many of them at their prayers; hundreds more were thronging in at the great archways. There were probably not less than seven or eight thousand in all, and there was suddenly a great hush as the Guardian of the Sanctuary, with an accursed infidel beside him, dressed in the detested Faringí dress, appeared entering the holy place. It was certainly rather a trying moment. I must confess a suspicion flashed across my mind, knowing how vexed the authorities were that the English Government would not interfere about Herát, that I had been brought into this danger with the set intention of exasperating the people against the English, and so aiding the cry for a religious war. However, though I most assuredly expected to be attacked when I left the mosque, I thought it right not to hesitate, and I walked in and sate down in the chair which the Mashír pointed out to me, and began to regale my eyes with a scene worthy of the *Arabian Nights*.

The quadrangle of the mosque in which I was seemed to be about 150 paces square. It was paved with large flagstones, and in the centre was a beautiful kiosk, or pavilion, covered with gold, and raised over the reservoir of water for ablutions. This

pavilion was built by Nádir Sháh. All round the
northern, western, and southern sides of the quadrangle, ran at some ten feet from the ground a row of
alcoves similar to that in which I was sitting, and
filled with Mulás, in white turbans and dresses. In
each of these sides was a gigantic archway, the wall
being raised in a square form above the entrance.
The height to the top of this square wall must
have been 90 or 100 feet. The alcoves were
white, seemingly of stone or plaster, but the archways
were covered with blue varnish, or blue tiles, with
beautiful inscriptions in white and gold. Over the
western archway was a white cage, which seemed to
be made of ivory, for the Muezzin, and outside it
was a gigantic minaret, about 120 feet high, and
as thick as the Duke of York's column in London.
The beauty of this minaret cannot be exaggerated.
It has an exquisitely carved capital, and, above that,
a light pillar seemingly ten feet high, and this and
the shaft below the capital for about twenty feet were
covered with gold. All this part of the mosque was
built by Sháh Abbás. In the centre of the eastern
side of the quadrangle two gigantic doors were thrown

open to admit the people into the adytum, or inner
mosque, where is the marble tomb of Imám Rizá,
surrounded by a silver railing, with knobs of gold.
There was a flight of steps ascending to these doors,
and beyond were two smaller doors encrusted with
jewels. The Mashír said, for at that distance I could
not see them, that the rubies were particularly fine.
The inner mosque would contain 3,000 persons.
Over it rose a dome entirely covered with gold, with
two minarets at the sides likewise gilt all over. On
the right of the Imám's tomb is that of Abbás Mirza,
father of Muhammad Sháh, and grandfather of the
reigning Sháh. Near him several other princes and
chiefs of note are buried.

Beyond the golden dome, in striking and beautiful
contrast with it, was a smaller dome of bright blue.
Here begins the mosque of Gauhar Sháh. The
quadrangle is larger than that of Sháh Abbás, and
at the eastern side is an immense blue dome, out
of which quantities of grass were growing, the place
being too sacred to be disturbed. In front of the
dome rose two lofty minarets covered with blue tiles.
All this vast building was in a blaze of lamps, and

was thronged by a vast concourse of people, and of that great multitude there was not one individual whose eyes were not bent upon me. The crowd fell into little groups, all talking of the intrusion, and looking angrily towards us. Even the Muezzin on the top of the great minaret in front of the western archway was gazing at me over the rail, and I could see him in a fixed attitude, as if in surprise. While I was looking at this wondrous scene, the Mashír showed to me the account of the daily expenses of the mosque, and pointed out that 751 pilgrims had arrived that day, and more than 200 had departed. During the whole year to that day, he added, upwards of 50,000 pilgrims had visited the shrine. Meantime, having sated my eyes with looking, and having sat some fifteen minutes expecting every moment to hear a shout of "Kill the infidel!" I got up, thanked the Mashír for the sight, and said it was worth while coming from England to witness, and then asked leave to go. At that very moment the people were consulting whether or not to kill both myself and the Mashír on the spot, and had we delayed a minute or two longer the result might have been death. As it was, the old man got up, and we left the mosque, returned through the long passages, and I bade him good-by and rode home. There was a very great crowd as I mounted, but not a word was said. As I rode to my lodging the city was lighted up by another great incendiary fire. An immense magazine of wood was burning just outside the Idgáh Gate, and the people were on the roofs of their houses looking at it. *

Next day happened the affray between the artillery-man and Dolmage, and on going out I was surprised to find a crowd of people assembled to see me mount. As my lodging was in a very retired quarter, and no one had ever before taken much notice of me, this

---

* I believe that I am the only European that ever went into the mosque of Imám Rizá at Meshed, certainly the only one that has entered as a European. It is possible that one or two Faringís may have got in in native dress, but I am not aware that such is the case. M. Ferrier talks of having walked about the quadrangle, but his description is just what might be given from hearsay, and after peeping in from the Khiyábán avenue. It seems strange that he says nothing of Nádir's pavilion, of the ivory cage, and the jewelled doors, and that he misdescribes several things that can be seen only from the inside.

looked odd. On Saturday the 18th, I had gone to bed rather early, and at midnight was fast asleep, when Rizá woke me by knocking at my window, and said Dolmage had come to say he must see me instantly. I jumped out of bed, undid the window, and let him in. Dolmage is a brave man, and has shown his coolness on many occasions; but he certainly looked on this occasion like the man who drew Priam's curtains in the dead of night. He then told me that he had been dining at the Vazír's, and found him unusually pensive and silent. When Dolmage was going away, the Vazír said to him, " Oblige me by doing a trifling thing. Put on Persian clothes for to-night, I will lend you a suit," and when Dolmage was going to turn it off in jest, the Vazír told him that there was very great excitement amongst the people, that he had received . upwards of thirty letters from the chief officials of the shrine, saying, in reference to the Mashír's bringing me into the mosque, that the dead body of the blessed Imám had been defiled by the presence of an infidel, and that unless he, the Vazír, took vengeance for the insult, they would take it them-

selves. The Vazír added that he so fully expected
an outbreak, that he and all his servants had been
up all night, and he hinted that, however anxious
he might be to save Dolmage, he felt that in a
popular tumult in such a city as Meshed on account
of the desecration of the mosque of Imám Rizá,
no Shiah would venture to oppose the fury of the
mob. In short, the Vazír said that our lives were
in most imminent danger, that the Mulás were
busy purifying the mosque, and that there was no
saying how that might inflame the anger of the
people. Dolmage, however, would not disguise himself, and said, " You know that I brought an
artilleryman through the city two days ago to prison
in spite of his comrades, and I will take the same
risk to-night." The Vazír then sent ten farráshes
with him to see him safe home, and he came at once
to me.

" So," said Dolmage, "you see we shall very
likely be killed. But, if they attack you, I will
come over directly to your help, and at all events we
will die defending ourselves. There's no chance of
getting away, and of course we wouldn't if we could."

" What vexes me most is," I replied, " that, if I do have my throat cut, every one will say ' Served him right ; what business had he to go into the mosque ? Besides, he ought to have remembered that he was on an important mission, when such an imprudence might have brought about a public difficulty.' This is what will be said, whereas God knows I am the last man living to wantonly offend any one's religious prejudices, and specially at such a time. I am sure you will bear witness to that, and that it never entered my head that the Mashír was going into the mosque. Do you know, I half think it is a regular plan to bring on a rupture between the Governments, and make an excuse for attacking the Afgháns ? "

" I should have thought that possible," said Dolmage, " if it had been any one but the Mashír, but he knows the power of England too well. No, he wants to break down the prejudices of the people, and he thought it would be a good opportunity to begin by taking you to the mosque. But I must go now; good-by, and for God's sake don't go out of the house, or you will very likely not come back.

On Monday the escort will be here, and then we can start."

As I had already taken leave of the Mashír and the other authorities, I had no occasion to go out on the Sunday, the day following this conversation, and on the Monday, Dolmage and I started for the Prince-Governor's camp, though the cavalry escort, with the usual slack discipline of Persians, never joined us till we had got some miles on the road. It was curious that when I took leave of the Mashír, I said I hoped I should see him again soon. " You will never see me again," he said; " I shall die here. I wish to die ; I came here on purpose, and I shall die." So it turned out, for a few weeks after I left, the poor old man did die suddenly. In fact, it is quite possible that the affair of the mosque may have hastened his end.

It was 10.30 A.M. on Monday the 20th of October, when we rode out of the Idgáh Gate of Meshed. Dolmage was on a fiery chestnut Turkuman, ready to jump out of its skin with freshness. The British Vakil and his son accompanied us, and after going a mile or so, we were joined by a Levantine in the service of the Sháh, a M. N——, who was riding a great, blundering Turkuman horse, seventeen hands high. This creature had been given him by a chief, and he much wished to sell him to me, though I would not have had him at a gift. But poor M. N—— was not a rider to show off a horse to advantage. He could not manage his great steed at all, and somehow it seized an old woman and bit her severely, whereupon he jumped off, and the horse began to strike out with its fore-legs at him, until he roared most lustily for assistance.

About half-past twelve we got to Turrágh, a fine village, with a particularly healthy air. Here we halted an hour, and were joined by 200 of the Hazárah Horse, under their Sartíp, who pressed me rather rudely to stop for the night at the village, which I felt inclined to do. Dolmage, however, said we had better go on, and we did so, leaving the Sartíp to his own devices, but followed by 150 of his cavalry. The road passed over an undulating country, with high hills on each side at the distance of a mile or two. On many of these hills were watch-towers. These, in fact, are common throughout Khúrásán, as are buildings of refuge in the fields, which are built with such low doors that a horseman could not attack a person inside.

At 5.30 P.M. we got to Sang-bast, a village six farsakhs from Meshed, which has been entirely built by the regiment of Naishapúr. The corps did not much like, I was told, being thus turned into masons, but Persian sarbáz are much more useful than soldiers in the West. The village has been newly peopled by the Hisámu's Saltanah, in order to be a check on the Turkumans. The Kadkhuda's house was assigned to me, and, being quite new, was free from vermin. The cold was severe, and there was no wood, but only dry grass to burn, which made a great blaze and smoke, and was out in a minute or two.

Next day we started at daylight, and rode six farsakhs more to Farímon. About four miles from the village, Nasrullah Khán, the chief of the Jámís, appointed to be my Mihmándár till I should reach the prince's camp, came to meet me with thirty horsemen. He was riding a splendid Turkuman horse, and he showed me the place where he got it cheap, by shooting its Turkuman rider. The night was intensely cold in the garden at Farímon, where we pitched our tents, and the water in my tumbler was frozen into a solid lump. Farímon is a small and very filthy village. Five regiments were encamped close by under the Muzaffir 'd daulah.

When I got up on the morning of the 22nd, I plunged my face into my basin and found that it was full of ice. Strong as he is, Dolmage was unable to sleep for the cold. The servants, half frozen, were long in loading the mules, so I started by myself, and Dolmage remained to look after the baggage. After galloping over some fields, and getting out into the road, I was joined by Nasrullah Khán and some horsemen. Presently we saw Dolmage galloping over the country to meet us. His chestnut horse looked to advantage, and went over some large jumps capitally. The distance to Kalandarábád from Farímon is only two farsakhs, the road winding to the south for the last mile or two. At length we descried the péshwáz, or Istikbál, coming to meet me from the prince, and as I was getting tired, I proposed a gallop across country to meet it. Off we set, and my little Kárábághí, as

usual, cleared everything in its way very cleverly.
Before long, however, we got into very rough ground,
with ditches and ridges, and innumerable holes made
by the jerboa. All of a sudden I heard a tremendous
thump close behind me, and looking round saw
Dolmage rising from the ground amid a cloud of
dust, and his horse stretched out full length. The
poor animal moved his head convulsively for a
moment, and then all was still, and the noble
charger, so full of fire and spirit a moment before,
now lay a lifeless lump. I immediately dismounted,
and running up to Dolmage found him much
bruised and cut, but with no bones broken. As for
the poor horse, it had just cleared a ditch, and came
on a second one before it could recover itself, so
it turned a complete summersault in the air, and
coming down with its head pointing in the direction
its tail did just before, broke its neck, and was dead
in an instant. Dolmage now mounted my Arab, and
in a few minutes we met the Istikbál party.

It was, indeed, something like a reception party,
consisting of more than five hundred horse, commanded by Safar Alí Khán, the Sartíp of the Sháh-

sevend Cavalry, and just promoted to the rank of
Amír Panj, or general of five thousand, for the
capture of the famous Muhammad Shekh.   This
Shekh was the most celebrated Turkuman leader
living, and in his life of eighty years had done more
mischief than almost any great pirate or brigand on
record.   At last, it being fated that he should take
his final ride, he started to chapáo some villages south
of Farímon, with several hundred picked Turkuman
freebooters.   But he had to do with the Hisámu's
Saltanah, who sleeps with his eyes open.   Wherever
the Turkumans went they found the alarm given,
cavalry on the alert, and themselves in danger.   So
after a long profitless gallop, all but eighty men left
the Shekh and went back to their own country, while
he resolved on a daring stroke.   Thinking that he
should probably find the Persians off their guard
close to the walls of Meshed, he rode in the direction
of Kwájah Rabiyah, and there Safar Alí Khán
came upon him with the Sháhsevend Cavalry, and
killed or captured seventy-nine men out of the
eighty.   The Shekh was slain, and all who were
made prisoners were executed.

Among the other men of rank sent out to meet me were also Muhammad Riza Khán, Governor of Rátkan; Ghulám Riza Khán, Commandant of the Merví Horse; Safar Ali Khán, Sarhang of Artillery; and Atá'ullah Khán, commanding a regiment of Cavalry. In short, had I been an ambassador, the prince could not have done more in the way of giving me a courteous reception, and I was glad of an opportunity to see such a large body of picked Persian cavalry manœuvring across country. All the horses I saw were fine animals, many of them quite equal to the horses of our English cavalry regiments. I was conducted, on reaching the camp, to a tent, where I was received by Nauroz Mirza, son of Riza Kuli Mirza, the Naibu 'l Iyálat, who was so well received in England by William IV. With him were the Adjudán Báshi, the son of Riza Kulí Khán, of Shíráz, and Ghulám Haidar Khán, nephew of Dost Muhammad, a very handsome Afghán nobleman.

On going to my own tent Dolmage told me that the Hisámu's Saltanah had directed him to tell me that I had arrived in a fortunate moment, as an express courier had just come in from the Sháh with the news

that the English Government had agreed to turn back
the Amír of Kabúl from Herát.   The prince further
asked me to wait upon him in two hours.   I went
accordingly, and found the Hisámu's Saltanah in a
large handsome tent, with every comfort about him.
The master of the ceremonies, on introducing me,
bowed three times to the prince.   My chair was
placed opposite the prince, but a yard lower, and right
across the tent.   No one sate in his presence except
myself. His manner was courteous, but dignified and
rather reserved.   He read a letter from the Persian
Chargé d'Affaires at Constantinople, saying that he
had received a telegram from Mirza Husain Khán,
then in London, announcing that Lord Russell had
undertaken to do justice, and had sent instructions to
Mr. Alison to turn back Dost Muhammad.   I could
not, of course, contradict this announcement, but I
felt sure there was a mistake somewhere. The prince
then entered into general conversation; asked me if I
would like to hunt, and offered me the use of his
beautiful English carriage whenever I wanted a drive.

Next day I rested, and on the 24th of October I
received a number of visits.   The first who came was

the Khán Názir, a nephew of the prince, holding, as
the title imports, the office of lord steward or butler.
His talk was all of the chase. Among other things,
he said there were tigers and panthers in the mountains near camp, and in fact all the way to Herát and
Merv, and that, the last time the prince went to Merv,
an enormous tiger was killed, and the prince offered
a large reward to any man in his camp who could
move the carcase. Hundreds tried, but there was
not a man strong enough to drag the huge beast
even a few inches.

After him came, among others, the Vazír of
Herát, Hasan Alí Khán, sent by Sultán Ahmed, the
ruler of Herát, on a special mission to the prince, by
which mission, if he did nothing else, he saved his
own body from the swords of Dost Muhammad's
followers, who would assuredly have made mincemeat
of him. He called himself a Kábulí, but he had a
vile Uzbek face, small, cunning eyes, high cheek-bones,
and a forehead " villanous low." His son, a boy of
fifteen years old, was with him. I contrived to keep
him from entering on business matters, but he gave
vent to a long tirade against Dost Muhammad, whom

he accused of ingratitude to the English. After half an
hour, as my servants, influenced no doubt by a retainer,
would not bring the pipe of dismissal, I was obliged
to retire, feeling too unwell to sit up any longer.
As ill luck would have it, my tent was pitched close to
the gun fired at morning and evening. This gun, to
the intense gratification of Dolmage, .who manufactured the powder, made a noise much greater than
might have been expected from its size, and many a
slumber of mine did it effectually dissipate, so that I
could not repair the loss for that night. Nor did it
improve matters that I found a venomous snake in
my tent among my clothes. It was brown, with a
flat head, and seemed to be a sort of adder. As
this was the third snake I had seen about, it did not
add to my sense of comfort. Further, the cold was so
intense that I really could not sleep for it, but for this
the prince promised a remedy, sending to say he
would have a Turkuman tent, with a stove in it,
brought out for me from Meshed. As for the officers
in camp, they were locating themselves in a very snug
fashion, having dug rooms in the ground, which they
warmed with large fires, and protected from the rain

by banks of earth and slanting wooden roofs. In one of these I visited Nauzar Mirza and another young prince, and found a difference of 20° between their cellar and the tents.

CHAPTER IX.

Second Interview with the Hisámu's Saltanah—Anecdote of the
Perso-Russian War—Gallant Behaviour of the Russian Regiments in the Retreat from Merv—Jafar Kuli Mirza—Description of the Camp at Kalandarábád—A Soldier's Idea of Celes-
tial Reliefs—The Herát Question—A Turkuman Ambush—The
Band i Farímon—Hawking with the Prince—Afghán Spies—
Attack on the Amír's Camp—Karíz i Budágh—Persian Jugglery
and Witchcraft—Arrival of a long-expected Courier—The
Author is appointed Her Majesty's Chargé d'Affaires in Persia,
and recalled to Tehran—Farewell Audience of the Prince—
The Horse of Allah Yár Khán.

On the 27th of October I had an interview with the
Hisámu's Saltanah, which lasted two hours.   He told
me that the revenue of Herát was 100,000 Herát
túmáns, equivalent to 80,000 túmáns of Tehran, or
38,000*l.*   Out of this the troops necessary for the
peace of the territory must be maintained, and these
could not be less than five regiments of infantry and
4,000 horse.   Then there are the civil charges; so

that, in point of fact, the revenues of the country are not sufficient to meet the expenses. Yúr Muhammad made up the deficiency by extracting 18,000 túmáns from Sístán, and a like sum from the Ghúrát. The conversation turning on the Perso-Russian war, it was mentioned that, after the insurrection headed by Pestall, the Emperor sent fourteen regiments to Paskiewitch, with an order to use them up. They were accordingly put in the van in every engagement with the Persians. At last, when the meeting of Abbás Mirza and Paskiewitch took place at Turkumancháí, the survivors of those three regiments offered to Abbás Mirza to kill Paskiewitch and join him. The Prince, however, was afraid to accept this offer.

Talking of the gallantry of the Persian soldiers, the prince said that three regiments, not having been relieved at Merv, were obliged to retreat, and were attacked by 12,000 Tekki, Sálár, and Sarakhs Turkumans. But the regiments, viz., that of Kárái or Turbat, that of Turshíz, and that of Naishapúr, marched on and did not leave one man in the hands of the enemy, dead or alive. They kept

close by at Farimon, and had eaten up the supplies
of the neighbouring districts to such an extent that
everything was very dear.

The tents were very well pitched, with the prince's
large tent in the centre, and those of the artillery
before him towards the Herát road.   The infantry
tents were pitched on the two flanks, and the cavalry
in rear.   There were the guard mountings, the post-
ing of sentinels, pickets, and all the other routine of
regular European armies.   It must be confessed,
however, that the sentries used to scoop out holes in
the ground of such a shape that I make no doubt they
lay down in them during the bitter cold nights, when
a wind was blowing that iced the life-blood in the
veins.   Also, the sentries would beguile the midnight
hours with long chats.   Some of these I could not
help overhearing, and they were droll enough.   On
one occasion a religious discussion took place between
several gruff voices, which seemed to turn on the
merits of various saints.   At last one voice, evidently
that of a recruit, from the diffident way in which he
addressed the others, asked if it was true that there
was no good in praying to Ali now ?   " Who told you

that ? " said another. " Hazrat Ali (on him be blessings and peace !) is always ready to hear. Are you a Káfir, that you doubt it ? " " Not so," said the inquirer, " *astaghfar allah*, may my sins be pardoned ! but I was told that his Holiness Ali had been relieved, and was off duty for the present ! "

The valley in which the village of Kalandarábád is situated is about twelve miles broad. The hills on the north sink low for about fifteen miles opposite to the village, and then rise rather suddenly to a height of several thousand feet, and just there there is a village on a spur of the mountains, to which it is not very safe to ride without a hundred good horsemen at one's back. Indeed, all along these northern hills the Turkumans constantly show themselves. On the south side the valley begins to undulate, just beyond the place where the prince's camp was pitched, and after a mile or two, low hills begin, which gradually mount to a range of peaks three or four thousand feet high, while both to the east and west of the camp are detached mountains, which thus included as it were the encampment in a sort of crescent. At the foot of those detached hills to the north are the ruins of two villages and a saráí, the inhabitants of which were carried off or killed in some Turkuman raid. The ground is everywhere covered with low bushes, among which were plenty of hares and sand-grouse, and we had some coursing close to camp, in spite of the myriads of holes made by the jerboas, which rendered falls by no means rare.

All this country might be rich and populous, but for the Turkumans. In my third interview with the Hisámu's Saltanah he descanted with much truth and feeling on this subject. " The desolation of Khúrásán," said the prince, " is wholly owing to the ravages of invading tribes, and above all of the Turkumans. To prove this, it is quite sufficient to examine the district in which my camp now is. From this camp to the frontier of the Turkuman country is about 200 miles in a direct line, and throughout that space will be found villages and towns, with their forts, their mosques, their baths, and houses standing, but utterly deserted, the population having been exterminated, or driven gradually south. Thus, in this very plain, which is from fifteen to thirty miles broad, there are no less than three lines of road from

Meshed to Herát. The furthest off passes at the foot of the northern chain of hills, and fine, solidly-built kárwánsáráis exist at regular intervals, and near them are the remains of villages. But owing to the ravages of the Turkumans, this line of road has been deserted for many years. The next road lies through the middle of the plain, and has been, for the same reason, similarly abandoned, and now all the traffic passes at the foot of the southern hills."

In connection with these remarks, the prince went on to speak of the reasonable anxiety of the Persian government to restore order and tranquillity in Khúrásán, and this led him to refer to the Herát question.

"The frontier of Persia," he said, "conterminous with the country of the Turkumans, is of such extent, that it is impossible to prevent the inroads of those marauders by simply guarding the passes. The Turkumans are so greedy of gain, and their avarice is so gratified by the sums which the chiefs and people of Bukhárá and Khaiva pay for Persian slaves, that nothing will prevent their kidnapping expeditions but the occupation of a stronghold in their own country by Persian troops. Such a stronghold is Merv, which commands the river that supplies the Taki Turkumans with water, and is sufficiently near to Bukhárá to make the ruler of that country more careful, were it occupied, of offending the Persian government by the purchase of Persian slaves, than he at present is. It is for this reason that Persia is so anxious to reoccupy Merv, and not simply because it is the country of a large portion of the Kájár tribe, and as rightfully belonging to Persia as any portion of the Sháh's dominions.

"But in order to occupy Merv, the possession of Herát, or an alliance with that State, is necessary, for the direct route to Merv is almost impracticable for troops, leading, as it does, through a waterless desert. Besides this, there are passes in the hills near Herát, through which the Turkumans have for ages come, and, crossing from the Herát territory into Persia, have plundered Tabbas, Kain, Turbat, and all the south of Khúrásán. When Herát has been in the possession of Persia, or when it has been under a friendly ruler, the garrisons of

Ghurián and Kohistán, near which fortresses the passes frequented by the Turkumans are, have given notice to our frontier posts of the approach of marauders, and then the inhabitants of the neighbouring Persian villages, after collecting their flocks, have kept within walls till the danger has passed. These facts explain the repeated movements of Persia against Herát, and show why she desires to keep some hold upon that province, for such a hold is requisite for the tranquillity of Khúrásán. But England persists in misunderstanding the policy of Persia, and supposes that the expeditions to Herát have originated in a weak vanity of adding to territories already too large to be easily governed, and too thinly populated to supply levies of soldiers for foreign aggression.

"For my own part," continued the prince, "placed as I am here to defend a province which ought to be the brightest jewel in the Persian crown, and seeing, as I do, the waste and desolation caused by the merciless hordes of the Turkumans in what was formerly one of the most populous and flourishing countries in the East, I am at a loss to understand the behaviour of the English. England professes herself to be the ally of Persia, and yet she pertinaciously opposes measures which are absolutely requisite to secure the Persian frontier. England assumes to be the determined enemy of the slave trade, and has gone to an enormous expense to liberate the African races, to whom she is no way bound save by the tie of a common humanity. It is surely, then, inexplicable that England should have never lifted a finger to save or rescue the hundreds of thousands of Persians who are carried off into slavery by the Turkumans. So far from that, England shackles and impedes every effort that the Persian government makes for the protection of its own subjects, and, by expelling Persia from Herát, and even discouraging a friendly alliance between the two countries, renders the tranquillity of Khúrásán impossible."

I must confess I thought there was a great deal of truth in the remarks of the prince, and my impressions on this head were deepened by seeing with my own eyes the horrible desolation which the Turkumans have wrought. Nowhere in Khúrásán is there any safety from these prowling wretches, as I learned by experience. The prince spoke to me several times about the risk of going on *shikár* expeditions without a guard, and one day I had proof that he was right. It was the 4th of November that, having nothing particular to do, I thought I would have a long ride to the foot of the northern hills, take the greyhounds and course. The first thing that happened was that, in jumping over a watercourse, my revolver went off, and the ball passed through the holster close to my toe. After going some miles we found several hares, and, in coursing them, got quite away to the hills. Presently my servant rode up and called my attention to a horseman a long way off, evidently watching us. On looking in that direction with a small pocket glass, one could see, a great way beyond that man, fifteen or twenty others, halted in a low jungle. On making this discovery, we turned and rode back to camp, and the prince sent out some scouts to see who the intruders were, but they were gone into some pass in the hills.

On the southern side of the valley there was, of course, greater security. My favourite ride in that direction was to the Band i Farimon, a corruption for Farídún, "the embankment of Farídún." This remarkable monument of antiquity is situated in the hills six miles to the south-west of Kalandarábád. Here a beautiful mountain stream comes wandering among swampy and reedy meadows down to a pass between rocks a thousand feet high. Nature had provided a leap for the water of some fifty feet, and here, many years ago, according to the legend, in the reign of the seventh king of the Píshdádyan dynasty, a stone embankment was thrown across. It is built of solid masonry, of stone and burnt brick, united by a cement which has become like iron, and is 100 paces long and ten broad. Against this causeway the stream rose to a certain height, and then found a passage down several tunnels of masonry, and so flowed out at the bottom of the embankment to fertilize the fields in the direction of Farímon and other villages. This important work had become dilapidated in the course of ages, and the Prince-Governor ordered it to be repaired, and set the regiment of Gerrús to work at it, under the superintendence of Jafar Kuli Mirza. I went very often to the spot and shot many fine wild duck along the stream, and one day the horsemen with me killed a wild boar, three parts grown. The traces of wild hog, of wolves and leopards, were to be seen in many places.

To the Band i Farímon, too, the prince took me on a hawking expedition. The hills about were full of partridges, but so wild were the birds that there was no getting near them, except with a hawk. The Persians are most fearless riders, and the prince, with his hawk on his glove, rode up and down the hills, where it was difficult for a horse to keep his footing. Then a covey of partridges would get up, and the hawk would chase them in an instant across a ravine which took us much time to cross. On these occasions thirty or forty partridges and a few tihús would in general be killed, and one day a single hawk killed nine birds in succession.

In these long rides and frequent meetings the prince's reserve wore off, and we, who had sate on chairs the first day in such a stiff fashion, with the breadth of the room between us, now breakfasted together, and played chess seated on the carpet.

The prince, in fact, soon found out that I had no intrigues to conceal, and that I wished well to Persia as honestly as he did himself; and the opinion he had formed on this head became conviction after a very simple incident. One evening, with a great deal of mystery, a man was smuggled under the walls of my tent, and I was informed that a secret messenger had arrived from Dost Muhammad, who wished to communicate with me. I asked if he had any letter, and on their telling me he had not, I said I could not communicate with him; that of course if Dost Muhammad sent me a letter I would receive it, but that there was no occasion for any mystery, and I did not wish to conceal anything from the prince. Most probably the whole thing was an attempt to find out whether I had any secret mission, and certainly when I reported it to the prince, he did not show any surprise, and looked very much as if he knew all about it.

But, on the 9th of November, a veritable messenger did come from the Amír, and was smuggled in again in the same absurd way. He was a ragged fellow

from Ghurián, and seemed in mortal fear, and when
he produced a letter from the Dost, he said, "If
I am detected, I shall be——" Here he drew his
hand significantly across his throat, and though I
told him there were no secrets at all in the letter,
I saw he did not believe me. The letter was dated
Herát, 11th of Jamádu 'l Avval, corresponding to
the 5th of November, and the Dost merely said he
had heard I had been ill, and wished to know about
my health. The fellow then asked me for some
money, and when I gave him a túmán, he disclosed,
in hiding it in his dress, another letter, which, no
doubt, was the really important one, and in delivery
of which he did probably risk his life. For whom it
was I know not ; as for the letter to me, I read it
next morning to the prince. It is possible that the
man who brought it may have been an Afghán spy ;
but I should hardly think any Afghán could have
managed to escape the notice of the Persian guard,
not only at Kalandarábád, but all along the road
from the frontier. The only piece of intelligence I
got from the man was a confirmation of what the
prince had told me a day or two before, that 6,000

marauders—Turkumans, Jamshídís, Tímúrís, and others—had chapáoed the Dost's camp, and carried off 2,000 camels and baggage animals, and several hundreds of prisoners.

My last ride with the prince was to the village of Karíz i Budágh, which he had lately restored and peopled as a check on the Turkumans. It lies about six miles to the east of Kalandarábád, in a fine situation, just where the valley sloped up to wooded hills, the beginning of the southern range of mountains. On the way the prince talked much of *shabdah bází*, "juggling," and magic. The conversation then turned upon witchcraft and calling up spirits, and the prince related a curious anecdote of what had happened to Farídún Mirza. Farídún had married his cousin, a princess, to whom he was very much attached. She died, and some years afterwards it was reported to the widower, then Governor of Khúrásán, that there was a certain Mulá, named Farzán, who had the power of calling up the spirits of the departed. The prince went to see him, and took Sultán Murád Mirza, then a youth, with him. On the wizard asking who should be called up,

Farídún Mirza named his wife, and after a few minutes the wizard said she had come. The prince then desired that a question might be put to her about a certain matter which no one but she and her husband knew. The wizard looked in a *tás*, or cup, and gave the right answer. After this the prince wrote on a slip of paper the name of Asif, the Vazír of Solomon, and, without showing the paper to the wizard, told him to call up the person named in the paper. Presently the wizard said the spirit had come! and without waiting to be questioned the spirit spoke in about the same words as Samuel addressed to the witch of Endor. " Why is my sleep disquieted? why have ye raised me up?" Farídún asked what was the name of God by which the throne of Balkís was brought to Sulaimán? The spirit answered, " It would be useless to thee, and of use only to one who wears the signet of Sulaimán."

On the 18th of November, the day after our ride to Budágh, an express courier, for whose arrival expectation had long been on the strain, came in. He brought me a despatch from Lord Russell, announcing that Mr. Alison had been summoned

to England, and appointing me her Majesty's Chargé
d'Affaires at the Court of Persia till further orders.
I was directed, therefore, to return to Tehran as soon
as possible.   Mr. Alison simply wrote that, as there
was nothing particular to do at Tehran, he thought
it a good opportunity to take his leave.   The despatch
appointing me Chargé d'Affaires, though dated the
24th of September, did not reach me till the 18th of
November, fifteen days after Mr. Alison had gone to
England, and must, therefore, have been delayed
somewhere.

As soon as this intelligence reached me, I waited
on the Prince-Governor of Khúrásán, and told him
I had been recalled to Tehran, and must proceed
thither as soon as I could make the necessary
arrangements.   Up to that moment the prince had
been buoyed up with hopes of the intervention of
her Majesty's Government in the affair of Herát,
and had relied on a despatch sent by the Persian
Chargé d'Affaires at Constantinople to his Government, announcing that Mirza Husain Khán had
attained the object of his mission to London.   It
was painful to witness the disappointment of his

Royal Highness when I told him the policy of her Majesty's Government was not to interfere with the Afgháns. He seemed literally stunned by the blow, and kept ejaculating, "Impossible! What is to be done?" At last he entered upon an exposition of the difficulties of his situation. He spoke first of the expense of keeping his army in the field, and said that it cost for his camp at Kalandarábád alone more than 600 túmáns a day. He then referred to the sufferings of the soldiers, owing to the weather, to the disaffection in Khúrásán, fostered by the presence of a large Afghán army on the frontier, and to the dangers of Turkuman attacks to which the Persian provinces were exposed by the withdrawal of friendly garrisons from the forts commanding the passes at Ghurián and Kohistán.

Lastly, the prince referred to my departure with regret, and spoke to me in a way that assured me of his friendship and regard. I, on my part, felt that if my expedition to Khúrásán bore no other fruit, it was something to have gained the good-will of such a prince as Sultán Murád Mirza, who for

twenty-four years has been engaged in state affairs
of such importance, and who has undertaken and
been successful in such memorable enterprises. I
had this consolation, therefore, in setting out on
my return to Tehran. But there was also another
thing which made me truly happy, viz., that the
prince, in kind consideration for my health, permitted Colonel Dolmage to accompany me. I had
great hopes of getting over my journey with his
friendly assistance, though otherwise I think I
should have broken down at the third stage. As
soon as Dolmage had obtained leave to go, he
started at once for Meshed to make his arrangements, promising to join me at Naishapúr. On
returning to my tent I found the prince had sent
for my acceptance his favourite charger, a horse
which had been purchased from the Teki Turkumans
by Allah Yár Khán, and presented by him to the
prince. It was what might be called a red dun,
five years old, sixteen hands high, of immense
strength, good in all its paces, and a magnificent
jumper. The smallness of its ears and the massive-
ness of its neck were remarkable, and it possessed

qualities highly prized by Persian horsemen. One of these was that it would not suffer a horse to approach it, but would kick it over instantly, while a man might lie under its hoofs without being harmed. It was a horse that ought to have been sent to England for stud purposes, and I regret that I did not bring it home.

CHAPTER X.

Departure from Kalandarábád — The Snow-storm—Ahmadábád—
Inhospitality of the Imám's Tenants — Kadamgáh — Parwíz
Mirza—Sagdih—Minaret of Khusrangird—The Touters of
Abbásábád—Anecdote of Páshá Khán—Herds of Deer at
Khairábád—Riding *Chápár*, and the Pleasures thereof—The
Runaway—Last Legs—A memorable Istikbál.

IT was in a deluge of rain at noon on the 20th of
November that I left the prince's camp. Nothing
could be more dreary than the scene. Thick
clouds rested on the mountains, the base alone of
the hills being visible. The wind was icy cold and
so strong that one was obliged to bend low in the
saddle to face it. The valley was one enormous
muddy pool, in the clay of which our horses' legs
sank a foot deep. When we reached, at 3 P.M., the
village of Farímon, we found the only lodging pro-
curable was a hovel in which no English squire

would put his dog. There was no cover for the horses, and they had to stand in the rain in a filthy yard, where my boxes also were deposited. When night came I found it impossible to sleep for some worthy troopers and their innamoratas in the next hovel, who drank, sang, swore, and quarrelled the whole night through. I could not help overhearing their conversation, and it was very much what might be expected in a *coup de gorge* house. In fact, if my neighbours were not themselves professed highwaymen, it was evident that they had acquaintances in that line.

Next morning, my servant Taki, who was rather a prophet of evil, informed me that the rain of yesterday had become snow. "There is a fine *burrán* (snow-storm) blowing," he said; "the people say we shall be frozen to death before we get a farsakh from this. As for the horses they are already dead with the cold. The Sáhib's things are all wet through with the rain of last night, and Dolmage Sáhib's orange-coloured horse is stolen." On receiving this pleasant information the first thing was to send out horsemen to look for the missing steed, which, after

payment of a few túmáns, was brought in. The next
thing was to get a cup of tea and to pack off the
reluctant servants with half the escort, and follow
myself in an hour with the remainder. The prospect
on getting out of the fort was truly terrific. The
snow was already deep, and the wind blew with such
force that the horses could hardly walk. In a few
minutes my beard was frozen into a solid lump of ice,
and my eyes were almost closed. It was only with
whip and spur that we could keep the horses at a
brisk walk, following one another in single file and
stumbling into holes and ditches, which were not to
be discerned under their snow covering.

"The Sáhib is well mounted," said one of the
horsemen; "he may, perhaps, with Nasrullah Khán's
son as his guide, reach Ahmadábád; but as for the
muleteers and those of our party whose horses are
weak, they may think themselves lucky if they get
to Farahgírd, which is half-way. And if, which God
forbid, we lose our way, there is not one of us that
will live out the night."

"What dirt is that thou art eating?" broke in
the young Khán; "as if I could lose my way within

a farsakh of my own village—I that have acted as
guide to the Khúrásán horse hereabouts for three
years! Besides, the Sáhib's destiny is good, and, if
it please God, this *burrán* will cease before the
evening."

These cheery words turned out true, and we had
no sooner got to Farahgírd, which is a small hamlet
perched on a hill, that looked in the snow and the
distance more like a dead camel than a village, than
the wind dropped, and we reached Ahmadábád at
2.30 P.M., having been seven hours in riding sixteen
miles. Ahmadábád is a fine village belonging to
Háji Kuli Mehdí Khán, in whose comfortable house
I took up my lodging. The route I had now taken
was the direct one to Naishapúr, from twenty to
thirty miles shorter than that by Meshed, and it was
one which, as far as I know, had not been travelled
before by a European. Finding myself in comfortable
quarters, I wrote several despatches and a farewell
letter to Dost Muhammad, in which I said that, by
the passes near Herát being left open, the Turkumans
were enabled to ravage the neighbouring provinces of
Persia, that their kidnapping expeditions were odious

to civilized nations, and that I was sure the English
Government would be pleased if he did what was in
his power to put a stop to them.

At 9 A.M on the 23rd of November, I left Ahmadábád.   It was bright but bitterly cold as we rode
along over the snow.   We crossed a number of low
hills, and saw many small forts and walled villages
at some distance, till, at two farsakhs from Ahmadábád, we came to Hasanábád, and one or two other
villages close to the roadside.   Thence the road
turned more to the south, and after another farsakh
we came to Bahrámábád, and then to a village on
a hill, and finally reached Dizbád, where we intended
to halt, at 2 P.M., the distance from Ahmadábád
being six farsakhs.   Here, to my disgust, no mules
were to be seen, and the villagers told us that they
had sent my things on, as there was no place for
me to stop in.   They said, too, that they were
ryots of *Hazrat*, " His Holiness," meaning the
Imám Rizá, and they would not receive any one in
their houses.   There was a dissipated looking Mulá
selling corn out of the village granary to the people,
and to him I appealed, but he would not aid me.

On this the horsemen with me began to talk in a threatening tone; but the villagers gave them frown for frown, and hard word for hard word, and, I believe, would have drawn swords and used their matchlocks on the smallest of provocations. In fact, the Khúrásánís are like the Afgháns, quite as ready to give broken heads as to take them.

There being no help for it, we remounted our weary horses, and rode on in the direction of Kadamgáh, and after three or four miles we came to the junction of the branch-road we were on with the grand trunk road to Tehran, and could see Kadamgáh about six miles off. Hereupon we put our horses to a canter, and got to Kadamgáh at 6 P.M., having ridden about forty miles from Ahmadábád.

Next morning before starting, I walked across from the post-house to the Ziyárát-gáh, or place of pilgrimage. This is a small but handsome mosque, bosomed in lofty trees, and built by Sháh Abbás. The object of reverence is a black stone with the impression of two very large and ugly negro feet stamped in it to the depth of two or three inches. It looks as if some one had been stepping on asphalte or bitumen, when in a softened state. "You see," said the Mutawalí to me, "what holy men there were in the old days. These are the footprints of the Imám Rizá, who tried to convert the fire-worshippers who lived here in his time. Their sacred fire was burning on this stone, and the Imám stepped on it and left the marks of his feet as a sign to them." "And pray," said I, "what was the effect produced on the Gabrs?" "Well," replied the Mutawalí, "the rock will not give forth water unless God will it, and the fire-worshippers repented not at the miracle."

After seeing the Ziyárat, I walked up a lofty hill to the fortress of Kadamgáh, from which there is a magnificent view over the vast plain of Naishapúr. The fort is inhabited entirely by Saiyids, who give themselves the airs which the sanctity of their descent entitles them to display. The fort of Kadamgáh is about 600 feet above the plain, and might be made a strong position. On the hill opposite are the ruins of a much more ancient fortress, said to have been destroyed by the Afgháns. Leaving Kadamgáh at 11 A.M., I reached Naishapúr at 3 P.M. The road was almost as good as a turnpike-road in England, the weather pleasant, and I was well enough to look about me and regret that a magnificent country, which two thousand years ago was comparatively populous, should now be so deserted as it is. As we journeyed, the leader of my escort beguiled the way with tales of the Turkumans, and pointed out a spot where an engagement took place between these marauders and the Persian cavalry, in which he was present. The Persians foolishly awaited the onset of the Turkumans, who, coming on at speed, overthrew them and killed forty or fifty. Just at that moment the Persian artillery opened at a very long range, on which the Turkumans withdrew into a gorge in the hills, where the Persians did not venture to follow them. This story was scarcely ended, when it came into my head to try if the horse the prince had given me, and on which I was riding, would stand fire. There were a number of crows on the ground more than a hundred yards off, and I drew my revolver and fired at one without the least idea of hitting it, but simply to try the horse's steadiness. As luck would have it, the ball hit the crow on the head, on which I put back my pistol, too wise to try another shot, while there was a general shout from the horsemen of " Wáh ! wáh ! the sáhib shoots better with a pistol than other people do with a rifle. We have seen shooting all our lives, but never such shooting as this ! "

On reaching Naishapúr, I was delighted to find Dolmage arrived. In the evening the Governor of Naishapúr, Parwíz Mirza, called upon us. He is the youngest son of Fath Ali Sháh, and must have been a marvel of comeliness in his youth, for he is still singularly handsome. He is also excessively witty and agreeable, and would have, were he to come to Europe, great success in society.

The villages round Naishapúr have been bestowed on refugee Afgháns, which very naturally excites great discontent amongst the natives of the province. Indeed, this part of Persia was in a most distressed condition at the time of my visit. The state of the finances of the province may be inferred from the fact that Dolmage having presented an order on the local government for fifty túmáns, the utmost that could be scraped together to meet the demand was twelve túmáns, and while that sum was being collected, several other claims were absolutely repudiated on the ground of "no effects."

It snowed dismally all day on the 25th of November. We halted, and I wrote despatches, rushing one moment into the air to escape the suffocating smoke, and, the next, piling on fresh fuel to save myself from being frozen. The 26th dawned with a bright sun, under which the snow was rapidly converted into slush. We left Naishapúr at 8.40 A.M., and reached the filthy village of Sagdih, distant four farsakhs, at 12.30. Here we halted to lunch, and Dolmage shot a pigeon at over a hundred paces. At this place he stopped two years before with General —— and his wife. During the night, hearing a scream, he fancied that robbers were upon them, and rushed to the room of his fellow travellers. There he saw Madame —— rolling in agony on the ground, and, on examining her neck, where the pain seemed to be, he found a spot swollen up as big as an almond and quite black. Thinking it was a snake-bite, he sucked out the venom, and

applied some remedies. In spite of this, violent
fever came on, and the patient was in some danger,
but, on examining the place by daylight, it became
evident that the bite was not that of a snake, but
most probably of the Argas Persicus.

From Sagdila we entered on four miles of deep
mud, and did not get to the half-way village, Shorah,
till 2.40 P.M., though we galloped hard after we
got out of the mud. From Shorah we rode for
eight miles through the chain of hills that separates
the plain of Naishapúr from that of Sabzáwar. The
highest of these hills seemed to be about 1,500
feet. On emerging from the hills, I galloped my
Kárábághí as hard as he would go eight miles to
the post-house of Rubát Záfarúni, and got in at
6 P.M., having done the forty miles from Naishapúr
in nine hours. The mules were four hours longer
in arriving. We left Rubát at 10 A.M., and got to
Sabzáwar at 3.30 P.M. on the 27th, and started
again from Sabzáwar at 9 A.M. on the 28th, and
in an hour came to the solitary minaret of Khusraugird, which marks the spot where the city of
that name once stood. This minaret is of brick,

and about forty feet high. The base has crumbled
away with age, and it will probably soon fall and
disappear. From this place to the fine kárwánsaráí
of Rihan, where we arrived at 2 P.M., we passed
through a plain, which has evidently once been
cultivated and populous. Now only a few villages
dot the horizon. We saw innumerable flocks of
sand-grouse and some wild ducks, but it was impossible to get near them. At 5 P.M. we reached
Mihr. Something, but what we could never discover, delayed the baggage until very late, and
the portmanteaux with my wearing apparel made
their appearance full of water. I could not help
having the faintest possible suspicion that they were
not the only portion of my belongings that had
been imbibing.

From Mihr, which we left at 7 A.M. on the
29th of November, the atmosphere warmed perceptibly till, on reaching Mazínún at 4 P.M., we found
it quite hot. The village of Sad Khar, which we
passed an hour after leaving Mihr, has its name,
"Hundred Asses," says the legend, because the
inhabitants in a former age resolved to transport

the minaret of Khusraugird to their own domain, and harnessed a hundred asses to carry it away bodily.

I had been too ill on my former expedition to see much of the country from Sháhrúd to Meshed, but this time, though very weak, I took every opportunity to explore. Mazínún is a curious place. The ruins are very extensive, and there are whole streets standing without a single inhabitant. It seemed odd to put up quantities of game in the very mosques themselves. The wolf and the jackal now chamber where mulás preached and crowds of men met to pray. Mazínún and Masnadábád, an adjoining town, were destroyed by Abbás Mirza, in consequence of the rebellion of a chief, who, having his head-quarters there, impeded the commerce of Khúrásán by his exactions.

At Mazínún our cavalry escort left us, and seventy matchlockmen and some artillerymen with a 6-pounder took their place. We started at 9.30 A.M., and at 11.45 reached an *áb ambár*, or reservoir, distant eight miles, where we lunched. The danger from Turkumans begins at this place, and a hundred gipsies joined us at it, to have the protection of our escort. Their fear was ludicrous when once or twice their beasts fell and they were apprehensive of being left behind. In about an hour more we reached the fine kárwánsaráí of Sadrábád, and twenty minutes afterwards the ruined bridge of Abríshm, the present boundary of Khúrásán. We reached Abbásábád at 5 P.M. Two miles before that station there is a spring of water with some bushes and low ridges of earth. This is a notorious spot for Turkumans, and many a prayer was muttered as we passed it. Half a mile from Abbásábád we were met by a number of boys who act as touters and come out to caravans to offer lodgings. The village was peopled by Sháh Abbás with Georgians, and their descendants speak a dialect which is very different from the Persian. The women are handsome, and are said to be not very virtuous, and they certainly have a fluency in abusing their husbands quite enviable.

The 1st of December commenced with snow, which changed into rain with a bitter cold wind, and in this we started at 9 A.M. The soil around Abbásábád is almost black, and there are traces of

volcanic action. The progress of our escort was so
slow that Dolmage and I rode on by ourselves, Riza
alone accompanying us to Miyán dasht. Eight miles
from Abbásúbád we came to a defile between low
hills, which is a famous resort of the Turkumans.
Dolmage recommended the Hisámu's Saltanah to
build a fort here, and it would certainly greatly add
to the security of the road. Two miles further on
is Al Aják, where we stopped to lunch and dry our
soaking clothes by a large fire. At this place we
found three fine-looking Afgháns, one of whom said
he had served in the Kháki Risálah, and spoke of
John Lawrence Sáhib. On the strength of his Indian
reminiscences he asked for money, and I gave him
a túmán. We reached Miyán dasht at 2 p.m. The
poor horses, greedily drinking after their fatigue, got
their mouths filled with leeches. The newly built
and neat post-house had been taken possession of
by the servants of Sartíp Riza Kuli Khán, brother
of the Shahábu'l Mulk, but they very civilly withdrew, when they heard of our arrival. The Sartíp
had with him 500 horse, and was going to join the
Hisámu's Saltanah. He told us that the Russians

had sent 8,000 harnesses for guns and troops in proportion to Ashurádah, and that the Persian commander-in-chief had gone to expel them! I guessed that he wished to amuse us with this little tale, and so it turned out. The night was intensely cold, and hundreds of pilgrims and travellers had to camp in the snow.

We left Miyán dasht at a quarter to 9 A.M. on the 2nd of December, and rode for eight miles along a beautiful level road, with a range of mountains on our left. Here, a year or so before we crossed, an unfortunate Persian nobleman named Páshá Khán was carried off by the Turkumans under peculiarly distressing circumstances. His brother, Alí Khán, who commanded the artillery at the battle of Merv, in October, 1860, received twenty wounds, and was cut down at the guns. Páshá Khán, like a true-hearted brother, started from Tehran to ransom him, and on reaching Meshed entered into negotiations with the Turkumans, which at last ended in their agreeing to give him back for 7,000 túmáns. Páshá Khán then set out for Tehran to collect the money, and was riding post, with only a servant or two, when he was attacked by a body of kidnappers, carried off, sold, and still remains in slavery. Alí Khán died of his wounds.

After two farsakhs from Miyán dasht, the road enters a defile four miles long, among hills. The partridges were very numerous here, and we saw men stalking them with paper screens, behind which they slowly advance to the game. The birds are not frightened at the screen, and when the sportsman gets near enough, he plants his masque and fires through it—otherwise it would be impossible to get a shot, as we found to our cost, for in spite of the danger of the place, Dolmage and I went a long way after several coveys, and never could get a shot within a reasonable distance. At the end of the defile is the village of Zaidah, under a lofty mountain, which is said to be the abode of demons, a reputation probably due to the wild beasts and snakes that infest it. A farsakh beyond Zaidah is Ibrahímábád, and four miles further the station of Mai a Mai, where we arrived at 3 p.m.

From Mai a Mai to Badasht, a distance of forty miles, is quite desert. We started at 4.30 A.M. on

the 3rd of December, with just moon enough to light
us to a solitary tree four miles from Mai a Mai.
Thence we plodded on in darkness that might be felt
for another four miles, when we reached an *áb ambár.*
Faint streaks of light then began to appear, and at
8.30 A.M. we got to the ruined village of Farahábád,
where we breakfasted, making a fire of withered
grass. The cold seemed to freeze one's very blood,
and I went on fast for some distance to warm myself.
At sixteen miles from Mai a Mai, we came to another
ruined village called Farrashábád, and at six miles
further we passed another *áb ambár,* or reservoir.
Between this and the ruined village of Khairábád,
which is another twelve miles on, we saw many herds
of deer, some of which passed the road so close, that
we were tempted to try if my Enfield could reach
them. We saw the ball strike close to the head
of one, and the whole herd set off like the wind.
There were also several coveys of royal partridges,
and a good many hawks and other birds.

After another four miles we came to the ruined
village of Badasht, where are poisonous bugs that
dispute the palm with those of Miyáni. At this

place the artillerymen and infantry left us, it being
only four miles to Sháhrúd, where we arrived at
3 P.M. The post-house was quite deserted, and as
our baggage had not come up, we could get nothing
to eat. Nor was there any means of making a fire,
and the cold was intense. Add to all this, that the
walls of the post-house were covered with an evil-
looking insect, and that we had no money left, and it
must be owned that there was ground for feeling
rather miserable. Indeed, even Dolmage's spirits
sank, and as for me, I was only less miserable than
when travelling to Khúrásán, in the horrible heat of
August.

Next day we halted, and the day after Abú 'l
Kásim, a merchant of Káshán, advanced thirty-five
túmáns to us, when unexpectedly a Ghulám came in
from Tehran, bringing me a supply of money   We
left Sháhrúd at 7.15 A.M. to ride *chápár*, or post, into
Tehran, leaving our baggage to come on stage by
stage. I was ill and weak, but Dolmage's help would,
I knew, carry me through the journey. He was
mounted for this first stage on a tearing, runaway
mare, that seemed never to have been ridden before.

We reached Dih Múla at 11 A.M., and after giving the horses a feed, rode on twelve miles, when we came to a clear stream, quite salt, that crossed the road. Just here we met a party of Goklán Turkumans carrying hawks as a present to the Sháh. They were wild, rough-looking fellows, and had they been going the other way, would doubtless have had much satisfaction in taking us as a present to the Khán of Khaíva. We reached Damghán at 2.30 P.M., having ridden the same horses all the way, a distance of forty-eight miles. Here I felt deadly sick, and should have broken down, but for strong doses of opium and brandy. We mounted again at 4 P.M. on fresh horses, and rode twenty-four miles further to Gushah, which we reached at 7 P.M.

After this ride of seventy-two miles I was sleeping pretty well, when an evil *Jin*, in the shape of a village cur, came to the door of the saráí, close to my bed, and awoke me with horrible howls, which he uttered periodically twice every minute. After bearing this calamity for ten minutes, I rushed from my bed to attack the wretch, but hearing me coming he fled, and lay perdue until he was certain I was again warm in bed. He then came back, and recommenced howling with redoubled vigour. Hereupon I rushed out once more, and raised such a din that the postmaster got up and pursued the caitiff fairly out of the hamlet. In spite of this the wretched cur came back, and finally deprived me of my hard-earned slumber.

At 7.30, on the 6th of December, we left Gushah. The morning was bitterly cold, and we looked rather wistfully at the snow-covered mountains, which we were to enter by the dreary pass of Ahúwán. We met, however, several caravans coming from the pass, which showed it was not closed. Still snow storms are so sudden and violent in this locality, that we were most anxious to get through, and galloped until Dolmage's great, lubberly steed was dead beat, and could hardly crawl. At Ahúwán, which we reached at 11.40 A.M., I got a villanous little pony that stumbled and would not go. By dint, however, of spurring, and with Rizá lashing him behind, I got him into a gallop, and kept it up till I was out of the pass, when the poor beast fairly broke down, and I had to walk to Semnún, where I felt so exhausted that I proposed a halt. Dolmage, however, urged me to continue the journey, and at 5.30 P.M. we started again, with moonlight to last us to Lasjird, where we arrived at 10 P.M. I had a capital horse, and finished the seventy-six miles better than I expected. The road at Surkhah, between Semnún and Lasjird, was so broken up, the mud so deep, and the water-courses so flooded, that but for the moonlight we should never have got through.

The morning of the 7th of December struggled feebly into light, with rain and a lowering sky. An irretrievable misfortune befell me before starting. My riding-boots being wet, I put them by the fire while I dressed, and when I came to pull them on, I found them hideously distorted and with great pieces burned out. Luckily Rizá had an old piece of carpet, which I tied round my legs, and in that picturesque attire started at 8 A.M. In addition to my other miseries I had now a bad cold, and but one very dirty pocket-handkerchief,* and was altogether a rueful figure as I rode along on a great, rough, bony animal,

---

* In riding express one of the miseries is the utter want of a change of linen or clothes of any kind.

under a pitiless rain.   Yet the ride was not without
objects of interest.   There was the curious rocky
defile passed through on leaving Lasjird, and then a
succession of crags of every colour and shape. Game,
too, was abundant, and numbers of partridges crossed
our road.

In the first two farsakhs we passed three bridges
over deep ravines, and after another farsakh came to
the village of Surkhah, and descended a long hill to
a tower, from which it is five short farsakhs to Dih
Namak. Thence Dolmage had to go on another stage
with the same horse he had from Lasjird.   We left
Dih Namak at 2 P.M., and after two farsakhs passed
the village of Ibrahímábád, and four miles further
Aradun, where I had lodged on my way out.   Thence
the road grew from bad to worse, being in fact a succession of muddy ditches, stones, and rocks.   Four
miles   before   reaching   Kishlák   the   Jájrúd   river
debouches from the hills, and divides into seven
streams, all of which have to be crossed repeatedly.
At this point of the journey Dolmage pointed out a
singular rock, which floods have grooved so as to give
it the appearance of a vast scallop shell.   Two miles

from Kishlák, as we were cantering our tired animals, that which was carrying Dolmage, a tall, black mare, came down heavily. Dolmage fell under it, but luckily escaped without any broken bones. We reached Kishlák at sunset, and halted, having ridden only fifty miles that day.

On, once more, we went at 8 A.M., on the 8th of December. The rain fell steadily, and the masses of clouds showed what we had to expect. Dolmage was mounted on a pigmy of a pony, that fell on its knees at every third step, and he, therefore, exchanged with Riza, and got an animal but a very little better. I had a thin galloway, whose appearance did not please me at all. The road for the first mile was through deep mud. On emerging from that I said to Dolmage, " I must try if I can get a canter out of my beast," and I forthwith stuck in the spurs sharply, and gave the animal a rather severe cut. To my utter astonishment it went off with a bound like an antelope, and I heard Dolmage shout in surprised accents, " A runaway, by Jove ! " and found myself careering madly at twenty miles an hour towards the Pass of Sardárí. After a little I managed to pull up, and made the galloway walk, and then tried to get it to take a gentle canter. But I soon found it had but two paces, a slow walk, or a tearing gallop, commencing with a series of buck jumps, which rendered it most difficult to keep the saddle. As it was raining fast I thought I had better get over the stage as quickly as possible, so, leaving Dolmage and my servant, I let the runaway have the rein, and was soon in the Sardári Pass, through which I galloped at full speed. On the other side of the Pass, I was delayed some time by mud a yard deep; but once clear of that, I galloped on, and reached Aiwán i Kaif a little after 10 A.M. Dolmage arrived about half an hour afterwards, mounted on a capital black mare, which, however, stumbled, from having no shoes. He had effected an exchange *en route*, but Riza did not make his appearance for another hour.

The postmaster at Aiwán i Kaif was an impudent Afghán, named Ali Mardán Beg, against whom Dolmage had warned me, and so, indeed, had the Ghuláms of the mission. They said they had generally to walk the stage from Aiwán, as the Afghán's horses never had a leg to stand on. The fellow came swaggering in, and sate down on the same carpet with me without being asked, which is considered great rudeness in Persia. I said, " All men are by nature equal, but there are artificial distinctions of which Persians are observant. If my Persian servant comes in and finds you sitting here, he may quarrel with you." On this the fellow slunk off. When asked if he had horses, he declared he had excellent ones; and, relying on his assurance, I gave up my fleet galloway. About 2 P.M. we called for our fresh horses, mounted and rode away, but had not got a hundred yards before both our animals were down on their noses, and it was quite evident that they would never be able to take us a furlong, much less twenty-eight miles. We, therefore, went back to the post-house to upbraid the Afghán, but he and all his myrmidons had absconded, and there was not a living thing to be found. The only plan now was to recover the tired animals from the last stage, and I succeeded in getting the black mare that had just come twenty-four miles. Dolmage's horse, however, would not go out of a hobble, and after going three farsakhs we came to

40—2

a village with a number of Iliyats encamped near
it. Here Riza went off the road to try if he could
get us fresh horses, was inveigled into a hut, and
attacked ; but being a strong, brave fellow, well
armed, managed to fight his way out with only a
few blows on the head and back from the cudgels
of his antagonists.

The last six miles to Kabúd Gumbaz were,
indeed, weary work. Even Dolmage's fine spirits
broke down, as his beast of a horse would not
carry him, and kicked ferociously when he tried to
lead it. At sunset we reached the station, and
found that the people sent to meet us from Tehran
had gone to Khátúnábád. There was, therefore,
nothing for it but to mount our weary jades, and
struggle through six more miles of deep mud,
ditches, and holes, in utter darkness, to the "Lady's
village." Here we rested for the night, sending
on Riza to Tehran that the Istikbál might be in
readiness to receive us. We had thus accomplished
260 miles in four days, which, considering the
wretched state of my health, was fair travelling.
Indeed, it was entirely owing to Colonel Dolmage's

aid and judicious treatment that I got on so well.

We left Khátúnábád at 7.30 A.M. on December the 9th, and plodded on twelve weary miles to Rhé, where the second Persian Mirza came to meet us with a note from Mr. Thomson, to say that the Istikbál would not be ready till two hours to sunset, and that he recommended us to go to the garden of the queen mother at Sháh Abdu'l Azím, once the property of Hájí Mirza Aghássi, and wait there. This we did, and at 5 P.M. we mounted and rode slowly towards Tehran. At Daulatábád, just outside Sháh Abdu'l Azím, the Istikbál made its appearance. It was commanded by an officer of the highest rank, the Sahámu 'l Mulk, general of the three regiments of Isfahán, and a relative of the late Sadr Azim. With him were the Kalántar of Tehran, and one of the Under Secretaries of State for Foreign Affairs. The French Mission, and the Turkish, both sent their representatives dressed in uniform, and there were many persons not belonging to the Corps Diplomatique, who also did me the honour to come out. The Sháh had commanded that

all possible honours should be shown to me, and, besides led horses, had sent a white Arab with housings
of gold studded with turquoises for my own riding.
His Majesty had also sent out his own pipes covered
with jewels, and the Sharbatdár of the household
to prepare coffee on the way. With the Istikbál
was a squadron of the cavalry of the guard, a very
unusual compliment, I believe. Near the gate of
the city some of the Sháh's running footmen joined
the procession. The Persian government, therefore, showed me every attention in their power,
and I shall always remember kindness which has
gone far to compensate for some cruel mortifications.

I have dwelt the more on this Istikbál, because it
was the last at which the members of European
Missions appeared. In a climate like Persia it was
always a great tax on European officers to take part
in what was originally a purely Persian ceremony,
and I myself had felt the inconvenience, when, as
Secretary of Legation, I went out to meet the French
Envoy, the Comte de Gobineau, and the Italian
Ambassador, M. Cerutti. Besides, accidents sometimes led to omissions, which had the appearance

of slights, whereas, if the ceremony were left entirely to the Persians, no misunderstanding could possibly occur amongst the Europeans about it. On the occasion of the Istikbál given to me, no Russian officer was present, and, as I had always been on the most friendly terms with the Russians, I thought it right to ask their Chargé d'Affaires why the members of his Mission were absent? It then turned out that due notice had not been given to M. Bartholomiei of what was intended, and in order to prevent, in future, mistakes which might have unpleasant results, it was agreed by all the heads of Missions that in future the ceremony of the Istikbál should be left to the Persians entirely, and the in-coming European Minister.

CHAPTER XI.

Reflections on being appointed to take charge of the British Mission
in Persia—The Burglary—Grande Tenue—First Audience of
the Sháh —Interviews with the Foreign Minister and the
Amínu 'd Daulah—Arrival of Servants and Baggage from
Khúrásán—Private Audience—Visit to the Sipáh Sálár—First
Despatches and successful Negotiation for the Telegraph—A
Merry Christmas—The Itizádu's Saltanah and the Nusratu 'd
Daulah—The Flash in the Socket before the Candle goes out—
New Year's Day—Successful Termination of the Affair of Mír
Alí Nakí Khán—Dinner to the Amínu 'd Daulah and the
Princes—Visits to the Sahámu 'l Mulk and other Dignitaries—
Frontier Disturbances—Habet! ferrum recipiat!—The Fare-
well Audience—The Diamond Snuff-box, or the Sháh's last
Words—The Farewell Dinner—Valete, non plaudite.

THE first thoughts of most men, perhaps, on obtain-
ing promotion are selfish—I confess mine were.
I had been playing a subordinate part for more than
a quarter of a century, aye from before the time
when I was Outram's assistant in Sindh, and now,

for a few weeks, I was to have a reign of my own. Poor human nature! vanitas vanitatum!

That foolish flutter over, I began to think seriously of my responsibilities. People in England know and care very little about Persia, or the officers employed there; but it seems to me there are few more responsible offices that an Englishman can fill than that of Minister at Tehran. Let a man be wicked, worthless, low, blundering, vulgar, what you will, in England, well, it's a pity, but he does not harm many people besides himself. The tone of public feeling is so good, that a false note jars at once. Perhaps, it would be extravagant to say that bad men in England, like the drunken Helots in Sparta, do more good than harm by their example; but it certainly is the fact that when vice makes itself noticed in English society, it deters and repels, rather than attracts. The case is very different with the Englishman in Persia, and, above all, with the representative Englishman who fills the post of Minister, because millions of people will take him as the test of Western civilization and Gospel truth, and will judge of it by him. Who knows anything of England in Persia? Who there has studied European literature, or read the Bible? To the Persians, to Central Asia, the British Mission at Tehran is England, and the lives of its members are a speaking commentary on the civilization and morality of the West.

Thoughts like these were flitting through my brain as I dozed unquietly after my *chápár* journey. I could not sleep, so rose at 2 A.M. on the 10th of December, the morning after my return to Tehran, and read through all the correspondence of the Mission, which had taken place since I left it for Khúrásán. I then began to consider what course I should pursue. I thought of many things, which I need not here record, but the most pressing and practical matter was that alluded to in the second precept of the Golden Rule for Bishops. I, therefore, immediately made preparations for three public dinners. On Christmas Day was to be an entertainment for all the non-diplomates; on New Year's Eve I was to receive the Persian Foreign Minister and his friends, and the Turkish Mission, and a week afterwards the Amínu 'd Daulah, the

Russians and the princes; and, lastly, there was to be a breakfast for the French Minister, whose health would not admit of his going out to dinner.

Now, in Paris or in London, dinners are easily arranged, but not so in Tehran, and I had not too much time that I could afford to expend it on such matters. I had first of all a difficult inquiry to make, which resulted in a despatch, that, with enclosures, ran to two hundred and fifty pages! I had, besides, a few police matters to look after. The consulate had been burglariously entered, and a quantity of effects had been stolen. The consul, Mr. Glen, was on sick leave in England, while another man was walking in his shoes, sleeping in his sheets, and eating with his spoons.

In the middle of my investigations arrived in unbroken succession all the *beau monde* of Tehran. With my head full of the invitations I had been issuing, of the instructions to be issued to the *maître de cuisine*, and of the conflicting statements made by Persian witnesses as to the robbery, I was meekly endeavouring to propitiate the Italians, Turks, French, Persians, Germans, and others who flowed in unin-

terruptedly, and discoursing in as many tongues as I
could muster, when suddenly I perceived that
there was something wrong. Conscious of the
extremest desire to make myself agreeable, I was at a
loss to know my fault, and it was not till the Gauls
had departed that the truth flashed across my mind.
Yes, too true, they came resplendent in *grande
tenue*, and I, that had not had one moment to think
of my outer man, was sitting in a plain black coat, that,
sooth to say, had before that dived to the bottom of
a stream in Khúrásán!

On Saturday, the 13th of December, I had my
audience of presentation to the Sháh. At 10 A.M. I
rode to the Ark with Messrs. Thomson and Watson,
and Dr. Dickson, and found the master of the
ceremonies at breakfast, and without his robes. My
coming a little too soon was no joke to him, though
he took it in very good part; for it is usual for a
horse from the royal stud, with a number of running footmen, to be sent when a minister or chargé
d'affaires pays his first visit. I was not aware of the
fact, and no one had told me, so the master of the
ceremonies must have trembled for his fee, which, on

such occasions, is sixty túmáns, about twenty-eight
pounds. At 11 A.M. we went to the Sháh, and
found his Majesty seated on a sofa, with a number of
the princes and grandees standing near the wall on
the other side of the room. The Sháh pointed to a
chair, and I sate down, and after a slight pause
made a short speech in Persian, saying that I had
been appointed chargé d'affaires, and that I hoped to
do my duty to the satisfaction of both governments.
The Sháh made a gracious reply, and then asked
me a number of questions about Khúrásán. I told
him exactly what I had seen, and bore testimony to
the devoted services of the Hisámu's Saltanah, and
my account seemed to please the Sháh. In about
a quarter of an hour, there being a pause, I rose,
and asked leave to go, and was glad to learn from
Messrs. Thomson and Dickson, who had had much
greater experience of Persia than myself, that it was
a successful visit, and that I came away just at the
right time.

On leaving the palace I found a horse from the
King's stud, covered with jewelled trappings, and
a number of attendants, waiting for me, and I then

rode to call on the Minister for Foreign Affairs, and the Amínu 'd daulah, and found them, as ever, most courteous and kind. Next day, the Foreign Minister called upon me, and among other things, said he was getting up a volunteer corps for Tehran! I took an opportunity of introducing the subject of the telegraph, and explained my views on it, laying much stress on the line being placed under the superintendence of an English engineer officer. Mirza Said Khán agreed with me in almost all I said, and, with the usual Persian politeness, assured me he would mention the subject to the King. I knew, however, very well what that meant, and that matters would remain exactly at the point at which they had stopped with Mr. Alison and Mr. Thomson, viz., in a vague promise that the Persian Government would, at some indefinite time, construct and work the line themselves, in which case, should it ever be accomplished, it would be continually getting out of order like that between Tehran and Tabríz.

Next day, the 15th, I had a very long visit from the Amínu 'd daulah, who spoke to me in the most friendly manner, and assured me of his support. I laid before him a new convention I had prepared for the construction of the line of telegraph from Kháni-kín, the Turkish frontier, to Tehran, and from Tehran to Bushire, and he pointed out to me certain modifications which he considered desirable. I then requested him to put it into elegant Persian, well knowing the effect of a well-turned sentence on the Persian ear.

The next subject we discussed was the claims of Mír Alí Nakí Khán. The Amínu 'd daulah said he liked the Khán personally, but he could not hold out to me any hopes that his claims would be settled, and he advised me not to agitate the question until I had obtained greater influence with the Sháh.

On the 16th of December, my servants, horses, and baggage arrived from Khúrásán, having been eleven days in performing a journey that Dolmage and myself had accomplished in four. On the 17th I went to the palace to a private audience, for which I had asked. The Foreign Minister and Yahya Khán received me. On going into the 'room where the Sháh was, I found his Majesty seated on a sofa, and my chair in the middle of the room. The Sháh made me bring the chair to within about six feet of him, and there I sate, with Mirza Said Khán standing beside me. As the Sháh did not speak, I began, and said his Majesty had, the other day, been pleased to ask me some questions about Khúrásán, to which I had not been able to give full answers, the audience being one of presentation. I had, therefore, asked for a private audience, in order to complete my statements. I then went through all the Hisámu's Saltanah's arguments about the value of Herát and Merv to Persia, and then endeavoured to show, on my own part, that if Persia would consent to be on good terms with Dost Muhammad, she might reap from an alliance with him all the advantages that she believed would accrue to her from the actual occupation of Merv and Herát. The Sháh listened with great interest, and then said to Mirza Said Khán, "Eastwick understands our case even better than we do ourselves, and he must write all this to his Government." His Majesty then spoke of Sístán, and said, with sound truth, that it did not belong to Afghánistán, and that the occupation of it by the Afgháns would be a source of danger· to the eastern provinces of Persia. I thought I had now a good opportunity of introducing

the subject of the telegraph, and began by speaking
of the great advantages of electric communication in
cases of sudden political difficulties. I then went on
to say that I thought it was a misfortune that the line
of telegraph from Tehran, proposed by the English
Government, had not been accepted by Persia. The
Sháh said, "You can talk to my Foreign Minister
about this." I replied, "Your Majesty, I have
already done so, and, in fact, I have a memorandum
in my pocket of the conditions which both of us
think fair and reasonable." With these words I pulled
out the convention and read it over. The Sháh
seemed struck with it, and desired me to give it to
him, saying he would lay it before his Council. I
said, "Your Majesty will, I trust, pardon me if I
bring to your remembrance the proverb that says,
'A thousand men have a thousand minds.' If this
paper be submitted to the Council, some will approve
of it, and some not. This will cause delay, whereas
the question has already been discussed for more than
a year. What is required now is a decision, and no
one is so capable of deciding the matter as your
Majesty." The Sháh smiled, and said, "Well, well,

I'll settle it myself." That very evening I received back the paper with his Majesty's autograph corrections, and thus a question, which for so many months had been the subject of such long and anxious negotiations, was satisfactorily arranged in a single day.

I was engaged all day on the 18th in writing despatches, going out only in the evening to call on the Sipáh Sálár. Next day, after writing a long despatch about the application of a certain act to Persia, I had an interview with the Amínu 'd daulah, when we talked over the new arrangements about the telegraph. In the evening the Turkish Minister gave me an entertainment. On Sunday, the 21st of December, I sent off a courier with my first despatches. They were twelve in number, and one contained the telegraph convention, according to which the line through Persia is now being constructed. It arrived in England the very day when, it having been announced that the Persian Government would make no concessions as to the construction of a line, an arrangement of another kind would have been proposed far more costly to England.

Christmas Day was a merry one to three of those who assembled at the Mission table, Dolmage, De Blocqueville, and myself. Dolmage and I, at least, had had enough of roughing it in Khúrásán, not to appreciate the luxury of being among friends under a comfortable roof. De Blocqueville, after more than a year's captivity amongst the Turkumans, was even more disposed to enjoy the contrast of bright days, after imprisonment gloomy enough to depress even a French Hussar. Sad indeed would it have been if one so fitted for society, the graceful rider and dancer, the clever artist and accomplished musician, should have been doomed to perpetual slavery among the hateful barbarians of the desert; yet for months there seemed no hope of escape. It was then that Dolmage, ever foremost in kind actions, began those efforts for the release of his friend, which failed indeed, but formed the prelude to the successful exertions of the Persian Government. Our Christmas party was a large one, and we mustered four ladies, two Italian, one Greek, and one French.

A few days afterwards, I went to call on the Itizádu's Saltanah, who, being the Minister of Public

Works, has the telegraph to Tabríz under his control, and so has been nicknamed the Telegraph Prince. His name is Ali Kuli Mirza, and Itizádu's Saltanah, "Arm of the State," is his title. He is a son of Fath Ali Sháh, and consequently great-uncle of the reigning Sháh, yet he is young-looking and full of life and spirits. His house teems with mechanical inventions. I recollected very well that when I called on him with Mr. Alison a year before about the telegraph, he asked how many millimètres thick the wire for our proposed line would be. Not expecting a French word in a Persian conversation, I was on that occasion puzzled for a moment to know what he said, and thinking he would very likely ask the same question this time, I was ready for him. Sure enough, after the usual compliments, out came the stock question with a little air of triumph, expecting to see me posed, followed by a slightly disconcerted look at my pat answer. Talking of Herát, the prince said he was in the Sháh's camp there when the news of the occupation of Kharak by the English arrived. Instead of this news causing dismay, there were general rejoicings, for the army was in such misery that they would have been glad if the English had taken the capital itself, provided they could only return to it.

I went next to Fíruz Mirza, whose title is Nusratu 'd daulah, and who is a younger brother of the Hisámu's Saltanah. Like all the sons of Abbás Mirza, he is a dignified and worthy prince. I enjoyed my visit much, for he was most friendly. His wife is said to be the most beautiful woman in Persia, and, to judge from her two daughters, I can well believe it. The prince sent for them both —girls of six and four years old—that I might see if their photographs were like. The elder girl was the beauty. She had the largest and most lustrous eyes I have seen. Among other things, the Nus-ratu 'd daulah said that formerly the Persian ministers strove to keep the princes of the blood out of em-ployment by working on the jealousy of the Sháh for the time being, but this policy was now out of date.

On the 31st of December, after working hard all day, I had to receive at dinner the Foreign

Minister, the Sháh's brother-in-law, and other grandees. As ill luck would have it, the Ainu 'l Mulk, the Sháh's brother-in-law, came an hour before the time. I must own I have a great aversion to the *mauvais quart d'heure*, but to have it quadrupled is really too much. Up to then, at Tehran, it had been the custom to give the Sháh's health *totidem verbis*, and not to make a speech; but after the extreme kindness and condescension of his Majesty in so readily and graciously accepting the convention for the telegraph which I had proposed to him, I thought I was bound to go beyond the ordinary rule. I, therefore, made a short speech in Persian, which, from the novelty of the thing, and partly, perhaps, because I felt in my inmost heart all I said, had a happy effect. I· had no sooner sat down than the Turkish Minister asked me for a memorandum of what I had said, and Mirza Said Khán declared that the speech should appear in the *Tehran Gazette*,* and he accordingly took the Sháh's pleasure on the subject, and shortly

---

* See Appendix V.

afterwards an account of the whole entertainment was printed.

New Year's Day passed in receiving visitors. It has always been the custom for some officers of rank on the part of the Sháh to wait on the British Minister on that day, and for the members of other legations to visit him, and nearly all the Europeans in Tehran follow the example. From morn to dewy eve the incense of innumerable Kalyans ascends, and beverages which cheer but not inebriate are handed round. The ceremony is right and proper, but it is exhausting to sit so many hours listening to decorous, but not lively, conversation, and I must confess I envied the spirits of Mulá Salih, one of my visitors, a man a hundred years old, who told an infinite number of good stories, and laughed at them till the tears ran from his eyes.

On the 3rd January, 1863, I had the honour of another private audience with the Sháh. I had resolved to endeavour to obtain a settlement of the long-pending claims of Mír Alí Nakí Khán. This nobleman had been many years a protégé of the British Government, and had performed services

which Lord Palmerston was highly satisfied with, so
much so, indeed, that he had presented to the Khán
a valuable diamond ring. During the war with
England, the Khán's house had been plundered, not,
it was thought, without the connivance of the late
Sadr Azim, or Prime Minister of Persia. The case
was one which ought properly to have been settled by
the Commissioners appointed after the Treaty of
Paris, but the Persian Commissioner would not dis-
cuss it. Ever since, it had been weighing on the
Mission, and had led to correspondence that would
fill a volume. Mr. Alison had, as I have already
stated, directed me to report upon it, and the English
Government had decided that it could not be dis-
missed, but must be regarded as an affair in which
the honour of the British nation was concerned.
My view of the matter was that so delicate an affair
could not be satisfactorily adjusted except by the
Sháh's free will and grace. After all, the Khán is a
Persian, thought I, and until he came under British
protection, he was a subject of the Sháh, and an
employé of the Persian Government. What Government in the world would like redress of a wrong to

be exacted for one of its own quondam subjects by a foreign Power?

I do not feel myself at liberty to mention what passed at the private interview with the Sháh, but I will simply state that I entirely succeeded, not only in settling the claims of Mír Alí Nakí Khán, but in what I consider to be far more important, in restoring him to the favour of the King. It may appear bad taste to refer to these successes of my brief tenure of office, and I do not know that even the fact of their remaining to this day wholly unacknowledged would justify me in mentioning them; but I am willing to incur the imputation of vanity, in order that I may here express my deep sense of that royal favour, which enabled me to bring to a happy conclusion what had been so long attempted in vain; and may show to demonstration that Eastern Governments are quite as willing to listen to reason as European, if they are properly approached. I shall only add that I received from the Khán a letter of thanks,* of which I

---

* See Appendix VI.

shall always feel proud, and that he was at once emancipated from restraints which had become almost intolerable.

On the 5th of January, I sent off another courier with despatches, among which was one announcing the settlement of Mír Alí Nakí Khán's affair. On the 6th, the Amínu 'd daulah, the members of the Russian Mission, and several princes of the blood came to dine with me. As there is no table of precedence in Persia, and as certain feelings that are very intense in other countries are not unknown in Irán, I had now to solve the most puzzling problems that had yet been presented to me. Thus I am even now in doubt as to whether the Sháh's uncle, or his grand-uncle, or his father-in-law, should have the precedence, the father-in-law being also Commander-in-Chief, and the grand-uncle Minister of Public Works. After all, perhaps, the most practical solution of such difficulties would be to have round tables made large enough, and I do not see why, in these days of useful invention, a circular table should not be invented to expand from the centre, *ad libitum.*

On the 8th of January I visited a number of Persian noblemen, and among them the Sahámu 'l Mulk, who was the chief officer at the Istikbál the Sháh was pleased to send for me. The house of this nobleman is a very handsome one, and I was much struck with the beautiful stained-glass windows. The art of making these decorations is carried to great excellence in Persia. Sahámu 'l Mulk is, of course, merely a title. The Khán's name is Mirza Ibrahím. He is of a very ancient family, and when I visited long before his baronial castle on the frontier of Mazandarún, I was astonished at its vast extent and the tokens of former magnificence around, though the castle itself is now a ruin. For seven centuries the ancestors of the Khán dwelt in that castle as lords of Belladi and Núr, and sometimes as independent princes.

From the Sahámu 'l Mulk I went to the Kalántar, who is a brother of Mirza Musa, the Vazír of Tehran, and an old comrade of Sir H. Bethune and Major Hart. He served in the campaign in which the former, then Lindesay Sáhib, put down the rebellion of Hasan Ali Mirza. "The forces of the rebel prince fought well, and had not the English Sáhib been there," said the old man, "the event might have been very different."

My time, among other things, was now much occupied with some serious disturbances which had broken out on the frontier between Persia and Turkey. These disturbances, as is well known, are of perpetual recurrence, and many years ago an expensive commission of English, Russian, Turkish, and Persian officers, was appointed to adjust frontiers and discover a remedy for a state of things which might lead to actual war between Persia and Turkey. Ever since then a boundary map has been in preparation. The difficulty is simply this, that the border tribes along the Perso-Turkish frontier prefer the plains of Turkey in winter and the mountains of Persia in summer. They go where they can find pasture for their flocks and herds, but while living in the territory of one State they often profess allegiance to another, and hence arises the question how they are to be governed. A permanent superintendence of the frontier by trustworthy officers appears to me the only means of settling the difficulty.

Another subject which engaged my attention was the commerce of Persia, and more especially of Khúrásán, on which I transmitted a report, which will be found at page 262 of the reports of H.M.'s Secretaries of Embassy and Legation, laid before Parliament in 1863. Persia produces the finest cotton, equal to any American, except only the Sea Island, and I cannot understand why so little reference has been made to the subject in England. No doubt the want of the iron road is a great obstacle, but it must be remembered that there is water carriage from Muhammarah, in southern Persia, and from the frontier of Khúrásán by the Caspian and the Russian canals, all the way to England. On the subject of railroads I was most earnest, and descanted on their advantages to the Persian Ministers; and in my commercial report a scheme for a line and an estimate of expenses will be found.*

---

* I am glad to hear that a scheme for a line of rail from Tehran to Baghdád is on foot. I feel convinced such a line would pay high interest. To say nothing of the hundred thousand pilgrims that travel yearly to Kerbalah and Mecca, the line would have a traffic all its own. As a Persian nobleman said to me, " Were such a railroad

But why dwell on labours, hopes, improvements attempted or accomplished? The fatal day was at hand. On the 2nd of February, as I was expecting the ratification of my convention for the electric telegraph by the English Government, it having been agreed to by the Persian, and signed with the seal of the Persian Foreign Minister, an order arrived, directing me to quit Tehran. Mr. Watson, who was with me when the order arrived, expressed much regret, and volunteered to carry to England my explanations, an offer which, in the weak state of my health, that rendered express travelling impossible, I was fain to accept. Mr. Watson likewise undertook to see Lord Russell himself, and make certain statements orally to his lordship, and he even provided himself with a sick certificate, that, under any circumstances, he might be able to continue his journey. But it cannot be

---

established, no man would ever consent to be buried, so far as his volition could affect such an arrangement, or to let his friends be buried in Persia. The dead who would travel to Baghdád would be five times more numerous than the living!" It must be admitted, however, that there would be no return tickets by these trains.

expected that, with ordinary men, zeal for another will outweigh personal interest. Mr. Watson seems to have encountered on his journey one of those cycloidal storms which are said to impel everything they meet in a circular direction; for, like the man in the song, "he turned him round and round about—and round about he turned."

I had now only to perform the painful duty of announcing my recall to the Persian Ministers, and requesting a farewell audience of the Sháh. With such a task before me, it was not so agreeable as it otherwise would have been to entertain the French Minister and his Staff at breakfast the morning after the order reached me. I was, in fact, quite deaf from the shock, and my stupidity must have been a sad contrast to the liveliness of his Excellency, certainly one of the most agreeable and accomplished of men. On the 4th of February, I went first to the Foreign Minister, and told him I had been recalled, and he promised to obtain an audience for me that I might present Mr. Thomson. I went next to the Amínu 'd daulah, who showed all the concern that a true friend would in such a case. "I take refuge with God!" said his Excellency. "What words are these? what can be the meaning of recalling you, when you have given such satisfaction to all? His Majesty the Sháh has a personal regard for you, and I am sure he will be hurt at this extraordinary measure. Besides, at this moment the siege of Herát is going on, there are matters of the utmost importance under discussion: it is not right that the British Legation should be left without an officer whose age and experience entitle him to confidence. I feel sure the Persian Government will request an explanation of this unlooked-for proceeding." Feeling anxious that there should not even be the suspicion of any misunderstanding on public matters, I thought it right to reply that it was entirely a personal affair, which regarded myself only.

On the 5th of February Mr. Watson started from Tehran with despatches. We accompanied him some way on the road, and drank a stirrup-cup of champagne at parting. On the 6th I went to the palace to my audience of leave, and presented Mr. Thomson. Dr. Dickson accompanied us. The Sháh's dress was most becoming, and he looked very handsome. He spoke in an easy, sensible, and earnest way, and without that stiffness and reserve which those who have been longer in Persia than myself have remarked. I said I had been recalled to England, and came to take leave. The Sháh replied that he was much surprised at this sudden recall of a Chargé d'Affaires with whom he was in every way satisfied. His Majesty then spoke of me in very flattering terms, and when Mirza Said Khán, who was looking very ill, had echoed his words, he inquired who was left at the Mission. I said, "Mr. Thomson." "Only Mr. Thomson?" asked his Majesty. "And Dr. Dickson," I said. The Sháh then repeated his satisfaction with my conduct, and said he hoped to see me return. He then asked me if I had understood the last message about Herát, and desired me to repeat it, in order that he might see that nothing had been omitted. I went through the points verbatim, and the Sháh expressed his satisfaction, and was pleased to commend my knowledge of Persian. He then commented on the message at great length, and expressed himself in the clearest way, and I feel bound to say his arguments seemed to me both able and just. Lastly, he inquired by what route I was going to England, and after some conversation on that head, I took my leave.

On the 9th I went to the Amínu 'd daulah to say farewell. He conveyed to me a most gracious message from the Shâh, to which I replied that I should ever retain a grateful recollection of his Majesty's kindness; but, of course, to my own Government I must stand or fall. So we parted, with deep regret on my side.

It had been usual for all Ministers and Chargés d'Affaires to receive some token of the Shâh's favour on departure for England. Leaving in the way I did, and after so short a tenure of office, I could not of course expect that the rule could hold good with regard to me. But on February the 10th, after I had been working all day in preparation for my departure on the 14th, and was just about to take my evening ride, a French officer, M. Rouillon, came in, and, while we were conversing, a long line of Persian servants entered the garden, and Yahya Khán, the Shâh's Adjudán-bashí, was announced.

I was so little prepared for the message he brought, that I was secretly vexed at being detained from my ride, but I began to talk on indifferent matters. The Khán, however, looked serious, and suddenly standing up, said he was charged with a message from the Shán. He was desired to express his Majesty's regret at my departure, and in token of his regard to present me with a diamond snuff-box, which his Majesty hoped I would value the more as being one which he had occasionally used himself.

On the 14th of February, I left Tehran, and the whole European community, and many Persians, did me the honour to accompany me for some distance. Mr. Thomson kindly drove me out the first stage on the road to Baghdád. We halted for the night at the village of Chahár Dáng, where Mr. Thomson gave me a farewell dinner, and drank my health in champagne. He afterwards sent me a beautiful Resht table-cover. Dolmage gave me a still hand-somer parting present, a Khúrásán ornament inlaid with rubies, turquoises, pearls, and emeralds. Colonel Pesce, senior European officer in the Shán's service,

in a letter, which will be found in the Appendix,
politely expressed the regret of the European
members of society at my departure, and sent me
a souvenir.   On the 15th, I took leave of all my
friends, and rode away on my solitary journey to
Baghdád.   As soon as I had left, the English Government ratified the convention which I had drawn
out, and which I had prevailed on the Sháh to
accept, and the line of telegraph is, I believe, now
in course of construction.   Of the advantages and
importance of such an alternative line to India, it
is not for me to speak.

---

* See Appendix VII.

THE END.

APPENDICES.

APPENDIX I.

(See p. 40, vol. I.)

LIST OF STAGES FROM TREBISONDE TO TABRIZ.

Names of Stations.	Distance in Hours.	Approximate Distance in Miles
Trebisonde to Jevezlyk	6	18
Istavros	8	22
Tuzunlu	4	14
Kyz Kalah	5	16
Hadrat	4	14
Baiburt.	6	18
Massat	6*	26
Khosha banou	8*	24
Erzeroum	8	28
	— 55	— 180
Hasan Kalah	6	18
Khorasán	8	25
Mulá Sulaimán.....	15	35
Kárá Kilissa........	12	25
Diadin	12*	35
Awajik	12†	30
Karajnih	7	28
Zoráwar	6	18
Khoi	7	20
	— 140	— 414
Tezwig	10	18
Shuster	7	18
Zobair	8	20
Tabriz	8	20
	— 173	— 490

* In some stages, on account of mountains, difficult defiles, mud, and stones, a greater time is taken to traverse a mile than in others.
† Frontier village of Persia.

LIST OF STAGES BETWEEN POTI AND TEFLIS, AND
TEFLIS AND TABRIZ.

Names of Stations.	Distance in Versts.	Remarks.
Poti to Chiladidi...	20	This distance can always be done by river in the little steamer.
Prince Micadza's .	25	Good house (private).
Village	35	Post-house.
Marand	11	Post-house and small town.
Village	18	Post-house.
Kutais	18	Town, capital of Imeritia, post-house, and hotel.
Simonette	18	Post-house.
Kuiril	16	Do.
Belog..	22	Do.
Molette	18	Do.
Suram	30	Do.
Gargarieff...	25	Do.
Gori	25	Post-house and small town.
Tarkanoff	16	Post-house.
Village	18	Wretched hovel, called a post-house.
Village .. .	18	Post-house.
Teflis	14	Capital of Georgia. Hotels.
	— 347	
Mekrán Tilsit	10	Post-house.
Kodi	15	Do.
Sarván	13½	Do.
Mughaulí	15	Do.
Sadrogli	22	Do.
Hasan Begli	25¼	Do.
Huzum Tálá. ..	17½	Do.
Istiboulak	17	Do.
Tcharupane	13¾	Do.
Delíján	18	Do.—Difficult pass.
Chabuklí, or Go-kchah Lake	20	Do.
Elenooka	14	Do.
Níjni Aktinskaia	15	Do.
Fontanken	12½	Do.
Erivan	16	Do.—Large town.
Kamarlu	27¼	Do.
Davalu	18	Do.

Names of Stations.	Distance in Versts.	Remarks.
Sadarak	18½	Post-house.
Koragne	22	
Buyuk Diez . . .	14	
Nakhshewán	20	Town.
Alandjakchai . .	20	
Julfah .. . ——.. .	15	Persian frontier.
	— 745¼*	
Galand Kayah . ..	20 miles.	
Marand . ..	26	
Sufiyán	18	
Tabriz	18	
	— 82 + 496 = 578 miles.	

* 745¼ versts = 496 miles.

APPENDIX I *a.*

(*See* page 179, vol. I.)

Tabriz, the ancient Tauris, was probably an old city when it became the capital of Tiridates III., King of Armenia in A.D. 297. Little, however, is known about it till A.D. 791, when Zubaidah, wife of Hárún'r Rashíd, the fifth Kaliph of the house of Abbás, beautified it so much as to obtain the credit of having been its founder. She is said to have called it Tavriz, "fever scattering," from the salubrity of the climate, but this is doubtless a mere legend. In A.D. 858, in the reign of Motavakkel, the tenth Abbaside Kaliph, the city was almost destroyed by an earthquake. In A.D. 1041, Tabriz was again levelled by an earthquake, and only those of the inhabitants escaped who had listened to the warning voice of Abu Tahir, the astronomer of Shiráz, who, being at Tabríz, foretold the danger. In 1392 Tímur took and sacked Tabríz, its then prince, Sultan Ahmed Ilkhání, flying at the approach of the great conqueror. After the decline of the house of Tímur, in the beginning of the fifteenth century, Tabríz fell under the sway of the Turkuman princes of Van; and Kárá Yúsif, one of that dynasty, died at a village close to the city in 1420. In 1500, Ismail, the first of the Safaví kings, took Tabríz from the Turkumans; but it remained under Persia only till 1322, when Sulaimán, the Sultán of Constantinople, made himself master of it, expelling Sháh Tahmásp, who then made Kazvín his capital. Again it was abandoned by the Turks, and again recovered, in 1584, by Murád bin Selim, or Amurath III., but won back to Persia by 'Abbas the Great in 1618, after his sanguinary victory at Shibli, in which the Pashas of Van and Erzerum, and the flower of the Turkish army, fell. In 1721 Tabríz was again in great part destroyed by an earthquake, and, according to one writer, 80,000 persons perished. To add to this misery, the inhabitants were attacked by the Turks under the Pasha of Van, and 4,000 of the enemy effected a lodgment in the city, but, after a desperate struggle, were all put to the sword; nor was it till 1725 that the town was surrendered, after 20,000 Turks had fallen in battle before it. But the Sultán had scant enjoyment of his new conquest, for in 1730 the invincible Nádír came, saw, and conquered. Since then, Tabríz, a city of Turks, capital of the Turkish province of Azurbáiján, where Turkish is the language spoken, has remained a jewel in the Persian crown, save during the short occupation by the Russians in 1828.

APPENDIX II.

APPENDIX II.

Pedigree of the Reigning Shah of Persia. (See page 184, Vol. I.)

FATH 'ALI SHAH, died in October, 1834.

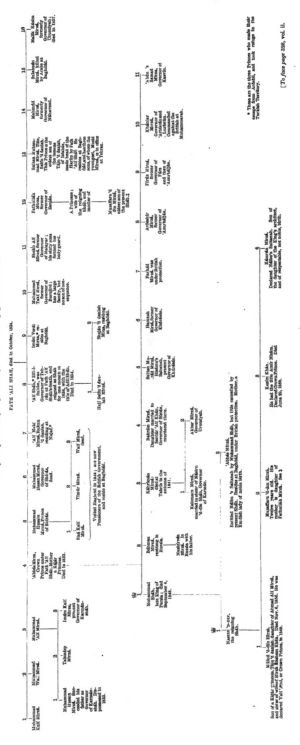

* These are the three Princes who made their escape from Ardabíl, and took refuge in the Turkish Territory.

[To face page 328, vol. II.

APPENDIX III.

(*See* page 188, vol. I.)

The following letter, written some years ago, from the late Dr. Bell, gives an account of that singular disease, " Fainting Fever," which was so prevalent when I arrived in Persia :—

" MY DEAR ——,—When I wrote to you last, I was by Mirza Baba's bedside. He was attacked by the disease which has proved so exceedingly fatal in Tehrán this year, and which, strange to say, has been most fatal in the strongest constitutions. I had lost two patients in whom I was much interested—a relation of the Imám Juma, and one of the French girls—by the same complaint, which completely baffled me, inasmuch as it is a disease wholly unknown, undescribed—viz , an ague which never comes out. There is no shiver, but a death-like coldness—no fever, and no sweating stage, and severe pain of the stomach, and oppression, which ends in blue cholera of the worst kind. I had several ill with the same complaint, when M. Baba was taken ill, and I succeeded in curing every one by a free bleeding, as soon as the chill came on. But all I could do, I could not persuade M. Baba to consent to be bled. However, we managed to get him over the first attack, and for three days he was quite well; but at the full moon he had another attack, which went on from day to day, growing worse, till the pulse ceased, and he was to all intents dead. I then bled him, which brought back the pulse, but it was too late, and he only lingered on three days more. Since then Mirza Sadik has had an immense number of similar cases, and I a good many, and I have not lost one by pursuing this treatment, which makes it doubly sad to have lost such a man through prejudice and timidity. As this pestilence is advancing fast upon you at Tabríz, if it has not already arrived, I think I cannot do better for you and your friends than tell you something about it; and as, since my first three cases, I am

not aware of having lost any patients (but three who were
past all hope). I may with benefit tell you how I always treat
it It is called by the Persians Tab-i-ghash, ' Fainting Fever,'
but it is, in fact, a mild kind of cholera. Its usual form is an
ague, in which—1st The cold fit is accompanied by extreme
oppression at the heart, and pain when pressure is made on the
pit of the stomach. This goes on for some days, when, at the
commencement of each ague, the patient becomes insensible, the
pulse is not to be felt, he neither shivers nor sweats properly.
and his skin is cold and clammy; if you bleed, no blood
comes; he has a few spasms, and dies mottled like a man in
cholera. 2nd. Sometimes there is pain and hardness of the
belly, and no ague; this the Persians fancy colic, but it is
the same complaint; the pulse gets weaker, the skin colder,
oppression at the heart greater, and the patient dies as in
cholera. 3rd Sometimes, with scarce any previous symptoms,
the skin is puffed up in an hour or two, and the man nearly
suffocated, with oppression of the chest, and dropsy. This is a
sort of inward sweating, where the perspiration does not come
out; I hear this is very prevalent at Burajird; this requires
bleeding freely, and calomel and jalap tartar in strong doses.
4th. But the commonest form is a daily ague, with pain and
swelling under the ribs of the left side, viz., in the spleen or
espoolse. 5th. More rarely, there is the regular purging and
vomiting of the blue cholera, with strangury, but spasms
only come on just before death. 6th. Often after eating water-
melon people are found dying or dead in their beds without
previous complaint; in children and infants it is very prevalent; without shivering, they become cold and insensible, only
recovering during the fever to fall again into a state of insen-
sibility, and dying in the same manner after two or three such
alternations. Now this is all the same complaint, and is to be
treated in the same way. My medicines are—1st, 7 miskals of
Epsom salts, 3 nakuds of green vitriol (sulphate of iron), 3 do.
of quinine, 12 drops of sulphuric acid (ark-i-Gugird), 1 bottle
of water, or 1 chirak: dose, a Persian coffee-cup full. 2nd, a
nakud of tartar emetic in a small cup of afshúrah limbu
(lemonade): dose, a tablespoonful every five minutes (emetic),

or two every half-hour, to cause perspiration. 3rd, pills of half a nakud of opium, and half a nakud of calomel each, to be made up with boiled rice.

" In the prevalent agues, without bad symptoms, four cupfuls of the mixture, at intervals of an hour and a half before the shiver, will cure well. But, if there be much tenderness at the pit of the stomach, it will not do so effectually without the aid of leeches to the left side 'of the pit of the stomach, fifteen (more or less) to be applied two hours before the shivering. The paler the lips and tongue, the greater the necessity for leeches. If the person be in the habit of getting bled often, it is better always to have him bled two or three hours before the coming on of the fit—fifty or sixty miskáls to be taken from him, till the colour of the blood changes, and then a few doses of the bottle will cure quickly.

" Whenever there is much oppression, and anxiety, and faintness, and paleness, and the shiver does not come fairly out, the patient should always be bled in the cold fit It appears like condemning the poor blanched, fainting wretch to death to bleed him in that state, and is sometimes fearful, as he becomes often faint with the first few miskáls. The blood comes thick, discoloured, and weakly, and he looks as if he were dying ; only have courage to take seventy or a hundred miskáls, and the blood flows freely, changes colour, and, no matter how bad the patient may be, his life is saved the instant the pain at the pit of the stomach and oppression at the heart ceases, and a few doses of the mixture will cure him. Remember, the more unfit to be bled he appears to be, the more he requires it. But when he *appears to require bleeding* (*i. e.* in a state of hot *fever*), it would be wrong to bleed ; give the tartar emetic and lemonade, a spoonful every ten minutes, till he bursts into a perspiration. During the sweating stage of fever, both bleeding and leeching will always do harm, but the mixture does good. In all these cases the mixture should be given from twice a day to every half-hour, according to the severity of the disease, the quantity of salts being increased or diminished according. to the state of the bowels. When the ague is broken there is often great sleeplessness and thirst for a night or two. Two of the pills should then be given at bed-time, and the patient should be provided with some lemonade. It is scarcely possible to cure children of ague at this season without leeches, and if these be properly applied, at intervals of three, five, or ten days, to the spleen, an hour or two before the fit, till the ague breaks, they have but little occasion for other treatment. As this is the result of my experience in three thousand cases, I have some confidence in the treatment I recommend."

APPENDIX IV.

(*See* page 201, vol. I.)

I am indebted to Mr. W. H. Ince, F.L.S., for having my attention drawn to the following account of the *Argas persicus*, or Poisonous Bug of Persia :—

VI. Argas. Latr. Précis des caract. gén. des Ins., p. 178.
Rhynchoprion Hern. Mém. aptérol., p. 69.

Histoire Naturelle des Insectes, par M. le Baron Walckenaer, Paris, 1844.

Mâchoires en sucroire, non engaînées par les palpes, et cachées ainsi que ceux-ci au-dessous d'une avance de la partie antérieure du corps ; dessous du corps granuleux, non écailleux, et d'une seule pièce ; pattes bi-onguiculées, non vésiculifères.

Ces animaux, dont M. Savigny a étudié avec le plus grand soin les caractères exterieurs, sont fréquemment parasites : deux d'entre eux vivent sur des oiseaux ; un autre, devenu célèbre sous le nom d'*Argas persicus*, fait souvent éprouver à l'homme des douleurs très violentes.

L'Argas persicus, au sujet duquel M. Fischer de Waldheim a rédigé un mémoire publié sous le titre suivant : De l'Argas

de Perse (Malleh de Mianeh), décrit par les voyageurs sous
le nom de Punaise venimeuse de Miana (in 4° Acad. de
Moscou, 1823),—a donné lieu à beaucoup d'exagérations de
la part des voyageurs.

Dupré (2), cité par M. Fischer, s'exprime ainsi au sujet de
ces insectes : " Il y a aussi une espèce de Teigne, nommée
dans le pays *Malleh*, qui est fort à craindre, parceque l'homme
qui en est piqué tombe dans une consomption qui le fait
dépérir à vue d'œil, surtout s'il ne se soumet pas sans restriction
au régime dicté par l'expérience ; c'est de s'abstenir de viande
ou de boissons acides ou fermentées. Le sucre est regardé
comme un grand spécifique contre la piqûre de cet insecte,
que l'on ne trouve pas dans les maisons nouvellement con-
struites, et que la clarté de la lumière éloigne, dit on, des
appartements."

Maurice Kotzebue (1), également cité par M. Fischer, en
parle en ces termes : " L'insecte dangereux que l'on appelle
la Punaise de Miana mériterait les recherches d'un naturaliste
exercé Il est un peu plus grand que la punaise d'Europe,
d'un gris tirant sur le noir, et parsemé sur le dos d'une multitude de points rouges. Il se cache dans les murailles, et
fréquente de préférence les vieilles. C'est là que les punaises
se trouvent en grande abondance, et que leur piqûre est la
plus dangereuse. Jamais elles ne se montrent en plein jour ;
elles craignent aussi la lumière : cependant la clarté des
lampes et des bougies ne les met pas toujours en fuite. Elles
infestent Miana depuis un temps immémorial, et se répandent
jusque dans les environs, où elles sont un peu moins dan-
gereuses. En hiver, elles restent immobiles dans les trous de
murailles, et, semblables à tous les animaux venimeux, c'est
dans les grandes chaleurs de l'été que leur venin a le plus
d'activité. Ce qu'il y a de plus merveilleux, même unique à
l'égard de ces punaises, c'est qu'elles n'attaquent pas les
naturels, ou du moins la piqûre qu'elles leur font n'a point de
suites plus graves que celle des punaises d'Europe, mais, en
revanche, elles font une guerre cruelle aux étrangers qui ont le
malheur de passer une nuit à Miana, et souvent elles donnent

la mort en moins de vingt-quatre heures. J'en ai entendu raconter deux examples :—

" Les Anglais de Tauris m'ont unanimement déclaré qu'ils ont perdu, à Miana, un de leurs domestiques qui fut atteint par ces terribles insectes. Il éprouva bientôt dans tout son corps une chaleur violente, tomba dans une espèce de délire, et expira enfin au milieu d'épouvantables convulsions.

" J'ai reçu d'autres informations non moins dignes de foi du Colonel Baron Wrède, qui a servi longtemps avec distinction en Grusinie, et qui, il y a quelques années, a été envoyé en Perse comme ambassadeur. Lorsqu'il passa à Miana, la saison était fort avancée ; ne croyant rien avoir à craindre des punaises, il y resta la nuit, mais avec la précaution de tenir une bougie allumée. Il n'éprouva aucun mal. Un Cosaque de son escorte eut le lendemain matin une tache noir au pied, tint des propos délirants et tomba enfin dans un accès de fureur. Les habitans conseillèrent un remède usité en pareil cas ; ce fut d'écorcher un bœuf et d'envelopper le pied du malade dans la peau encore chaude. On eut recours à cet expédient, mais cela ne servit de rien, et le pauvre Cosaque mourut dans une douloureuse agonie. On assure que ce moyen réussit ordinairement, mais il faut que le malade reste pendant quarante jours sans prendre autre chose que de l'eau sucrée et du miel. Comme je l'ai déjà dit, les naturels de Miana prennent sans danger ces punaises dans leur mains. Quel bonheur que ces formidables insectes ne se mettent point dans les habits ! Car ils se seraient bientôt propagés dans toute la Perse."

46. Argas de Perse (*Argas persicus.*)

Corps ovalaire allongé, plus retréci en avant que celui de la punaise des lits, avec laquelle on l'a comparé ; tout le dos garni de petits grains blanchâtres, comme chagrinés ; le bord très-peu ourlé, un peu énchancré, bilatéralement en avant ; couleur d'un rouge sanguin clair, parsemé sur le dos de points élevés blancs ; pattes pâles. (Fischer.)

Arg. pers., Fischer, Notice sur l'Argas de Perse, p. 14, fig. 8, 11 de la pl. unique.

C'est la punaise venimeuse de Miana des voyageurs, et dont o'i a tant exagéré les accidents. M. Audouin rapportait à l'*Argas persicus* l'espèce représentée par M. Savigny (Egypt, pl. ix., f. 6), et que nous avons reproduite d'après lui (pl. xxxiii , f. 0).

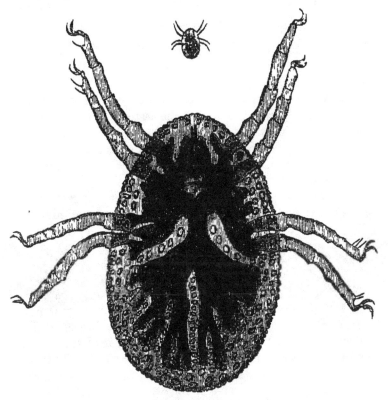

JAMES SMITH, F.L.S., delt.

[This diagram has been enlarged from the actual specimen by means of the camera lucida. This specimen is oval, whereas that given by Walckenaer and Gervais is truncated.]

APPENDIX V.

(See p. 310, vol. II.)

The following extract from the *Tehran Gazette*, the Persian *Moniteur*, contains the only notice of a European entertainment at Tehran which ever appeared in that journal:—

[Translation.]

[*Copy.*]

As Wednesday, the 10th of the month of Rejeb (1st of January, 1863), was the eve of the festival of the English new year, Mr. Eastwick, the Chargé d'Affaires of the English Government, gave a dinner-party, and in accordance with the friendship between the two Governments, invited a number of the Persian Ministers.

The entertainment was of the most elegant and recherché description, and every one of the guests enjoyed himself thoroughly.

The party did not break up till after five hours, being prolonged by pleasant conversation after dinner.

The Chargé d'Affaires of the English Government made himself most agreeable, and showed his respect and regard for his Majesty the Sháh in a truly gratifying manner. For example, at dinner he proposed his Majesty's health in the following words: " I have to ask the Ministers of the Crown and the gentlemen present to fill their glasses and to fill them to the brim. It is well known that in the old times there were kings of Persia great and renowned, and monuments of the glory of some of them remain even to the present day; but I venture to predict that the fame of the Sovereign who now occupies the throne will be more solid and lasting than that of any of his predecessors, for his reign has been stamped with the marks of true progress—such as the founding of colleges for the study of all sciences, and the introduction of the Electric Telegraph, and other similar discoveries. I heartily wish his Majesty a long and prosperous reign, and I call on all present to join in that wish."

In reply, the Minister for Foreign Affairs said (before drinking the health of the Queen), "Although the friendship between the Persian and English Governments has been based on a foundation not to be shaken, yet whenever the English Ministers have exerted themselves to strengthen that friendship it has grown with their efforts, and this has been the case on some late occasions; especially Mr. Eastwick, who is now at the head of the Mission, has displayed the most perfect good feeling in a manner which even surpasses all that has gone before, and the result is that the friendship between my august master and her Majesty the Queen of England has reached a culminating point. It is right, therefore, that the happiest feeling should reign here this night."

When the Minister for Foreign Affairs had sat down, the Ameen u Shourah said, "As I know the friendly sentiments which the Sháh feels for his Royal Highness the Prince of Wales, heir-apparent to the throne of England, I 'drink to his Royal Highness's health."

The Chargé d'Affaires then said: "I beg to thank the noblemen and gentlemen here assembled, for the way in which the Prince of Wales's health has been drunk, and I would remind them that Persia, too, has now an heir-apparent, and that he also is a prince of the highest worth and promise. I ask you, therefore, to drink to the health of the heir-apparent of Persia."

APPENDIX VI.

(*See* p. 313, vol. ii)

[*Translation.*]

MEER ALI NAKI KHAN *to* MR. EASTWICK.

Rejeb 24th, 1272 (*January 24th*, 1863)

It is requisite that I should give expression to my feelings of extreme gratitude and thankfulness to the British Government for its kindness, protection, and support, and to yourself for the trouble and friendly interest which you have taken in my case, because none of the former Ministers ever took such pains, nor did they succeed in making any arrangements regarding my claims, and during the last few years I have suffered very great hardships. Now, however, praise be to God, by the favour of the exalted British Government and through your kindly exertions, my case has been brought to a satisfactory and suitable termination. This measure, which redounds to the credit of the English Government, has been carried out by you, and yesterday, Wednesday, the 14th day of the month, I had the honour to receive a " khelaat " (dress of honour) from his Majesty the Shainshah, and I was further honoured by being presented to his Majesty, who was pleased to treat me with the greatest condescension. I am full of hope that the royal favour will continue to increase day by day. I make this brief communication to you for the purpose of stating how deeply grateful I am to the English Government for its support and protection, and to you for your kindness and friendship.

APPENDIX VII.

(*See* p 324, vol. ii.)

Farewell letter from M. Pesce, senior European officer in the service of the Shah, who speaks of the general regret of all the Europeans in Tehran at Mr. Eastwick's departure.

Teheran, 11 *Febraro,* 1863.

STIMATISSIMO SIGNOR EASTWICK,

E da molto tempo che avero l'idea di presentarle un' esemplare del mio Album fotografico della Persia, e per diverse circostanze, nelle quali la mia volontà non vi ha preso parte, non ho potuto finora sodisfare a questo mio desiderio; ora pero che Lei abbandona questa terra, forse per non ritornarvi mai piu, mi prendo la liberta di offrirle un Album della vidute della Persia, debole mio lavoro, che certo non corrisponde all' infinito suo merito; ma che pero incontrera dalla di Lei parte tanta indulcenza, d'accettarlo in attestato del inalterabile stima e rispetto che le professo, e come ricordo di questi luoghi, ov' Ella ha trascorsi tre anni circa; e se dal suo canto non provi alcun rammarico nell' allontanarvisi, sia pure certa, che quasi la totalita degli Europei di Teheran sentono un vivo dispiacere della sua partenza, e restera loro, maisempre impressa, la di Lei bonta, e le belle qualita che la distinguano.

Nella lusinga di rivederci ben presto in questa, o in altra terra qualunque, la prego di gradire i miei auguri di futura prosperità; e gli attestati della più inalterabile venerazione

Di Lei
Devotissimo ed obbligatissimo Servo,
L. PESCE.

9 783752 592344